BOOK THREE

THE FAE REALM SERIES

SACRIFICE

CATHLIN SHAHRIARY

Sacrifice

The Fae Realm

by Cathlin Shahriary

Cover design by Indie Solutions by Murphy Rae

Formatting by Alyssa Garcia at Uplifting Designs

Copyright ©2018 Cathlin Shahriary

This is a work of fiction. The names, characters, places, and incidents have been used fictitiously. Any resemblance to actual persons, living or dead, is entirely coincidental and intended by the author.

To Haley,
Your what-ifs keep me inspired.

Author Note

Sacrifice is the third book in the Fae Realm series, but also a prequel of sorts. While Fate (book 1) and Exile (book 2) focus on Ianthe's journey, in Sacrifice, Ayanna goes back to tell the story of before Ianthe was born, and more importantly, of the love that led to Ianthe. It is recommended that you read the first two books before reading this one, but not necessary.

SACRIFICE

PROLOGUE

AYANNA RESTED HER hand over her belly, knowing she wouldn't be able to hide the truth much longer. Either a slightly protruding baby bump or someone's Fae magic would reveal the secret she was hiding, and she had to escape before it was too late.

As much as she loved Corydon, she didn't love the man he had become since assuming his father's seat on the Unseelie throne. The power, responsibility, and need to be the uncontested ruler were all changing him. He was no longer the man she had first met and fallen in love with two years before. Had it really been so long? It felt like she had only been there a couple months, but she sighed knowing a few months could equal a year back home. She knew her birthday had mostly likely come and gone in the time she'd stayed; she very well could have been nineteen already and not even known it. *Nineteen and soon to be a mother—too young.* She focused her thoughts on her baby, using her love and protectiveness to fuel her determination.

She rubbed her hand against her flat stomach. "Don't worry, my precious baby, your mommy will protect you. I will do whatever I have to do to keep you safe. I'm sorry you will never know your true father, but trust me, this is for the best."

She dressed quickly and started braiding her golden blonde hair. She was glad, then more than ever, that Alvina had listened when she insisted she didn't need anyone to help her dress anymore. If that woman ever found out… She shuddered to think of it. Alvina would probably insist that it would be better for the baby to be raised by a pure Unseelie like herself, and Ayanna couldn't let that happen. She would die before she let anyone take her baby away.

She slipped the knife she had smuggled from the kitchen into her right boot then plucked her necklace off the vanity, the midnight blue one he had first given her. She carefully put it on, tucking it underneath her tunic. It made it easier to leave knowing she still had a piece of him with her, something that might help protect her. She checked her pack to make sure she had all the necessities and quietly closed the door. Tiptoeing her way through the castle, she hoped her plan would work and she and her baby would soon be free.

CHAPTER 1

2 years and a few months earlier

AYANNA SIGHED AS she stared into the Oregon night sky, taking in the view out the window at her aunt's cottage. Sure, she was incredibly grateful that her aunt had taken her in after her parents' accident, but the adjustment hadn't been easy. To go from living in the city, surrounded by friends and neighbors she had known for a lifetime to the secluded woods and small town her aunt lived in was tortuously boring. She yearned for something to distract her from her pity party.

She knew her aunt had meant well. Grace had tried so hard to make Ayanna's seventeenth birthday a good one. She baked a homemade red velvet cake, bought her niece's favorite chocolate chip cookie dough ice cream, and rented a few romantic comedies for them to watch together. It was a good birthday, but it was also a reminder of what was missing from her life. Grace had made a scrapbook filled with pictures of Ayanna's mom's life from when she and Grace were little girls, her marriage to Ayanna's father, and holidays and time spent together, up until their last visit with Aunt Grace. It was incredibly thoughtful, and she was so thankful to have that piece of her parents, but it also made her heart ache. She wished she could have been a better daughter while they were still alive, or that she could just hug them one more time. So, after two movies, she had called it a night and headed to her room, where she now sat staring out the window, wallowing in self-pity, and wondering how her life would be different if her parents were still alive.

A sudden movement near the edge of the woods yanked her from her thoughts. She peered closely into the moonlit yard. *There!* She saw it again—a dark shape was weaving through the trees near the edge of the clearing. She pressed closer to the glass, her heart pounding in her chest, eager to see what might be lurking in the yard. Whatever it was, it was large…too large to be a dog or a wolf. Finally, it stopped moving near the large oak tree, and Ayanna opened the window as quietly as she could. The warm summer breeze tousled her hair as she leaned slightly out of the window to get a better look. A large black stallion stuck his head into the clearing, his snout and mane illuminated in the moonlight. She sat frozen in awe. He was so majestic. She wondered if he had gotten loose from someone's property or if he was truly wild.

The midnight stallion nibbled on the grass and wildflowers by the tall oak tree while the breeze blew through Ayanna's hair. Suddenly, he lifted his head. His nostrils flared, sniffing the breeze, perhaps looking for better things to eat or sensing danger. He drew in a deep breath and swung his head in her direction. She gasped as his bright violet eyes met her light blue ones. She had never seen eyes that shade before. He stared at her and nickered softly in the wind, as if trying to talk to her or call her closer. She remembered the times her mother had taken her horseback riding as a girl. It had been quite a long drive to the stables, but her mother always took the time, said the horses called to her, and there was nothing quite as peaceful as being granted the love and trust of such a large creature. She smiled as she remembered the wind in her hair and her legs sore from the saddle, the wild feeling of power. She could almost hear her mother's laughter echoing in her ears. She instantly ached to interact with a horse once more, to maintain that connection to her mother.

"Hello there, boy," she cooed softly into the night air. He took another couple steps into the clearing. He was a magnificent specimen, much larger than the horses she remembered seeing on any of the nearby ranches or properties. Again, she wondered where he had come from. "Stay right there," she commanded, hoping he would listen.

As quickly as she could, she left her room and crept down the stairs, hoping Aunt Grace was already asleep. She stopped at the landing and listened, searching for any sign that Grace might be awake, but only silence greeted her. She slipped on her boots and opened the front door. Quietly closing it behind her, she stole into the night in her pajamas—a pink tank top and white pajama shorts with red hearts on them. Her golden hair flowed around her in the breeze. She didn't think the horse would care what she looked like, but she was sure with her clunky Doc Martens, the outfit would be somewhat humorous. She turned from the door, praying the horse was still there.

He was.

He had stepped farther into the clearing but was still near the edge of the woods, where he stood pawing at the ground impatiently. When she stepped off the porch and onto the ground, the gravel crunched under her feet and his head swung toward her again.

"Hey, boy." She wished she'd had the forethought to grab an apple or a handful of sugar cubes from the kitchen. She approached the stallion cautiously, knowing the slightest movement or sound could spook him and send him running back into the woods where he came from. He stared at her curiously and whinnied softly. "It's okay, boy. I'm not going to hurt you. I just wanted to come say hi," she called out quietly to the horse.

He pawed at the ground again, but his gaze studied her as she approached. She stopped a few feet away, giving him room to run if he so desired.

"Hi there, handsome." She stopped and held her hand out in front of her, allowing him to be the one to make the final move. His nostrils flared again as he inhaled her scent. He stepped closer. *Jesus.* He was even larger up close, and her heart pounded against her ribcage. His coat was a shiny jet black, catching the moonlight around them. His eyes were even more mesmerizing up close, such a striking shade of purple. The stallion stopped right in front of her outstretched hand, placed his muzzle right next to her palm, and inhaled again. His breath tickled her fingers and she giggled. He turned his head slightly to eye her curiously again before relaxing and pushing his muzzle against her hand. She laughed as he attempted to nibble at her with his lips. When she withdrew her hand, he whinnied in protest. She smiled, bringing her hand up to stroke the side of his face. She watched him closely for any sign of spooking, but he simply pressed his face into her hand. Stepping closer, she stroked the side of his muzzle down his neck. His coat was so soft, such a contradiction to the hard muscles she could feel underneath, rippling with each movement. He was a magnificent beast.

He stepped a bit closer and pressed his face into her neck, inhaling again. She released a full belly laugh, feeling such joy in that moment. "Well, aren't you a little flirt?" He whinnied softly in agreement and she wrapped her arms around him then rested her head against his neck. "Best... birthday...present...ever," she whispered. He leaned into her as if returning her embrace.

A twig snapped in the distance. She yanked her head up and stepped away from the stallion, feeling his muscles tense underneath her. They both froze, breathing, listening. There was another snap, the unmistakable sounds of something moving in the woods beyond them. The horse neighed at her insistently and nudged her gently with his muzzle, shoving her toward the house. She wasn't sure what was going on, but she could read panic in his eyes, and that was enough to get her moving. He nudged her again, more forcefully, as if to urge her to hurry. She ran to the house, only turning back once she had reached the porch. The horse neighed loudly before rearing up on his hind legs, as if commanding her to go inside. She stepped onto the porch and grabbed the door handle, opening the door before she turned back again to see him land on all four of his feet, snorting loudly, angrily. He had transformed from her gentle giant into a fierce warrior. With one last glance in her direction, he turned around and raced off into the woods.

She stepped inside and closed the door, locking it behind her. She stood there for a few minutes, breathing heavily from her sprint home, her heart racing, her veins filled with adrenaline. She could still feel his silky coat under her fingers and his warm breath against her neck. She quietly took off her boots, crept upstairs to her room, and climbed into bed. When she fell asleep, she dreamed about her beautiful stallion.

She awoke the next morning, convinced her encounter with the midnight creature had just been a dream. During breakfast, she told Grace about it and asked her about horses in the area. Grace reaffirmed Ayanna's assumptions: there were no wild horses nearby, and the nearest farm that had horses was quite a ways away.

Aunt Grace stared at her for a few minutes, studying her. She looked like she had something to say, opening her mouth, only to close it a moment later. She ran her hands through her curly brown hair. "Ayanna, there's something you should probably know. I know it won't mean as much coming from me as it would from your mother, but…"

"Umm…if you're about to give me some parental advice, I feel I should tell you I already know not to talk to strangers and to look both ways before I cross the street. I also got the birds and the bees talk, along with all discussions about womanly body changes a few years ago from Mom. So, you don't need to. Don't worry," Ayanna interrupted, hoping to stave off any embarrassing conversations.

"Ah, if only it were that simple." Grace sighed. Ayanna quirked an eyebrow curiously. "You see, my dear, this may be rather hard to believe…" She paused, unsure of where to go from there, unsure how her news might be perceived.

"I'm listening," Ayanna said reassuringly.

"Well, the women in our family have always had a gift that can be passed on from generation to generation. Your mother did not receive this gift, but I have it, as did our mother. You see, there is real magic in this world, and many things you may have been brought up thinking were just fairy tales…well, they're based on some truth."

Ayanna bit her bottom lip, and her puzzlement at where Aunt Grace was going with all this must have been apparent on her face.

Grace huffed. "I'm doing a horrible job at this. It's been so long since my mother sat us down and had this talk with your mom and me. This is probably going to be really hard to believe, but you have to trust me on this. I wouldn't lie to you, not about this. Have you ever heard of Fae, fairies, or fair folk?"

Ayanna shook her head no, and then stopped. "Wait, do you mean like Tinkerbell?" she asked.

"Sort of. Fae are ancient creatures full of magic. They live in a realm parallel to our own and have access to our world. They are very beautiful, very dangerous creatures, definitely not like Tinkerbell, unless you're talking about pixies. There are many kinds of Fae and even Fae creatures that come from their world. Most humans don't see Fae when they roam our world because they have glamour, which is sort of like a magical disguise that helps them blend in with humans, making them appear normal. Now, for some reason, the women in our family are sometimes burdened with the gift of Sight after their seventeenth birthday. It allows us to see beyond the Fae glamour to what they really look like. While other people see them as unbelievably attractive humans, someone with Sight will be able to see the Fae's sharp, angular features, pointed teeth and ears, and strange glowing eyes."

The iridescent purple eyes of the stallion flashed through Ayanna's memory, but she shook it away telling herself it must have been a dream.

Grace continued, "While sometimes this 'gift' skips a generation, it's quite possible that you may have Sight. You must be extremely careful, because Fae do not take kindly to humans with this ability. Some see it as a threat and may wish to harm you as a result. You must not let them know you can see them as they truly are. Come to me at once if you notice anything strange, do you understand?" She grabbed Ayanna's hand, holding it tight and staring her straight in the eyes to convey the seriousness of the situation.

"I understand, Aunt Grace. I'm pretty sure I only dreamed of the horse, but I will be careful and you will be the first to know if I see anything strange. I mean, I may not even have this 'gift' if my mother didn't, right?"

"You're absolutely right, my dear. I just want you to be safe."

She squeezed Aunt Grace's hand. She wasn't sure what to think of the conversation; it was a rather strange idea. Surely if her mother had thought this might eventually be Ayanna's reality, she would have mentioned it before, or at least read her bedtime stories about Fae.

"Is it okay if I go out to pick blackberries today?"

"Of course, just don't wander too far until I have this horse situation figured out." Aunt Grace patted Ayanna on the shoulder before picking up the breakfast dishes and carrying them to the sink.

Ayanna strolled upstairs and changed into a pair of jeans and a neon pink tank top since she was going to be traipsing through the woods in the summer heat. The tank top would keep her cool while the jeans would protect her legs from prickly bushes and unwelcome insects. She quickly tied her hair up with a matching hot pink scrunchie then ran downstairs. She was curious to investigate the horse situation for herself.

She kissed Aunt Grace on the cheek and filled up a canteen with water before she laced up her Doc Martens, snagged a basket, and set out on her way. Her boots crunched loudly on the gravel drive, reminding her of how real her dream had felt. As she approached the tall oak tree, she stopped short. Sure enough, there in the soil by the tree were hoof prints, large enough to fit that of her midnight stallion. She hadn't been dreaming after all. She squatted down and ran her fingers along the indentations, remembering the silky feel of the horse's coat.

Without thinking, she followed the hoof prints farther into the woods. She gasped and came to a halt. Where she had just been following horse prints, she now discovered boot prints. *Maybe someone tracked the horse to bring it back? Or perhaps the rider was hiding the whole time I was with the horse, watching me from the safety of the trees, spying on me?* That thought caused a chill to rush down her spine. She hoped no one had been spying on her. She looked closely, noticing where the boot prints appeared, the hoof prints seemed to disappear. She explored farther into the woods, following the boot prints until they once again met horse tracks and raced away. She was so busy tracking the prints that she didn't realize how far she had strayed from the house until she noticed her unfamiliar surroundings. She knew she should be cautious, but her curiosity was winning. *I guess if I get too deep into the woods, I can just follow the horse and boot tracks back. It's not that big of a deal.*

She wasn't sure how long she had been walking, maybe twenty minutes or so if she had to guess, when she saw sparkling blue water through the trees. She stepped into a small clearing with the most majestic pond. It was rather large, and the water was unusually clear and blue. Most ponds she remembered seeing in the area had a murky brown-green tinge to them, but not this one. There was soft grass leading up to the shore and a few rather large boulders she could see herself sunbathing on. It almost felt like the pond where Princess Aurora first meets Prince Phillip in the movie *Sleeping Beauty*. All that was missing was the woodland creatures to gather around her. She chuckled at the thought.

The water looked so cool and inviting, and Ayanna was so hot from her hike through the woods—she just couldn't resist. She set her basket down by a large boulder and studied her surroundings, making sure she was completely alone. Then she unlaced her boots, stripped down to her bra and panties. *It was practically a bikini anyway,* she reasoned, tossing her clothes next to the basket and dipping her toes into the water. It was so refreshing, she sighed happily before immersing herself in the cool water. She swam lazily for quite some time, enjoying her relaxing surroundings when a cough interrupted her leisurely laps.

"I didn't know any mermaids lived in this pond."

Her arms immediately went to cover her chest even though she was still in her bra as she turned her head toward the masculine voice. She noticed a pair of dark brown leather boots standing on one of the large boulders, and her gaze followed the almost knee-high boots up to soft brown pants and a forest green tunic. It was an interesting outfit to say the least, but that wasn't what made her jaw drop. She had moved on from his broad chest to his magnificent face. He had a firm, chiseled jaw with a perfectly strong, slightly pointed nose, and then there were his eyes, which were an incredible shade of violet Ayanna had only seen once before, on her midnight stallion. He was more gorgeous than any model she had seen. His skin was like a smooth, slightly flushed porcelain, and his hair hung in sheets just below his shoulders—a blonde so pale it appeared white, with hints pale silver in the sunlight. Best of all, he looked to be in his early twenties.

"I...um...I..." she mumbled until a deep, rich laugh erupted from his perfectly kissable mouth. It was the best sound she had ever heard.

"I was kidding." He smiled. "Although you do look like a siren temptress in that water." She blushed, clutching her arms tighter around her chest and sinking into the water for more cover. "I'm sorry. I didn't mean to interrupt you. I just happened to stop at my favorite spot, and imagine my surprise when I found you here," he continued.

Her eyes widened in panic. *Have I unknowingly hiked onto someone else's property?* "Crap, I didn't know this land belonged to anyone. I'm so sorry," she replied, staring up at him.

"I'm not…sorry that is." He smirked flirtatiously. "In fact, you're a lovely addition to my spot and are welcome back at any time—although I do have to say I don't remember seeing you around here before."

"Oh, well, um…I moved in with my aunt earlier this year, and I haven't hiked out this far before. I guess I never really saw the point, but now…" She smiled. "I may have changed my mind about that."

He chuckled in response, and his laughter became her new favorite sound. A breeze swept through, sending chills down her exposed skin and reminding her that she was barely clothed. She blushed furiously.

"Um…do you mind…"—she made a little twirling motion with her finger—"so I can get out and get dressed?"

He reached down and plucked her shirt off of the rock next to him. She held her breath, waiting to see his response. He could be a perverted jerk and not turn around, leaving her to either freeze in the water or show him what she was hiding, or he could be a gentleman. She knew which one most guys at her school would be. This guy, however, was not like most guys. He blushed when he realized what he was holding meant about what she was—or wasn't—wearing. He placed her shirt on the rock.

"Oh…yeah, of course," he mumbled nervously. He smiled boyishly and hopped off the boulder, giving her a bit of privacy.

She stepped out of the water near the boulders and glanced over at the boy. To her surprise, he was facing the woods instead of the pond. She dressed quickly while still peeking at the mysterious boy with pearly hair and violet eyes. When she was fully clothed, she called out to him, "You can turn around now. It's safe." She smiled as she sat on a dry part of the boulder, and she enjoyed watching him lithely stride toward her. She found his attire very strange, but didn't want to ruin their easy banter and friendliness by asking him about it. *Maybe he's foreign or likes being different and has his own unique style.* She held her hand out in front of her as he approached. "I'm Ayanna, by the way."

"Ayanna? What a beautiful name." He took her hand in his and awkwardly shook it. "My name is Corydon."

"Core-ih-dun?" she asked, verifying that she pronounced it correctly, and he nodded encouragingly. "I haven't heard that one before. It's different…unique. I like it."

He smiled. "I could say the same about your name. I don't know if I've ever met an Ayanna before."

"Probably not—well, at least not around here. It's an Eastern African name meaning beautiful flower." She blushed slightly as she met his striking eyes. She held his gaze, mesmerized by the unique violet hue. His eyes almost seemed to darken to a royal purple the longer she stared.

"Very fitting," he replied, her blush deepening as he held her gaze for a few moments longer than appropriate.

"So, um…how long have you lived around here?" She fidgeted, running her fingers through her wet locks to untangle them.

"My whole life. Mind if I sit?" he asked, gesturing to the empty space on the rock next to her. *Okay, so not foreign after all*, she thought, which was odd because she sensed a slight accent that she couldn't place.

"Go right ahead," she replied as his lips tugged up along the corners. "So, do you go to school?"

He paused. "Not anymore. I used to have a private tutor, but I no longer require his direct instruction."

"So, you were, like, homeschooled?"

His brow furrowed slightly in the middle as if he were trying to unlock a puzzle. "I suppose you could call it that, but it was years ago," he answered vaguely. Ayanna took that to mean he was probably college aged, but maybe didn't go to college. She didn't have long to figure out what that meant before he fired a question her way. "What about you?"

"I'm going to be a senior at Ashford High School."

"So, that makes you…" He trailed off, unsure of how to complete his thought.

"Just turned seventeen." She grinned.

"Well, happy late birthday to you." He nudged her with his elbow and a spark of electricity fired across her skin at the contact.

"Thanks. What about you? How old are you?" The question seemed innocent enough, but he paused. Strangely, she could almost see him calculating in his head.

"I guess around 20." He shrugged, as if guessing at one's own age was a common thing. Ayanna discreetly reached down and pinched herself just to ensure this bizarre conversation with this good-looking guy was actually taking place. She felt the sting of her pinch, reassuring her that she was, in fact, not dreaming. Almost as if sensing her slight discomfort, he changed the subject. "So, since I haven't seen you around here before, what brought you out today?"

She brightened. He'd be the perfect candidate to ask questions about her midnight stallion. "Well, last night I thought I had the strangest dream, but I don't think it was a dream after all."

"Is that so?" he asked, clearly amused with the start to her story.

"Have you seen a black stallion running around these woods?" He quirked an eyebrow and she pressed on, fearing he might tell her she was wrong. "Well…last night I saw this midnight black horse in the clearing by my aunt's house. He was beautiful in the moonlight."

"Beautiful, huh?" he replied with a grin, seemingly chuffed. She couldn't tell if his grin was only to humor her, or if he knew something he wasn't telling her.

"He had a wild look in his eyes." She paused, wary to mention that the animal's eyes had been the same shade as his. "But he was very friendly. He might even be someone's horse who got away. He let me pet him, and he had the softest coat ever—it was like a baby rabbit."

"I don't know if this very manly stallion would like being compared to a baby bunny," he joked. This time she nudged him with her elbow and felt the current run through her skin again.

She rolled her eyes. "So, anyway, I asked my aunt about him this morning, but she gave me a super strange look, so I thought maybe I dreamed him. However, when

I went outside earlier, I found horse tracks exactly where I had stood with him. With the excuse of picking berries"— she pointed toward her empty basket—"I followed the tracks, and they led me here, which is how I found your secret place."

"Interesting…" Corydon replied, his hair hanging forward and hiding some of his chiseled features while he studied her hand where it lay between them on the rock.

"So, have you seen a horse like that around here?" She held her breath, waiting for his reply.

"Maybe…" He continued staring down at her hand but then flicked his eyes up to gauge her reaction.

Her eyes widened. "Oh my god! I'm not crazy! Unless you're messing with me—you better not be messing with me about this."

He finally lifted his head, his lips tipping upward in amusement. "You're not crazy. He's a wonder around these parts of the woods, a fearsome, majestic beast who has been known to roam the forest at night." There was almost a hint of pride in his voice as he described her midnight stallion.

"Oh, so you know him quite well then," she teased.

"I guess you could say that…" He smirked, reaching up to tuck his hair behind his left ear.

Ayanna noticed that her arms were starting to turn a light shade of pink. *Damn*, she thought, realizing she must have forgotten to put on sunblock before she left. As much as she didn't want to leave him, she knew she should probably head home to avoid further sunburn, because a little pink would definitely deepen by that evening without the help of any more exposure. "Unfortunately, I should probably go before I turn extra crispy."

He placed his hand on her pink forearm. "I had no idea you could burn so quickly."

"The curse of the pale," she joked. He removed his hand tucking his hair behind his ear, but the heat from his touch remained.

"It's been entertaining getting to know you, Ayanna. Do you think we could meet up again? I'd love to spend some more time with you."

"I'd like that too." She met his gaze and stared into his eyes, seeing nothing but sincere interest, and perhaps the start of a friendship.

"I don't think I can get away tomorrow, but what about three days from now? Same place, around noon?"

"It's a date—I mean…I'll see you then," she stammered, unsure if he would take her words the wrong way. She hopped off the rock and turned to face him straight on. She took a moment to study his sharp features until her eyes halted on his left ear, where his silvery blond hair was tucked. Her breath caught in her throat. She had only seen ears like his on *Star Trek*, and while they were definitely pointy, on him they seemed to fit. Like a bullet, her aunt's description of Fae hit her, and she staggered back a few steps.

"Are you okay?"

She was sure her eyes had widened. "I…um…just remembered something—I have to go," she called out, leaving the pond at a sprint.

"Ayanna, wait!" His voice echoed off the trees around her, but she was afraid of what she would do if he caught up with her. She pushed herself to run as quickly as she could without tripping over rocks or tree roots. She glanced back, and much to her relief, he wasn't following her. Could Aunt Grace have been right after all? Could Corydon be Fae? And if he were, how would she ever face him again?

She pondered all of these questions, but more interestingly, she found herself disappointed at the thought of never seeing him again. He had been sweet and kind, nothing like how Grace had described the Fae. Perhaps Grace could be wrong, or had been talking in generalizations. Corydon could be an exception to the rule. Then another thought occurred to her: if she did decide to see him again, how would she explain her sudden departure? She couldn't let him know she knew who—or rather, *what* he was. She knew she should certainly keep that bit of knowledge to herself to give her the upper hand. She was so lost in thought that only a few minutes later did she realize she had left her basket at the pond. *Damn.* She'd have to come up with something to tell Aunt Grace, and she would have to go back for it…eventually.

CHAPTER 2

GRACE LOOKED AT her strangely when she walked in. She was sure her appearance was cause for concern. "Everything okay dear?"

"Oh…um…yeah. I'm…uh…I'm fine," she huffed in between breaths. She was winded from running all the way back to the house, so she stopped to gather her breath and her story. "When I was out collecting berries, I heard a large animal and it scared me. I dropped the basket and ran all the way back here."

"A large animal? What kind of large animal?" Grace looked genuinely concerned.

"I don't know, I just heard it making noises and took off. I didn't want to hang around to find out in case it was dangerous," she lied.

"What kind of noises?"

"Uh…like…a huffing sound, and it was shuffling through the woods, so it sounded like it was really big… maybe a bear…"

"A bear? We don't have any bears around here."

"I don't know, Aunt Grace. I was too scared to stick around and find out." She hated how her voice snapped. It wasn't Grace's fault her story was unbelievable, but it was the first thing she had thought of to explain why she'd returned without her basket and berryless.

"I know. I'm sorry, sweetie. I just…sometimes the woods aren't safe, as you just learned for yourself. We don't have bears or other large predators, but there are other creatures…Fae creatures, and they aren't like the ones we're used to. I haven't had any problems in the area around the house before, but there's a first time for everything, so be careful out there, okay? Let me know immediately if anything like this happens again." Grace's brow furrowed and she chewed on her lower lip as she turned away from Ayanna.

"Will do," she replied, striding toward the small library of books Grace kept in the study. Guilt seeped into Ayanna's conscience. She felt horrid for lying and causing Grace unnecessary concern, but what else was she supposed to do? She thought briefly about telling her the truth, but that might be more worrisome than the threat of some unknown wild creature. Besides, Corydon didn't seem like he was the evil Fae Grace had described. She decided for now she would keep him a secret and do her own research. She had a few days until she was supposed to meet him again, time to decide if she would go after all. She figured she should get all her facts straight before revealing anything to Grace.

She browsed the shelves more closely than she had in the past. She remembered looking at them when she first arrived, noting that the titles ranged from books about herbal remedies to Fae folklore. She used to wonder why Grace had books full of fairy stories, but now she knew why. Perhaps these weren't just tall tales, as she had initially concluded. She chose a few from the shelf and carried them up to her room. She knew Grace wouldn't mind, but she didn't feel like answering any questions about her sudden interest in all things Fae.

Several hours later, she had learned quite a bit about Fae, including that they could be both good and bad. They were also known to manipulate people and take human energy for their own use, usually through touch of some kind. There were also different types of Fae and Fae creatures. She tried looking up anything she could about her mysterious midnight stallion in case he was a Fae creature, but she only found information about kelpies, horses that lived in the water and lured humans toward the shore until they could drown them. She shivered; perhaps some of what Grace had told her had been true. Kelpies definitely sounded like dangerous creatures.

She thought back to her interaction with Corydon. He knew she was human, yet he didn't seem to want to hurt or use her. He seemed nice, like a normal teenage boy, except for the clothes he wore, but those made sense now, along with his hair color. She had never seen anything quite like it, so pale and shiny, like moonlight. She sighed. She wasn't sure what to do about him. Thankfully, she had a few more days to figure it out. She spent the rest of the evening enjoying dinner and watching TV with Grace, acting like nothing had changed when, in reality, everything had.

That night, she read next to her window with one eye on the book and the other searching the area for the black stallion. At one point her head nodded, and as she jerked herself awake, she knew it was time to call it a night. She glanced longingly out the window one last time and she smiled widely. There he was. He was standing so still at the edge of the wood and seemed to be staring straight at her window, watching her. She waved to him, and he whinnied, shaking his head up in a sort of nod in reply. As she rose from her seat, he pawed the ground and turned around, racing off into the forest. The realization that she wouldn't be able to touch him or interact with him was thick in her throat as she climbed into bed, and that night she dreamed of visiting him in the forest, of riding the stallion to the pond and finding Corydon there waiting for her.

When she awoke the next morning, she sighed heavily; part of her longed to return to her dream. She showered, changed, and went down for breakfast, where she was surprised to see her berry basket sitting on the kitchen table, full of berries.

"Wh…where did you find it?" she asked Aunt Grace, her voice shaky.

Grace turned from where she was flipping pancakes at the stove. "On the porch when I stepped out this morning."

"The porch?" Ayanna asked, the surprise evident in her voice.

"Mmmhmm." Grace nodded, flipping another pancake in the pan.

"But…how did it get there?"

"How, indeed?" Grace turned, arching her eyebrow.

"Don't look at me. I told you I dropped it in the woods."

"Yet here it is full of berries." She motioned toward the basket sitting in front of Ayanna.

"Well…maybe a neighbor found it and brought it back."

"A neighbor?" Grace's eyebrow arched even higher.

"Yeah…I mean, it's possible."

"I suppose…" Grace sighed, seeming unconvinced but

willing to drop the subject for the moment.

Ayanna reached over and plucked a blackberry out of the basket, popping it into her mouth and savoring its sweet juice. When she reached her hand back in, it grazed something soft. She pulled the basket closer to her, peering inside, and she found the most magnificent purple flower she had ever seen tucked underneath the berries. Its petals had royal purple tips bleeding into lavender, so soft and delicate and feminine, a color almost too vibrant to be real. She brought the flower up to her nose, inhaling the fragrance. It smelled unlike anything she had smelled before, almost as if someone had mixed winter snowflakes with a hint of berries.

Grace turned with plates full of pancakes, catching Ayanna with the flower up to her nose. "Where did you get that?"

"It was in the basket." She sighed dreamily. "I didn't know you had flowers like this around here."

"We don't." Grace frowned. "Are you sure you didn't see anyone yesterday?"

Ayanna's stomach sank. She hated lying to Grace, but fear kept her from sharing the truth. "Nope. Just whatever creature I heard in the woods but didn't stick around to see." She stared at the flower to avoid Grace's scrutinizing gaze. Admiring the violet, she had a flash of recognition—it was the same shade as Corydon's eyes. She smiled to herself. It would make sense for him to be the one to have found her basket. She had dropped it when she was running away from him, but to pick the berries up and leave the flower…that was very thoughtful. She had planned on looking for it the next time she went to the pond. She had still been debating whether she would see him again, but this sealed the deal for her. She had to see him.

She finished breakfast with Aunt Grace in an awkward silence. It was the first time she had felt even slightly uncomfortable around Grace, and guilt swirled under her skin. *Should I tell Grace about Corydon? No, she'll forbid me from seeing him, and besides, he didn't seem evil like she thinks all Fae to be.* Ayanna battled internally before deciding she would keep him a secret until she learned more about him. He didn't know she knew the truth about who he was, and she was going to use that to her advantage the next time they interacted.

The next couple of days crept slowly by. She longed for time to speed up, which was perhaps why it seemed to trickle by. She used that time to devour all the books about the Fae that she could find in Grace's study. Grace seemed glad that she was educating herself and taking their conversation to heart when most other people would probably have dismissed it as a crazy woman's rant. At first, Ayanna worried Grace would see through her true intentions behind learning more about the magical beings, but she ultimately had nothing to fear. Grace viewed knowledge as a power you could wield in your favor and reading as the ultimate weapon to arm yourself. It was a belief she loved to impart upon Ayanna every chance she got, so she was more than happy to supply her with the books she found to be most beneficial, and of course, Ayanna was happy to oblige.

She did venture outside quite a bit, many times sitting on the porch or lying out in the sun while she read. She often stared off into the woods, wondering if he was there. She had yet to see her midnight stallion again, and her thoughts often wandered back to him—was it merely a coincidence that she hadn't seen him since the last time she saw Corydon, or were the two linked somehow?

The night before she was supposed to meet him again,

she made sure to eat the last of the blackberries so she would have reason to venture back into the woods. She smiled to herself, replaying their last interaction while she lay in bed until she fell asleep dreaming of him, his violet eyes, silver white hair, chiseled jaw, and high cheekbones that reminded her of Johnny Depp in *Cry-Baby*.

When she awoke the next morning, she was still thinking about how Corydon was even more handsome than Johnny Depp, if that was possible. Of course, that was also when her doubts started creeping in. If he was so gorgeous, what would he want with a lowly human like herself? She wallowed in insecurity for a few more minutes before deciding the best plan of action would be to go in with her guard up. She changed, making the conscious decision to put on her blue polka-dotted bikini underneath her clothes. She didn't want to swim in her underwear in front of him again. Then she slipped a pair of jeans and a lavender tank top over her swimsuit. She pulled her honey blonde hair into two loose braids, one at either side of her head, then applied a quick coat of waterproof mascara and a light dash of blush before trotting downstairs.

Before her foot even hit the final step, she could smell the bacon in the air. Grace was already at the table eating when she took her place at her plate of bacon and eggs. "You know, you don't have to cook for me every morning, Aunt Grace. I can survive on cereal."

Grace smiled sadly. "I know, dear, but I thought…" She paused, trailing off.

Ayanna knew exactly what her aunt thought. Her mother had been a stay-at-home mom and had almost always cooked a nice family breakfast for them before her dad headed off to work and she left for school. It was sweet that Aunt Grace was trying to keep some things consistent for Ayanna, but cooking her breakfast every morning wouldn't change the fact that her parents were gone.

She reached over and squeezed Grace's hand, which rested on top of her fork. "I know you did, and it's sweet that you want to be like my mom, but you don't have to. I'm fine with whatever. I can have toast, or a bagel, or cereal." She noticed Grace's frown increase. "I mean, if you didn't cook breakfast before I came here, it's okay. I can fix food for myself."

Grace's eyes softened, understanding how hard things had been for her niece. "I know, but just humor me, okay? I only have you one more year before you head off to college." She squeezed Ayanna's hand and released it.

Ayanna smiled. "Okay, but I'm serious—I know some mornings before school it can be tough, so don't feel like you have to cook breakfast every morning. I'm really fine with whatever."

Grace paused with her fork raised near her mouth. "I will take that into consideration."

Ayanna studied her aunt closely while she ate. Grace still looked young, only two years older than Ayanna's mother, but the last year had definitely taken its toll on her. She looked a little more worn, a few fine wrinkles making their presence known. Her chestnut brown hair was still a wild mass of curls that never seemed tamed, like they had a mind of their own. She was wearing a maroon tank top and a tie-dyed gypsy skirt, and her style had always been what Ayanna would classify as bohemian hippie, exactly the type of clothes a woman who sells herbal remedies, salves, and homemade candles with healing properties would wear. The first time Ayanna had caught her aunt outside in the clearing on a full moon dancing around in a circle at midnight, it really hadn't shocked her. Ayanna smiled, remembering how much her mom loved to talk about Grace's free spirit, the yin to her mother's yang, as she used to say. She finished her breakfast lost in thought and memories.

Grace collected their plates and took them to the sink to wash them, and Ayanna helped her rinse and dry without even being asked. It was a comfortable routine the two of them had established. She was still working on convincing Grace of the benefits of a dishwasher, but she didn't know if she was making any progress. When they finished, Ayanna casually mentioned that she would be going berry picking again. Grace tensed, her body freezing right in the middle of drying her hands on the dish towel.

"I'll be careful, I promise," Ayanna said quickly, attempting to assuage Grace's hesitation.

"I don't know, Ayanna…"

"It'll be fine. I'm sure whatever animal was there is gone," she lied smoothly.

Grace's lips flat-lined before she finished drying her hands with a little more force than necessary. She walked over to the junk drawer and rummaged around for something before facing Ayanna again.

"Fine," she acquiesced, thrusting the object she had retrieved from the drawer out toward Ayanna, "but you're taking this with you."

Ayanna took the object, studying the old metal and engraved wood of the handle before unfolding the knife blade. It was the most ornate and deadly hunting knife she had ever seen in person. The designs on it were foreign and intricate, and the silver blade had similar, strange symbols carved onto its surface. She met Grace's eyes; there was a warning in them. She may not have known exactly what Ayanna had planned, but she knew her niece wasn't being entirely truthful about her last journey into the forest.

Ayanna nodded. "Deal." She flipped the blade closed, slid it into her pocket, and filled a canteen with water before giving Grace a hug and a kiss on the cheek. "I'll be back in a few hours," she called out as she grabbed the berry basket off the counter, tossed her canteen inside, and walked to the door. She stopped to lace up her boots over her sock-covered feet. Once out on the porch, she grabbed the towel she used to sunbathe in the yard and slung it over her shoulder before heading out. Nervous energy buzzed underneath her skin, causing her to quicken her steps toward the tall oak tree. She was amazed to see that some evidence of her midnight stallion was still there in the dirt, along with her own hurried footprints heading back toward the house.

She followed what she could until the prints disappeared under the foliage and rocks of the woods. When there were no more signs to follow, she paused, unsure where to go next. A slight unease crawled over her skin at the thought of getting lost in the strange forest. She took a few more steps forward then a peculiar sight caught her eye: a tree a few yards away had a violet flower stuck to one of its branches. She approached it cautiously but smiled widely when she saw that it was a duplicate of the one that had been left in her berry basket. It was tied around the branch with a piece of rough twine. Her heart fluttered. Corydon must have left it there to help her find her way back, which also meant he was the one who had returned her basket. She placed her right hand over her racing heart as warmth filled her chest. He wanted to see her again, wanted her to find her way back to him. She traced the delicate petals with her finger before continuing along the animal trail now visible through the grass and underbrush.

She followed the path, only veering off onto another one when a violet flower tied to a branch with twine caught her eye or to stop and collect some berries along the way in case she got hungry later. She would make a point to gather more on her way back to ward off Grace's suspicions. Her pulse thundered the closer she grew to the clearing with the pond. She studied her surroundings on the path he had left for her, eager to memorize the way so she wouldn't have to depend on anyone else next time, and so she could easily navigate her way home if need be. As she reached the edge of the clearing, she paused despite every limb of her body begging her to go on, as if drawn to him like a magnet. She took a few calming breaths, not wanting to be some lust-filled fool, but rather a levelheaded girl with power-ful knowledge on her side. She reminded herself that she needed to keep her guard up. As handsome as he was, he was also a dangerous inhuman creature she should not un-derestimate. She needed to keep her wits about her despite what her body and betraying heart wanted. She needed to get more information out of him, discover his intentions before she let anything get out of hand.

She stepped quietly out from behind the trees. He was there; of course he was there. He was sitting on the large rock they had sat on together the last time, but he didn't look happy. His head was bowed, cradled in his hands. His pale hair was draped behind his back, the front locks half tied back with what appeared to be a strap of leather. His porcelain skin appeared slightly paler than before, which was odd since it was summer. He should've been getting tanner, just as her own skin had darkened from her time in the sun. Maybe it had something to do with him being Fae.

His clothes were also different this time. Gone was the strange, old-fashioned tunic, although now that she knew what he was, it didn't seem so odd. In its stead was a plain forest green t-shirt paired with black leather pants and boots. She studied him, noticing his pointed ears were on full display. They reminded her of a Vulcan's ears on *Star Trek: The Next Generation*, one of her favorite TV shows. *Star Trek* had been her dad's favorite show when he was younger, and he was thrilled to continue the tradition with her when *TNG* started. Now, she watched it with a twinge of sadness, knowing he was no longer around to share it with her, but somehow feeling his presence with her when she did. She was lost in thought as she attempted to approach quietly, ruining it when a large twig snapped under her foot.

Corydon's head snapped up instantly, his hand reaching for something at his side, his eyes searching. When they landed on her, he dropped his hands and pushed himself off the rock, striding toward her.

"You came." His breath was heavy with relief.

"I did. Was I not supposed to?" she teased.

"I wasn't sure after you ran off last time," he explained with a trace of sadness.

"Oh, that…um…well, I hadn't realized how late it was and I really had to get home before I got into trouble," she lied. She didn't want him to know she knew the truth about what he was yet.

"So fast that you dropped your basket?" he asked, raising his brow.

"Uh…" *Shit.* "I guess I didn't want to waste any time to stop and pick it up."

"Because that whole minute would have made *all* the difference." Sarcasm and disbelief dripped off his words, but she attempted to play it off.

She shoved him playfully with her free hand. "Hey! It does make a difference when you're trying not to get grounded. You know how parents can be…" She trailed off, unsure if he did know how human parents could be.

"I guess you're right about that," he replied with a snort. "My father is quite demanding when it comes to being on time." He smiled, and she breathed an internal sigh of relief.

"Thanks for bringing it back to me, by the way." She plucked a berry from the basket and popped it into her mouth, his eyes tracking the movement as he licked his own lips. She reached in for another one and held it out toward him between her fingers. She did not expect him to lean forward, his mouth hovering above the blackberry before his teeth gently scraped against her fingertips, his lips closing around the berry as he ate it from her hand. She swallowed hard, feeling hot, her cheeks flaming. She watched him chew and lick the last of the sweetness from his berry-tinted lips, and his violet eyes seemed to swirl with ribbons of royal purple. His gaze was hungry, and she didn't think it was for more berries.

She reached for the canteen from her basket and took a long drink, trying to cool her runaway thoughts, but his gaze only seemed to grow hungrier. *Shit. What the hell am I doing?* she wondered, realizing half of her was thrilled to read the interest in his eyes and the other half was slightly terrified. It was like playing with a burning match, waiting to see how long you could hold it until you got burned.

"You're welcome." He smiled. "I was just about to take a swim. Would you care to join me?"

She glanced at the water, a slight breeze rippling across its surface as if to invite her in. When she returned her eyes to Corydon, he was pulling his t-shirt over his head. Her breath caught in her throat upon seeing his delicious chiseled features continued down his body with a beautifully sculpted back. His muscles were tight and lean, defined but not huge. She wondered if this was particular to him or if all Fae were built to be appealing, perfect specimens of beauty. He turned his head and caught her staring. She blushed furiously and glanced down at the ground, but not before she saw his wicked smile. He liked that she was practically drooling over him. She kept her eyes glued to his feet as he removed his boots. When his pants dropped, she thought she was going to hyperventilate. *Do Fae wear underwear?* Just the thought had her spinning around to give him some privacy, even as curiosity begged her to take a peek.

When she heard the splash of the water, she knew it was safe to look. As he stood, his pearly white hair slicked back on his head, his Fae features seemed even more pronounced. She dared not stare at his ears in case she might give herself away. He didn't know she had the ability of Sight, and she was not about to divulge that information when she didn't know his true intentions.

She fidgeted with the hem of her shirt. She had worn her bikini so she could enjoy the water, but now she hesitated. Insecurity was a wicked beast, sneaking into the corners of the mind and feasting on her confidence. She bent down and unlaced her shoes, removing them and her socks before she strolled toward the pond. She dipped her toes into the water, which was so cool and luxurious on the hot summer day.

"Are you coming in?" he called out. "I promise I won't bite." He grinned wickedly, his sharp teeth flashing in the sunlight as if to contradict his words, and she shivered. "Come on, the water feels great! Although it would feel better if you were to enjoy it with me," he coaxed.

Gathering her courage, she stepped back from the shore and unbuttoned her jeans, sliding them down her legs. She stood, feeling slightly exposed, unconsciously tugging the hem of her top down to cover the tops of her thighs. She locked onto his gaze, which was glinting with hope and anticipation. She drew her eyes back down to her legs. There was nothing wrong with them. She had always been slender, and she was more conscious of the fact that her breasts were small, no more than a handful really, but in proportion to her frame. She froze, unsure of whether to just step in with her shirt on or go ahead and pull it off.

Sensing her uncertainty, Corydon turned around and she heaved a sigh of relief, quickly seizing the opportunity to whip off her top and step into the pool. She dipped her hair back in the water, conscious of her makeup, not wanting to have raccoon eyes later from her mascara. "Thank you," she whispered, swimming toward him.

"I'm glad you came." The corners of his lips tilted up in a shy smile. "I don't get many visitors around here, and it's nice to have someone to talk to."

"I know what you mean," she replied, thinking about how since summer began, she really only had her Aunt Grace. Sure, she would see kids from school when she went into town, but none of them were what she would consider friends. Acquaintances, yes, but not friends, not like she'd had before she moved there.

"Did you do anything exciting these last few days?" he asked, lightly moving his hands along the surface of the water.

"Let's see…yesterday I almost fell off the trapeze during my performance with the traveling circus, and the day before that I qualified for the Olympic curling team."

He tilted his head back and laughed, his voice echoing off the trees. "You have been busy."

"Yes, I barely had time to make it here today. I had to squeeze you in between my debut with the American Ballet Company and my final flight lesson to get my pilot's license," she continued, staring at her nails as if being there with him was dull in comparison to her glamorous life. A moment later, a wave of water smacked into her face. He splashed her again, his laughter brimming at the indignant look on her face.

"Oh, you'll pay for that," she growled, splashing him in return with as much force as she could muster. Soon they were battling, throwing water back and forth as they both dissolved into giggles. She paused when she no longer heard his voice mingling with her own and looked around. He was nowhere to be seen.

"Corydon!" she called out, turning around and around, hoping to find him. "Cor! Where are you?" she yelled, her heart thundering as her panic grew. She was about to yell once more when a hand wrapped around her ankle and pulled her under. It was a brief yank, instantly released once she was submerged. She came up sputtering for air to see him now inches in front of her, smiling, but his eyes crinkled in concern.

She smacked his bare shoulder. "That wasn't funny, asshole."

"Perhaps not to you, but from here it was quite entertaining."

She huffed and crossed her arms, sticking out her bottom lip in a pout.

He plucked her protruding lip with his thumb. "No pouting. Just admit it—I got you."

She huffed again. "Fine, you got me." She rolled her eyes, reluctant to admit true defeat.

He grinned triumphantly before his smile fell and he arched his brow in a puzzled manner. "Why did you call me Cor?"

"Huh?"

"When you called for me the second time, you called me Cor."

She knew what he was talking about but found it hard to answer his question. "Um…it just slipped out?" Her voice betrayed her by rising at the end as if it were a question instead of an explanation. She bit her lower lip. "A nickname of sorts, I suppose." She worried he may hate it, but honestly it just had come out without her thinking about it.

"I like it." He smiled, relieving her fears and she smiled in return.

They swam for quite some time, talking, sharing childhood stories, although there were times when Corydon would hesitate or pause in the conversation as if he were editing his answers beforehand; most likely he was not including anything that would give him away as something other than human. His stories were filled with adventures and mischievousness caused by him and his brother. His only slipup was mentioning a castle, and of course she called him out on it, eager to see how he would explain it.

"I don't recall any castles in the U.S.," she mused.

"I didn't grow up around here."

"No shit, Sherlock," she taunted, but he didn't take the bait, his brow furrowing. It then dawned on her that he most likely wasn't used to some of her slang, but he didn't question it. Perhaps he could hear the sarcasm in her tone and took it as a signal that further explanation was needed.

"I lived in Europe for quite some time, where my dad bought an old castle. We lived in it while he was restoring it." He seemed pleased with himself for his quick explanation, so she let him have it and nodded as if that explained everything. She didn't point out that it was a contradiction to what he'd told her when they first met—that he had lived around there all his life. She wondered if that meant there was a way to enter Fae somewhere in these woods. If there were, it would explain how he could have lived around there his whole life but still lived in a castle.

He asked her about why she'd moved there, which led into questions about what happened to her parents. She was so caught up in their discussion that she didn't notice how long they had been in the water until her skin turned pruney. She watched him climb out of the water, drops cascading from his hair down his back to his waist. Her eyes widened as the drops continued down and then she looked away, blushing furiously. Well, I guess that answered her question—if Fae wore underwear, he certainly didn't have any on right then. After she heard the rustle of his clothing stop, she crept toward the shore, quietly hoping he wouldn't notice until she was dressed. She turned her back to him as she pulled on her jeans over her wet bikini bottom.

She was reaching for her top when she felt warm hands on her waist. She gasped, wrapping her arms around herself for cover.

He stepped around her, tugging her hands away. "Why do you cover yourself?" She didn't answer, uncertainty swimming in her eyes as he looked her up and down. She supposed being in her bikini top and jeans was better than just standing there in her bikini. "You're beautiful," he whispered, running his hands down her neck to her shoulders and arms. She closed her eyes, savoring the moment, basking in his compliment, but she still reached for her tank top the moment he released her. He sighed in resignation, allowing her to finish dressing.

They sat on the large boulder by the pond, snacking on berries and talking until she noticed the position of the sun. She had been gone a while. If she didn't return soon, Grace would worry.

"I have to go," she murmured reluctantly. He reached his hand toward her face and brushed back a few wet strands of hair, tucking them behind her ear.

"I know." He smiled sadly, as if he also did not want to see their time together end. "Will you come again?" Hope laced his words.

"When?" she asked.

"A week from today?"

She tried to hide her disappointment. Why would he want to wait an entire week to see her again? She had felt the connection with him growing stronger throughout the day. He was nothing like she thought he would be, and certainly not anything like how Aunt Grace had described a Fae to be. "Sure," she replied, the corners of her mouth tugging down.

"I'm sorry it can't be sooner, but I have to go out of town and won't be back until then. If I could, I would meet you here every day."

She smiled, her insecurities dissolving into hope. "A week from today, then." She stood and paused for a moment, unsure of how to end the conversation. He stood as well, pulling his boots up toward his knees.

He walked toward her and grabbed her hand, pulling her in toward him before he wrapped his arms around her in a hug. She sighed contentedly and placed her head on his shoulder, breathing him in. "I'll be thinking about you," he whispered in her ear before he released her.

"I'll count the days," she replied before gathering her

things and heading back to the path marked by flowers.

"One week, Ayanna. You better be here!" he called out, as if she would miss the date. She waved her fingers at him over her shoulder in reply.

She smiled and hummed as she walked back to her house, stopping along the way to gather berries so her story wouldn't be questioned. The whole time she thought about him, the secret she would keep.

Chapter 3

AYANNA SPENT THE next few weeks falling into a routine of sorts. She devoured all the books on Fae folklore that Grace owned, desperate to learn more about the mysterious boy she was infatuated with. She kept him her little secret, afraid if she told Grace the truth, her aunt would forbid her from seeing him again. Thankfully, Grace just seemed so grateful to see her happy for once that she was afraid to question it. So, they both remained in blissful ignorance. Once a week she would sneak away to meet him at the pond, which she now referred to as their spot. The same flowers remained wrapped around the trees with twine, never seeming to wilt or fade, always sweet smelling and vibrant as if freshly picked. Occasionally, she would also wake up to find one on her windowsill. She wasn't sure how he was able to get it to the second story, but she was sure magic had something to do with it.

When they met, they sometimes swam, and other times he brought books of beautiful poetry and read aloud to her like a scene straight out of a romance novel. They usually snacked on berries or she would pack a small picnic lunch, and they always talked. They talked about everything, from their favorite colors (his was blue, hers purple) to their secret hopes and dreams (he wanted to give up his family duties and escape the pressure his father was putting on him, and she wanted to go to college but wasn't sure what she wanted to study yet). He became her best friend, the person she told every secret to, except the big one—that she knew what he was. Most of what he said was truth, but she could still sense that at times he was censoring himself, careful of what he revealed or rewording things to fit her perception of him.

She looked forward to their meetings, and aside from the occasional playful touch or goodbye hug, he hadn't really made a move on her, seeming to enjoy her companionship above all else. Every time she saw him, he looked as if he carried the weight of the world upon his shoulders, but the more time they spent together, the lighter he became, quicker to laugh and play, and when he let his guard down, his joy was contagious. More than anything, she wished she could always make him happy, as happy as he made her feel. She was so grateful to have a friend other than Aunt Grace that the insecurities she'd felt during their second meeting quickly dissipated. She realized he truly enjoyed her company, and she could be herself. Of course, there were still times when she wondered what it would be like to have more, what it would feel like to run her hands over his chiseled abs, trail her fingers through his long hair, or taste his sweet lips, but she kept those thoughts to herself, unwilling to share them for fear that it would ruin what they were building.

During that time, she only saw her mysterious midnight stallion once. He studied her from the clearing but fled before she could sneak downstairs and outside. She would occasionally leave sugar cubes or apples out by the tall oak tree and they would disappear, but she could never be sure if he took them or it was some other animal. She would also hike to the pond on her own to swim, part of her hopeful that Corydon may show up on his own, but he never did. She even took Aunt Grace one day (praying Corydon would be nowhere in sight) since Grace had been asking where she was hiking off to and why she was wearing her swimsuit. Aunt Grace seemed suspicious about the flowers tied to the trees to mark the path, questioning her quite persistently about their origins. Ayanna lied, saying she'd found the flowers discarded on the forest floor on the other side of the clearing one of the days she was picking berries and thought them too beautiful to leave there, tying them to the trees as a way to mark the path. Grace didn't seem completely convinced but let the matter drop, and for that Ayanna was grateful.

Grace enjoyed their afternoon together, but wasn't a big fan of swimming. She was glad to see where Ayanna was spending her time, but still required her niece to take the hunting knife with her, just in case. Ayanna was grateful for the freedom, a respite from lying to Grace, and that Grace didn't seem too keen on returning for a swim any time soon.

She was so wrapped up in her blossoming relationship that she was disappointed when she discovered that summer vacation had passed the halfway point. Time was trickling away from her. She debated many times whether or not she should tell him that she knew what he was. The more they talked, the worse she felt about keeping it a secret, until one day she decided to just be honest. He seemed to care for her as much as she cared for him and never once had given her any hint that he was anything like

Aunt Grace had described Fae to be. He didn't want any-thing from her, never used her in any manner, and never even projected an air of superiority over her.

When she awoke on the morning of their next planned visit, she decided it was the day she would come clean. She only hoped it didn't change anything. She made a couple sandwiches and grabbed her backpack, a towel, the berry basket, and the hunting knife. She kissed Aunt Grace on the cheek and informed her that she was heading out for a swim and would be back later in the afternoon.

"Be safe!" Grace called out as she practically sprinted out the door. She could barely contain her excitement. Her nerves were butterflies fluttering in her stomach and chest, causing her pulse to race the closer she got to their spot. When she approached the clearing, he was there waiting for her, shirtless, sitting on the large flat boulder, beautiful face tilted up toward the sky. His hair glimmered in the sunlight, appearing as if he were a sea nymph basking in the sun. She studied him for a few minutes, noting the new, slightly dark circles under his eyes and the deep breaths that filled his smooth, porcelain chest. He inhaled, holding the breath in his lungs before releasing it in a heavy sigh, and her brow furrowed. She wondered what was weigh-ing him down. He never once glanced her way or even opened his eyes as she walked toward him. He continued his deep breathing, even when she slung her bag on the ground next to the rock and took the seat beside him. The only acknowledgement of her presence was the way his body leaned slightly toward hers, as if unable to resist her pull, until their shoulders touched. She sat there drinking him in for several silent moments until he spoke.

"I have something to tell you, and after I do, you may not want to see me again, but I can no longer keep it from you." He sighed, cracking his eyes open to study her reaction.

Her heart stopped and she drew in a sharp breath before releasing her reply. "I have something to tell you too."

His eyebrow quirked in response, and he sat there for a few moments, gauging whether she wanted to go first or not. Part of her did want to tell him first, but she needed to know what he was confessing. There was no way she wanted to tell him about her Sight if he was about to break her heart. The realization that the only way he could break her heart was if she had already given it to him struck a chord within her. She licked her lips, her mouth seeming dry. "You first," she whispered.

"I need to do something first," he whispered in return, his body turning to face her. He placed his hands on her shoulders, turning her so she faced him head on. She watched as his pupils dilated, the violet swirling with a deep plum. He licked his lips as his gaze landed on her mouth, her breath coming in short spurts as she watched his chest rise and fall just as quickly as her own. He slid his hands across her shoulders, up her neck, cupping her face. He traced his thumb across her bottom lip. Her heart stopped, waiting for his next move to start beating again.

He leaned in, his eyes closing the closer he came as her own eyelids fluttered shut in anticipation. His hands slid to the back of her head and neck, leaving lightning in their wake. He pressed his lips against hers tentatively, rubbing them back and forth. She gasped at the sensation, the electricity running under her skin, and he seized the opportunity to deepen the kiss, his mouth now devouring hers. Their tongues met in a smooth motion that soon became a frantic dance. Her hands immediately sought those luscious locks, feeling their silkiness between her fingers before finding the back of his head to press him closer. Without releasing her hold, she attempted to pull his body toward her, but he remained firmly in place so she went to him, pressing her body against his, climbing over his legs until she knelt between them, only releasing her firm grip when his mouth left her lips to trail down her neck. She panted as his hands moved down her back, pressing her into his chest. She could feel the heat radiating off his skin and sank into him. His lips moved back up her neck, seeking her mouth again, and she sighed happily when they found it. He kissed her so deeply that she felt it in her bones. He seared himself onto her soul, and she knew she would never be the same.

When he pulled back, her lips followed his movement, aching to continue the connection, but he drew her body back as well. Her eyes felt heavy with desire as she reluctantly opened them. He smoothed her hair back from her face and leaned forward to rest his forehead against her own. "Wow," he whispered breathlessly.

"You can say that again," she replied

"I didn't know it could be like that."

She smiled. "If you haven't kissed anyone before, you certainly have me fooled, because that was some skill, buddy."

He blushed slightly. "It's not that…I mean, I've kissed girls before…" He sighed. "Just not human ones."

Her eyes widened. Even though she already knew what he was, it was a shock to hear him admit it aloud. "Cor… I…"

He put his fingers on her lips to silence her. "I need to tell you something, and if you no longer wish to see me after I tell you, I will be heartbroken, but I will understand."

His eyes were heavy with sadness, and she realized how afraid he was that she would reject him once she knew the truth. It was sweet to see him as vulnerable as she felt around him. She opened her mouth to reassure him, but his fingers pressed onto her lips, warning her to let him finish.

"I'm not like you," he stated, and she wanted to shout at him that he was like her in every way that mattered. "I'm not human." She hated how insecure his usually cocky voice sounded, as if this one little difference was all that mattered and would be the death of their relationship.

She yanked his fingers from her lips and squeezed them in her hand. "I know."

This time it was his turn to be shocked. He scooted back from her, his eyes widening and then narrowing into slits within the span of a heartbeat. "You know?" His voice waivered. "You *know*?!"

She didn't understand where his outburst was coming from. She had been hoping her confession would reassure him that she wasn't going anywhere, and it certainly had never occurred to her that it would enrage him. He threw her hand down and pushed himself off the rock, beginning to pace in front of her, talking to himself and pulling his hands through his hair. She only caught bits and pieces of his tirade.

"Of course she knows, you fool…must be Rodric… I'm a fucking idiot…caring for a human girl…some sort of sick joke…" Finally, he stopped and spun toward her. His gaze was almost predatory as he approached, and she felt like a field mouse being hunted, her own flight instinct rising to the surface. She had never seen him like this, and it scared her. She worried she'd made a mistake in telling him the truth, but it was too late to back out now. She scooted back as far as she could on the rock, attempting to put space between them. His arms came down on either side of her, caging her in, and his fingers wrapped around her wrists, pinning her hands to the boulder in a vice-like grip, his eyes a storm of violet lightning.

"What do you know?" he growled, his voice full of accusation, but she had no clue what he was accusing her of.

She swallowed hard, her pulse ratcheting against her wrists. "I know you're not human," she stated, wincing as his grip tightened on her wrists.

"Then what am I, *Ayanna*?" His voice dripped with venom, his fingers digging into her skin so hard she was afraid he might leave bruises behind.

She flinched from the pain. "Cor, you're hurting me," she pleaded, her eyes watering against the pain in her wrists and in her heart. *Who is this monster?*

It was as if her words broke the spell that had taken over him. He instantly dropped his hands, drawing back sharply, his eyes filling with disbelief and apology. "I…shit…I'm sorry, Ayanna." Several tears spilled over her cheeks and he reached to brush them away, but she recoiled. He knelt in the grass in front of her, giving her some space, his eyes full of regret. "And here I thought it was my confession that would scare you away," he said quietly, attempting to jest, but the seriousness of his reaction was not lost on either of them. "I didn't mean to hurt you."

"I…" She trailed off, unsure of what to say in response. She worked to quickly rebuild all the internal walls he had knocked down with his kiss.

He took a deep breath, his teeth clenched. "I need to know what it is you know and how. I didn't mean to put my hands on you in that way, but I need you to be honest with me and tell me the truth before I lose it again." He took another deep breath, his body still drawn tight.

"I will, Cor, but I need you to calm down. I can't talk

to you while you're like this. It scares me," she confessed, her voice small and shaky. While he looked genuine and regretful, it did not excuse his behavior. He walked away for a few moments, seeming to rein his anger before returning to kneel back in front of her. She rubbed her left wrist to soothe the sore skin and when she met his eyes again, they were brimming.

"I never meant to hurt you. I've just been so lonely and then I found you and you were like a balm to all my wounds. You brought me such happiness, but I keep thinking once you know the truth about me, you will leave and take all my sunshine with you."

"But I already know. I knew from the moment I saw you," she replied.

"Knew what exactly, and how?" he probed, his voice tinged with a growl.

"I knew you are Fae." She met his eyes defiantly, using her desire to prove him wrong about her to fuel her fire.

His eyes widened, staring as if she were the most fascinating thing he had ever seen. His hand reached for her face again, and this time she did not move away. His anger was gone, and he was back to looking like the young man she had started falling for. He brushed away the trails of her tears from her cheeks and she closed her eyes, briefly relishing his touch. "How?" he inquired, dropping his hand from her face and reaching to take her left hand instead.

"That's what I wanted to tell you earlier—I have the gift of Sight. I can see you." She reached up with her right hand and tapped the pointed tip of his ear. "Your ears were the first thing that gave you away."

"I don't look like a normal human boy to you?" His brow drew down in frustration.

"Were you trying to look like a normal human boy?" she wondered, smiling at the thought of him trying to impress her with his glamour.

"Of course! And a good-looking one at that." He tilted his head down, staring at their hands. "I thought that was what you liked about me," he mumbled.

She raised her free hand and tilted his chin up until he met her gaze, uncertainty swimming in his eyes. "I liked you because you were you, no one else, and you've always looked like you to me—long white-silver hair, pointed ears, violet eyes, sharp teeth, chiseled jaw and cheekbones, slightly pointed nose and chin." With her finger, she traced each of his features she'd been able to see since the beginning. Then she stopped, her own brow furrowing. "Why? What did you want me to see?"

His eyes held awe as he stared at her. He grabbed the finger on his chin and brought it to his lips, kissing it. "Doesn't matter." He laughed jubilantly, pressing kisses to the palm of her hand. "So, you're telling me I've looked like this the whole time, you've known I am Fae the entire time, and yet you kept coming back?"

She smiled proudly, her chin lifting in triumph. "Yep." She popped the P sound at the end of the word to accentuate her point.

His smile lit up his entire face. "You don't know how happy this makes me. I was so worried you'd never want to see me again when I told you, and here you knew all along. So, what do you know about Fae, besides the fact that you can see what we truly are?"

She gave him an overview of what she had learned from all the books she had read in the last few weeks—that there were many different kinds of Fae and each kind had special, magical abilities that varied even within the same kind of Fae. She knew each type was marked by their eye color, but that didn't mean they were completely the same, and they aged slower than humans but were not immortal, causing her to briefly wonder how old he was. She'd read that there were two courts, the Seelie and Unseelie, which were split based on their beliefs about how to use their powers and the value of human life. She could have used that one as an opportunity to see which side he was on, but after his display of anger, she was hesitant to learn the truth and preferred to live in denial a little while longer. While she talked, he corrected some of her misconceptions (Seelie and Unseelie did differ in their beliefs about humans, but they were born into their court, not able to choose a side) and laughed at others, declaring them completely inaccurate.

The longer they talked, the more she began to let her walls crumble again. At some point, she brought out the lunch she had packed for them, feasting on peanut butter and jelly sandwiches, fruit roll-ups, crackers, and juice boxes. He savored her food as he always did, eager to try new things, especially ones that were foreign to him, like the fruit roll-ups. As time crept by, his outburst seemed more and more foreign and out of character. It didn't mean she would forget it, but at the same time, she refused to let it define her feelings for him. *He did release me once I said something*, she rationalized.

After they ate, they lay down on the grass under the shade of a copse of trees and talked some more. She rested her head in the crook of his arm, using his shoulder as a pillow while he played with her hair. He answered some of her questions, but not all of them, and she avoided the heavy topics, deciding they had been through enough for one day. There was always the next time. His voice was like a soothing lullaby as he talked about his family. His mother had died giving birth to him and his father was a powerful man, one to be feared and respected at the same time, but he was most fond of talking about his brother. He recounted many stories about their childhood hijinks. It was during one such story that Ayanna drifted off to sleep.

"Ayanna…darling, wake up," he whispered in her ear. She felt him shift underneath her. Her cheek was pressed to his warm chest, her arm thrown across his body, his leg tucked under hers. She blinked her eyes open slowly, reluctant to leave his warmth but embarrassed to have practically sprawled herself across him in her sleep. The first thing she noticed was how low the sun had sunk into the sky. It jolted her into action and she jumped up, gathering her things and shoving them into her backpack.

"I have to go. Aunt Grace will worry," she apologized.

Corydon rose and walked over, pulling her into his arms. He pressed a chaste kiss on her lips, but with enough pressure that she knew he was restraining himself. He smoothed her hair back, which she was sure had become quite a mess since she had napped.

"I'm sorry I fell asleep," she told him.

"I'm not."

"But I wasted our time together."

"You were beautiful while you slept, and I enjoyed every second of holding you in my arms." His sweet words eased her embarrassment.

"Will you be here next week?" She bit her bottom lip, unsure of where they now stood since they had crossed the line from friendship into something more.

"I wouldn't miss it for the world." He hugged her tightly and kissed her neck. She sighed before she released him. She grabbed his hand and squeezed it, holding on to him until the very last second while she slung her backpack over her other arm and picked up her basket.

"I'll see you then." She squeezed before releasing him and walking away. She ran toward the woods and the path that would lead her home, turning back to wave goodbye before she fled from his view. He was still standing there watching her with an intense expression that had her wishing she could read his mind. *Read his mind! Shoot! I forgot to ask him about his magical abilities.* She wondered what his power could be all the way home.

Grace was understandably worried when she returned later than usual, but she just explained how she had fallen asleep while she lay out after a swim, which wasn't a complete lie.

Grace hugged her and smoothed her hair down, murmuring, "I just worry about you."

"I know, Aunt Grace. I'll try not to let it happen again."

Grace accepted her promise and turned her attention back to cooking dinner: spaghetti with homemade tomato sauce and fresh basil, one of her favorite meals. They watched TV that evening, and Corydon's episode of anger was quickly forgotten as she recalled their conversations about Fae and the kisses they'd exchanged.

Later, when she was ready for bed, she glanced out the window, searching for the horse, but when he was a no-show, she blew a kiss to the moon, hoping it would somehow make its way to Corydon.

CHAPTER 4

THE NEXT WEEK she kept herself busy by helping Aunt Grace with her herbal remedies, a mixture of salves, poultices, and herbal blends. Some of the plants she didn't recognize. They were foreign and beautiful like the violet flowers Corydon left for her. She held up a beautiful but odd-looking flower. Its petals were the colors of a warm sunset, the centers a darker red, blending out into a pale pink like the darkening night sky. She touched the pointed tip of one of the petals and it pricked the pad of her finger like a thorn, stinging and drawing blood. "Ouch," she hissed, bringing her finger to her mouth.

"Careful with that one," Aunt Grace warned over her shoulder, a little too late. When Ayanna didn't immediately reply, she turned. "Did it get you?" Ayanna nodded in reply. Grace gently tugged Ayanna's finger from her mouth and pulled her to the sink to wash out the wound, wrapping a piece of cloth around it until the bleeding stopped. It didn't take very long as the cut was only a shallow prick.

"What kind of flower is that? I've never seen anything like it before."

"It's not from around here," Grace replied curtly, returning to her position at the kitchen island.

Ayanna was a little taken aback by Grace's short answer; she had never been so abrupt with her before. She could sense that Grace didn't want her to press the subject further, but her curiosity was too great. "Where is it from then?"

Grace didn't respond, continuing to grind some herbs with her mortar and pestle.

"Aunt Grace?" Ayanna pressed again.

Grace sighed. "You're not going to let this go, are you?"

She smirked in reply, shaking her head.

"It's from Fae." Grace looked down at the herbs on the island, her eyes focusing on the flower that had just pricked Ayanna and lingering on a couple other foreign plants.

Ayanna gasped. "Fae? What do you mean from Fae?" She picked up the flower again to study it. No wonder it reminded her of the flowers from Corydon.

"I mean it comes from the Fae realm."

"But…but…how do you have it?" She felt the delicately soft petals, taking care not to touch the sharp tips.

Grace sat down at the table and Ayanna followed. "I have a contact," was all she said.

"A *Fae* contact?" Ayanna clarified.

"Yes."

"But I thought…you said…they were dangerous. You said the Fae shouldn't know who we are and that we see who they are." Ayanna dropped the flower, an ache of betrayal radiating from her heart. She hated to be deceived.

"I was trying to protect you, my dear—I still am. Most Fae are dangerous. Most of them seek to use and manipulate humans for their own purposes, and surely you've read about this in those books I've seen you devouring." Grace's eyes flicked toward Ayanna, her gaze almost accusatory, as if she knew they both had been keeping secrets.

Ayanna swallowed and nodded, a slight trembling starting in her hands. She pressed them against the table to hold them still.

"You are better off if you have nothing to do with them. I was making generalizations based on the majority of the population." She reached across the table for Ayanna's hand and held it. Ayanna sucked in a breath, hoping Grace couldn't feel her shaking. Grace continued, "Just like most of humanity is good and yet there are still some evil people, the opposite is true with the Fae—while most of them are evil, there are still some who are good. I have been fortunate enough to meet one of the good ones, an Unseelie, if you can even imagine it." She smiled, as if the very idea were hard to believe, and based on what Ayanna had read, it was. For the most part, the Unseelie Fae were described as evil beings that fed off human torment and suffering. Ayanna held her breath, waiting for Grace to continue.

"I met Enora about a year after I moved here, and over time, she has become a close friend. She lives a ways out in the woods, in Fae land. I stumbled across her while I was picking herbs one day. Of course, at first I did not let her know I knew what she was, and we talked. She told me she was also a healer, so we talked about natural cures and remedies, offered to share knowledge with each other. After that, we met several more times and built a friendship. It was hard to remember what she truly was at times, because she never acted the way my mother and the books had led me to believe she would."

Grace's story hit closer to home than she could have possibly realized. It was as if she was describing Ayanna's encounters with Corydon, minus the kissing.

"So, I kept an open mind and we grew closer. She told me what she could about her kind and would bring me plants from her lands, sharing their medicinal properties, and I shared my knowledge of our plants with her as well. I came to learn that as a healer, she was considered somewhat of a black sheep by the Unseelie Fae. They needed her, yet they despised her because her ability was contrary to the harm they caused. Both of us feeling like outsiders created a deep bond of friendship." Her eyes bore into Ayanna's. "I still see her from time to time. She always comes to the house discreetly so our meetings are not noticed by humans or Fae. She's promised to keep my secrets, just as I keep hers. The last time she came was shortly after your arrival. You were so lost in your grief that I doubt you remember. I asked that we postpone any future visits until you'd had enough time to heal, until I could figure out if you would inherit the Sight and had the opportunity to explain things to you. She would prefer to keep to the shadows for now. She's hesitant to trust any more humans, even if you are my family. Our friendship is a dangerous thing to have, and she knows how much I want to keep you safe.

"Now, I don't want to you to feel like I lied to you about the Fae. I told you how most of them are. I don't want you to hear this story and think they are all like Enora, because they certainly are not. Enora is a rarity, my dear. You *must* keep you guard up, especially while you are out there hiking around those woods. I'm glad you took me to the pond, to see where you've been wandering off to." A blush crept across Ayanna's cheeks, but Grace continued. "However, sometimes Fae, or creatures from their land, wander into the woods. I haven't been to where they cross over, but I know it's out there, and not as far away as I would like. I've seen things"—she shuddered—"things I would prefer you never lay eyes on, darling, so be careful." With that last warning, Grace stood, leaving the kitchen where Ayanna still sat contemplating all that had been revealed.

When the day arrived for her to meet Corydon, she tried to contain her excitement around her aunt, but she was sure she was doing a poor job of it. When she could finally make her escape, she practically ran toward their spot in the woods, not even bothering to collect any berries this time. When she reached the clearing, she paused to smooth her appearance and calm her racing heart before she stepped out of the shadows of the trees.

Her eyes immediately sought his form, which was usually waiting for her on the large boulder, but this time the spot remained empty. "Corydon?" she called out, searching the area for signs of him, but she found none. Their spot was empty. She swallowed hard, holding back the multitude of emotions battling inside her chest. *Maybe he's running late*, she thought, trying to convince herself. Eventually she decided instead of sitting and pining for him, she would go for a swim.

She swam for quite some time, but he still didn't show up. Waiting as long as she could with no appearance or sign from him, she heaved a sigh as she gathered her things and prepared to leave. She pulled her pink scrunchie from her hair and left it on the boulder—a token, so if he happened to show up later, he would see that he missed her.

As she stepped away from their spot, she glanced one last time toward the pond with a final drop of hope dissolving within her, leaving her feeling as empty as the clearing around the pond.

Grace noticed the shift in her mood when she came home, but Ayanna tried to play it off as a mild case of heat exhaustion. The disappointment lingered like stones in her belly, but she claimed she was just tired. She retreated to her room after dinner, changed into her pajamas—a blue tank top with blue and green plaid shorts—and just lay on her bed, staring at the ceiling, thinking, running over and over the possibilities. She wished she could turn her brain off, could stop thinking about it, but nothing she could hold her attention, not the TV, not her books, nothing. She sighed and got up to get a drink of water, hoping it might help calm her.

As she was filling up her glass, she glanced out the window above the sink. She drew in a sharp breath, almost dropping her glass. Framed in the moonlight and closer to the house than ever before was her midnight stallion. She took a drink before rushing over to throw on her shoes and race out the door. She ran toward him, only slowing when she got close enough that moving too fast might spook him.

"Hey there, boy. I've missed you," she whispered on the night breeze.

He whinnied softly and strutted toward her, so she stopped and held her hand out. When he reached her, he nuzzled into her palm, lightly nipping at it with his lips. She snickered before running her hand against the smooth fur along his face and neck. He stepped closer, bringing his head to her neck, where he breathed in deeply. It was almost as if he craved her affection and wanted to hug her in return.

They stood like that for several minutes before she stepped back, gazing into his violet eyes. "It's been a while. Where have you been?" She stroked his muzzle as she spoke. "Never mind, it doesn't matter. I'm just glad you're here now. I needed this after today. I can't believe he didn't show up." She sighed then continued to tell the black stallion all about her dismay and fears with Corydon standing her up.

He was a very attentive listener; of course it probably helped that he couldn't talk back. After she finished, he nickered at her before turning and trotting toward the tall oak tree.

"Wait! Don't leave me yet," she called out, but he kept going until he disappeared into the thick of the woods. Yet another boy had disappeared on her that day. She stood there for several minutes, hoping he would return, but he didn't. She sighed and turned, walking back to the house, but then an achingly familiar voice called her name.

"Ayanna?"

She froze in her tracks, unsure of whether to blow him off like he had done to her that afternoon or to turn back and hear him out. Her pride said to give him a taste of his own medicine, but her heart begged her to stay. She was so wrapped up in emotions, she didn't even bother to ask what he was doing there so late at night, how long he had been standing there, or if he had seen the stallion as he came in. In the end, her heart won, and she turned around. "What do you want, Corydon?" Her voice was ripe with irritation. Just because she'd decided to stay didn't mean she had to take it easy on him.

"Can we talk?" he pleaded. He was standing near the edge of the clearing a few yards to the right of the oak tree, and his voice bled such trepidation and vulnerability as he stepped forward into the clearing. His pale hair was pulled back into a ponytail, making his features appear sharper in the moonlight. The dark sky did nothing to conceal the shadows under his eyes. He looked as if the weight of the world was sitting upon his shoulders again, and she hated that look. She hated that she saw it on him more and more frequently. She wanted to take some of his stress away, but he was so tight-lipped about everything that she was clueless as to what was the cause.

"We can, if you'll be honest with me," she replied with a bite in her tone.

He sighed heavily while he jogged toward her. "I have been honest with you."

She held up her hand to halt his steps and his words. "Not completely, and don't even try to deny it. You're hiding things from me. I know you are, and I thought I was okay with it, but when you didn't show up today, it hurt me. I was worried, left with no way to know if you were all right, and more than that, I felt like I wasn't enough for you, Corydon." She used his full name to stress the importance of her words.

He moved her hand out of the way, gently grasping it within his own and invading her space. His eyes were soft and full of tenderness, but his face was hard and serious. "You are *more* than enough, Ayanna. Never feel like you are not." His other hand laced through her hair, cupping the back of her neck. He used both to pull her inches forward until their lips met and he pressed a hard kiss against her mouth. "Trust me, I have never met someone like you.

I'm so sorry I didn't show up today. I had obligations for my father that I couldn't avoid. He kept an eagle eye on me today, as if he knew I have been sneaking away." He ran his hand down her neck then repeated the motion at the top of her head, threading his fingers through her hair. She swore if she were a kitten, she would've been purring. He pulled her against his chest, wrapping his arms around her and placing a kiss against her hair. "I missed you," he whispered.

She practically melted into him, wrapping her arms around him and squeezing him in return. She pulled back a few moments later to gaze into his eyes. "I missed you too, but I still want some questions answered."

He swallowed. "I understand, and I will do my best, but there are some answers you are better off not knowing. Some things I will only reveal if it is necessary. This is for your own protection, and when it comes to keeping you safe, I will not budge."

She could tell her response could make or break the fragile relationship they were building, and she wasn't ready to see it break. "I'm not happy about it, but I under-stand."

"Let's go sit, so we can talk."

She glanced toward the porch, knowing it would be the most comfortable spot, but she couldn't risk Aunt Grace discovering them, so she tugged him by his hand over toward the tall oak tree. They sat under it in the soft grass, and she leaned back against its trunk. He sat next to her, tightening his grip on her hand any time she moved to release it, almost as if he needed her touch to remind him she was real, and she felt the same way. It was hard to believe this was real.

"So, you've got questions," he prompted, tugging her

from her thoughts.

She gathered her courage to ask him the things she'd been scared to ask when she first revealed that she knew the truth.

"How old are you?"

"In Fae years or human years?" He smiled.

"Is there a difference?"

He laid her hand on top of his lap, palm up, and traced her life line with his fingers.

"Time is a fickle thing, especially when you have a longer perspective than others, or when it comes to crossing the realms. It moves more quickly here in the human realm, which effects our age in terms of human years, although Fae generally tend to live centuries."

Even though she already knew Fae lived longer lives from her own research and reading, her heart ached at the thought that her lifetime would be only a small blip in his timeline.

He continued, oblivious to the inner turmoil he'd stirred in her. "So, while it is a week for you between the times we meet, for me it's only almost two days. The plus side is that when I spend hours with you, I'm only sneaking away for a few minutes or hours, depending on how long we spend together." His eyes studied every miniscule movement of her expression, waiting for her reaction.

"When you couple our time differences with longer life spans, Fae age a lot more slowly. A few years after a Fae reaches maturity, the aging process is almost frozen until they hit their first century. So, while I appear to be in my early twenties in human years, I'm actually sixty-three in Fae years."

"Sixty-three?! Holy shit. You're sixty-three? Wait, how

old does that make you in human years?" She shoved away from him, rather appalled with herself for having feelings for someone so much older. "Do I even want to know what that is in human years?"

He shook his head. "Not if your current reaction is any indication." He reached for her, and when she didn't respond, he scooted closer, his shoulder bumping her own. "Please remember that our life span is in centuries, so while sixty-three seems like an old age to you, it's relatively young for a Fae. I'm still a ways away from the first quarter of my life."

She liked the way his logic worked, because when he worded it that way, he was around her age—still a ways away from the first quarter of life. "Okay, I see what you're saying." She relaxed against his shoulder but chewed on her lower lip, worried she really wouldn't like the answers to her other questions.

"I'm afraid to answer any more questions," he whispered, as if reading her mind. She swung her head toward him, her gaze sharp and slightly accusatory. He sighed. "I will answer them, I'm just afraid. I'm afraid you won't like my answers, or they will scare you away. I'm scared after this conversation you will convince yourself you're better off without me, and truthfully, you probably are, but the selfish part of me hopes you will still want to see me once you know who I really am."

Her heart cracked with his confession. She hadn't considered that he would be nervous to reveal the information, but it made sense. "How about I promise to stay and hear everything you have to say? Will that make things easier?"

He nodded but then hung his head, staring at the ground. She placed a finger under his chin and tilted his head up until their eyes met. She stared into his purple eyes and could almost read every emotion he was experiencing within their swirling depths. "I cannot promise that your answers won't change things. I wish I could, but it would be a lie. The truth is, I'm just as terrified of the answers you're about to give me, but I know who you are in here." She placed her hand over his heart. "And I will keep that in mind when you share with me what I've been avoiding discovering, because the truth is, I really don't want your answers to change the way I feel about you."

His heart picked up speed underneath her palm. "And how do you feel about me?"

She licked her lips. She needed to be honest with him if he was being honest with her. "I care about you…a lot. You've become my best friend, and I look forward to the days we spend together." She blinked and looked at her hand on his chest, unable to maintain eye contact while she made her confession. "I think…" She took a deep breath, gathering her courage. "I think…I'm beginning to fall for you."

This time it was his fingers that tilted her chin as he captured her lips in a passionate kiss, as if he were trying to convey his emotions through his actions and not his words. When he pulled back, he breathed a thank you against her cheek and kissed her there. He did not say any more and part of her was a little dismayed not to hear how he felt, but she understood. He was arming himself, putting up his walls in case she rejected him. The power was completely in her hands.

She took a deep breath and ran her hand along his jaw, savoring the touch in case it was the last, in case what he told her changed everything she thought or felt about him. She took a few moments to gather her courage and ask the question she most feared to hear his answer to. "Are you Seelie or Unseelie?" Her heart pounded, and it felt as if a charm of hummingbirds were fluttering around in her stomach.

He visibly flinched, and she knew what his answer was without him saying a thing. "You should know that being Unseelie or Seelie does not make a person who they are. It may define our nature, but does not determine how we will act." He was stalling, prepping her for what he was about to confirm. He drew in a deep breath then exhaled and said, "I am Unseelie."

The truth washed over her like a bucket of ice water. The hummingbirds morphed into sparrows as she choked down her flight instinct. Everything she knew about Unseelie Fae bounced around in her brain while he sat silent and still as if he didn't want to spook her into running.

Finally, he put his hand on her knee and she startled. He retracted it, placing it over his own heart, as if her reaction had physically wounded him. "You know who I truly am, Ayanna. You're one of the few people who know the real me, and me being Unseelie does not change the man you were falling for. I've been Unseelie all along." His eyes begged her to be open-minded.

She considered his words. As much as the thought of him being Unseelie scared her, she would've been lying to herself if she hadn't considered it before. She had, she just hadn't wanted to admit it to herself, but he was right—it didn't change who he was. He was still the same guy he had been the week before.

"You're right," she replied, still processing the truth.

"What else?" He sighed heavily.

"What type of Fae are you? What can you do?" This was the other question that had her losing sleep at night.

"I can't tell you that...yet."

"Why not?" Frustration simmered under her skin, making her snap.

"It's…complicated. I can tell you that I can't manipulate your emotions or what you see, and I don't feed off your energy or feelings."

It put a little bit of her fears to rest; at least he wasn't using her or toying with her emotions, but she still wondered why he was hesitant to reveal this piece of the truth. "Will you eventually tell me?" she asked.

"Yes, when I know you won't leave." He stared directly into her eyes so she could read the truth there.

"What difference does it make?" She shrugged.

"All the difference in the world." His words were cryptic and vague, which frustrated her to no end, but she was glad for the information he had revealed.

"Okay, I think I'm done for the night." She pushed herself up and away from him, brushing off her shorts as she rose.

"That's it? That's all the questions you have?" He followed her, rising from the ground as well.

"Those are the important ones. Why? Is there something else you feel you need to tell me?"

He hesitated; she could read it in the way he paused and wouldn't quite meet her eyes. There was more, quite a bit more he was afraid to tell her. She held her breath, waiting for him to confess, but instead he shook his head. Disappointment sat heavy on her chest. She'd thought he was going to be completely honest with her. She would have to keep her guard up around him if he was still keeping secrets. There was one possibility she hadn't considered before, but now it struck her like an arrow to her heart.

"Is there someone else? A girlfriend or a fiancée or

something like that you're not telling me about?"

His eyes widened, wounded. "No! How could you think that of me?"

"Well, geez, I don't know, *Cor*, maybe it has to do with the fact that you're still not being completely honest with me. How am I to know what it is you're still hiding?" She seethed, her blood simmering under her skin.

He paled slightly, succeeding in fueling her panic. "It's nothing like that. It's just…you're safer not knowing." She wished the words reassured her as he had intended, but they did not. He reached for her as if to embrace her but she crossed her arms against her chest, so he let his arms fall limply to his sides.

"All right, well, thanks for telling me what you could. Good night." She turned for the house.

"Ayanna?" His voice cracked with emotion and she paused then turned back, unable to resist. "Will I see you next week?" He held his breath, waiting for her reply.

"I'm not sure." She chewed on her bottom lip, her fingers fidgeting with the hem of her shirt. "I…I need a little time to process all this."

His face fell. "I understand, but please know that I will be there waiting, next week and the week after that and the week after that, in case you decide you want to see me again." With each word, his face hardened a little in determination.

She started walking again, eager to get away from him while at the same time a little depressed to leave his side. It was a confusing mixture of feelings.

"Wait!" he called out and she paused again, turning back toward him.

He pulled at something behind his head, and when he

got it, his hair fell in silvery shimmering sheets, looking every bit like the mystical being he was. He lifted his hand out in front of him, her pink scrunchie dangling from his fingers. "You left this." She smiled, but it didn't reach her eyes. She was glad he'd found it and knew she had shown up when he had not.

The minute he held it out, she knew she couldn't take it again. It would only remind her of him and of this exact moment. "Keep it," she replied. It would give him something to remember her by. Her throat felt thick at the thought of never seeing him again, making it hard to swallow. Before she could second-guess her actions, she sprinted to the house and climbed the porch steps. She snuck inside and turned back once more before closing the door. He was still standing in the same spot, his body hunched over, shoulders heavy with defeat. He rubbed his fingers over and over her scrunchie before bringing it to his lips and finally tucking it safely, almost reverently, into his pocket.

She lay awake in bed for hours that night, waiting for sleep to take her, replaying their conversation and the newly acquired information over and over in her head. It was a constant loop that part of her wanted to shut off so she could forget it all, while the other part craved the replay, hoping it would work itself out in her head so she could reach a decision about whether to see him again, but the only thing that eventually came to her was sleep.

CHAPTER 5

THE NEXT WEEK crept by slowly. Every day she ran through the pros and cons of seeing Corydon again but was still unable to decide. She debated asking Grace for advice, but she knew her aunt would freak out if she discovered she was seeing a Fae, especially an Unseelie. She mentally went through their last conversation over and over again, attempting to reconcile the boy she had been falling for with the new information she had learned. She asked Grace as much as she could about Unseelie Fae and her friend Enora without drawing suspicion. The more Grace talked about Enora, the more Ayanna felt like perhaps Corydon was also an exception to the rule. While his anger-filled outburst still lingered in the back of her mind, it was easy to dismiss it as him battling his Unseelie nature.

The morning of their next date dawned, and she still had not reached a decision. It was a battle between her head and her heart, but she didn't know which one she really wanted to win. When she got dressed, she unconsciously slid her bikini on under her jeans and a well-worn David Bowie tank top. It wasn't until she was completely dressed that she glanced into the mirror and realized what she had done. She smiled tightly, accepting that her heart had won the battle and, despite her trepidation, she would soon see Corydon again. She skipped down the steps, feeling lighter now that her decision had been made.

While they ate breakfast, Grace observed her shift in mood and appearance. "Going for a swim today?" she asked with a curious smile.

"That's the plan," Ayanna replied, lifting the spoon to her mouth and taking a huge bite of granola with fresh berries.

"Have you looked outside recently?" Grace quirked her eyebrow above her steaming mug of tea, watching as the spoon Ayanna had raised with another bite froze a few inches from her lips. She slowly chewed what was left in her mouth and shook her head in reply.

"I'll think you'll need to take a rain check," Grace explained, pointing toward the kitchen window.

Ayanna dropped her spoon into her bowl and sprinted from the table to the kitchen window. The sky was completely overcast with charcoal grey clouds. "No, no, no," she murmured as she rushed to the front door, throwing it wide open. How had she not noticed it had rained last night? The evidence was everywhere—the wet damp grass, the gravel soaked with puddles, and the sky that looked like it wasn't done. She sighed and hung her head, her shoulders slumping forward. What would she do now? If she didn't show up, he might think she'd decided to never see him again.

Grace came over and wrapped an arm around her. "Cheer up, buttercup. You can go swimming another day.

Maybe tomorrow?"

How Ayanna wished it were merely an issue of waiting another day to swim, but she couldn't tell Grace, so she let her believe that was the root of her despondency. They stood there for several minutes, staring out at the dark clouds as a crack of thunder echoed through the air, Grace's arm draped around her niece. Ayanna leaned her head against Grace's shoulder, soaking in the much-needed comfort.

"How about we run into town today, maybe pick up some books from the library and rent a couple movies? We could have a little movie marathon."

"That sounds like a great idea." Ayanna sighed. Grace gave her a squeeze and released her, gathering her things so they could head to town.

The whole time they rode in Grace's beat-up, blue, 1973 Chevy truck, Ayanna worried about what the approaching storms meant. Was it a sign that she shouldn't meet with Corydon after all? Would he still show up in the rain? She bet he would, unless something kept him away like the last time, although he'd seemed pretty determined to fight for her. Would he give up when she didn't show up that day? She nervously chewed her bottom lip as all the doubts and questions swirled through her head.

"It will be okay, sweetheart. It's just a little rain," Grace soothed. Ayanna was so lost in her thoughts that she hadn't realized it had started raining. It was only a light drizzle, but her heart picked up speed and her breaths came in shorter, panic stirring under her skin. It had been raining that night when her parents left for a dinner party at their friends' house and never returned home. In that moment, it felt like she was right back there—opening the door in the rain to let the two police officers inside, hearing them apologize, seeing the look in their eyes that spoke of death and regret at bearing the responsibility to break the news to her. Their voices were etched into her memory as random strands of conversation heard over the pounding of her heart.

"...*car careened off the wet pavement...struck a tree head on...*"

"...*deaths were instant...didn't suffer...*"

"...*anyone we can call?*"

She'd sat there on the couch, numbly listening over the ringing roar inside her ears. Somehow through the icy shock, she had been able to mumble that Aunt Grace's phone number was listed on the fridge. The officers had stayed with her, sitting in awkward silence until Grace showed up at the door. The minute she'd lain her eyes on Grace, the tears had started, because she finally felt safe enough to break down. She'd sobbed as Grace cradled her in her arms, rocking her, soothing her, their tears mingling into each other's. She hadn't even heard the officers leave, feeling so lost, clinging to Aunt Grace as her lifeline.

Her heart ached and her chest burned. She felt like she couldn't catch her breath. Grace took one look at her and paled, pulling over safely to the side of the road. "Ayanna, baby, breathe. It's okay. We're okay." Grace held Ayanna's cheeks, wiping away tears the girl hadn't realized were falling, centering her back in the present and not in the memories of her parents' deaths. "Draw in a deep breath, breathe with me," Grace coached as she pulled in a controlled breath, held it, and released it. They had done these exercises before; this wasn't the first time Ayanna had experienced a flashback-induced panic attack. Thankfully, Grace had had enough foresight to get her counseling after the accident, so they were well equipped to deal with them.

It took a lot of self-control and refocusing, but eventually she could return her breathing to normal.

"You okay? Want to wait it out?" Grace asked, rubbing her back in a comforting motion.

Ayanna took a few more deep breaths, evaluating her options. While part of her wanted to wait, she also knew the only way she was going to get through this was to experience enough driving in the rain that her brain would stop equating it with fatal car crashes. What had happened to her parents was an accident, and driving or even riding in a car in the rain was something she needed to come to terms with. She couldn't miss school any day it rained. "I'm good." She sighed, grabbing Grace's hand and giving it a squeeze. "Thank you, Aunt Grace. I don't know what I would do without you." She smiled sadly.

Grace squeezed her hand in return. "I feel the same way. I love you, my most favorite niece."

Ayanna rolled her eyes. "I'm your only niece."

"True, but you'll always be my favorite." She winked before starting the truck again and getting them back onto the road.

They spent some time at the library and then picked up movies and snacks before heading back to the cottage. The rest of the afternoon they spent curled up with good books and watching movies with a bowl of popcorn sitting between them. It was relaxing and for the most part helped her keep her mind from dwelling on standing up Corydon. She wondered briefly if he had shown up, even when the light drizzle had turned into a downpour. Had he waited there soaked to the bone, hoping she would show up? Or had he known she wouldn't come? Did he think it was the rain that kept her away or her feelings about him?

When the skies finally cleared, it was too dark for her to hike to their spot, and she doubted he would still be there anyway. After Grace went to sleep, she crept down the stairs and sat out on the porch in the cool evening air, staring at the stars. She wished there was a porch swing, as it would be the perfect thing to curl up on outside. Maybe she could learn how to build one for Grace. Surely it would be something they would both enjoy. She could just imagine it, both of them curled up with a mug of coffee, watching the sunrise, or sipping hot cocoa as the leaves turned to a golden yellow and russet orange. She closed her eyes, relishing the happy visuals, and when she opened them again, she smiled. It seemed she had been doing that a lot more lately—smiling. A few months before, she probably could never have visualized being happy there out in the middle of nowhere, torn away from the life she used to know, but she was. The ache of missing her parents seemed to ease a little every day, and finally having a friend to talk to was a soothing balm to her soul.

The stars were gorgeous out there. There was nothing quite like it. In the city, the street lights seemed to dim the sky, making the stars seem like elusive things millions of miles away that occasionally peeked through. Here in the woods, the stars were so bright they almost seemed alive, as if you could build a ladder tall enough to pluck one like an apple from a tree. They were mesmerizing, and she was so lost in thought she didn't notice her stallion approaching the clearing. He snorted loudly, pawing at the ground as if to say, *Look at me! I'm here!* She startled, surprised by his presence. Her heart skipped and she put her right palm over her chest as if she could press hard enough to calm it.

"Oh, hello handsome," she called out, pushing off the

porch and walking toward him. Her toes hit the cold wet grass, and she realized she was barefoot. Her soles sank slightly into the muddy ground, but she didn't care enough to go inside and grab her rain boots. In a way she relished the feeling, for it reminded her that she was alive and this moment with her mysterious stallion was real. She focused her gaze on the horse but stepped gingerly, aware of the rocks and sticks that could poke her feet. The jet black beast approached her just as carefully, as if she were the skittish horse and his actions would startle her and send her running away.

"I just realized I don't know your name," she confessed as she reached toward his mane. He pushed his head into her, eager for her attention, and she laughed at his neediness. "I definitely should name you, if we're going to be this close. Let's see…what shall I call you? How about Cookie?" He snorted in reply.

She giggled. "Guess not then. Maybe something a little more masculine?" He neighed, and she imagined he could actually understand her. "Maverick?" He pawed the ground. "Chocolate?"

She pressed her hand over her mouth, attempting to smother her laughter. He lifted his head so his violet eyes pierced hers, almost narrowing in response to that name. She dropped her hand, letting out a booming laugh.

"Okay…Stan?" He snorted lightly. "Well, I suppose I'm no good at names. I definitely don't want to call you Horsey." He nickered in agreement. "Hmmm…Black Beauty?"

He showed her his teeth.

"Snowy?"

He snorted loudly and backed away from her, turning back toward the woods.

"It was supposed to be ironic! Wait! Don't go!" Her heart sank. Her stallion had been insulted by her attempts to name him. He would leave and she may not see him again. "Please don't go," she pleaded. "Come back, please. I'll think of a better name. I promise!"

Her mind spun, trying to think of good horse names. "Artax!" she called out, recalling the name of the horse from her favorite childhood movie, *The NeverEnding Story*.

The stallion halted, but didn't turn around.

"Come here, Artax!" she shouted, but he didn't turn, just stayed with his back end toward her, almost giving her the cold shoulder, but she would take that over him retreating. "I'm trying here, I really am." She stepped hesitantly toward him. "Come on, give me a break. It's not my fault I don't know your name. It's not like you came with a collar and a tag, you know."

She shrugged. Perhaps it was a stupid endeavor, attempting to name her mysterious new companion.

"I think I'll just call you Midnight because you're black as night. Would that be okay with you?" He looked over his shoulder, almost studying her before he turned back around, strutting toward her. "All right then, Midnight it is. So, what are you up to this evening?" She stroked his flank, feeling his soft hair underneath her fingertips. "Were you just having a stroll through the woods?"

Of course, he didn't answer her back, but just having him there to talk to was comforting.

"Did you enjoy the rain today? I bet you did. I bet it cooled you off rather nicely. I, on the other hand, hated the rain. It ruined my plans." She stroked his neck and leaned into him. "I was supposed to meet someone and I couldn't because of the rain. I just hope he knows that's the reason I couldn't make it." She gazed into his eyes. "See…we had a bit of a fight, I guess you could say, and showing up today was supposed to be the way I showed him I was sorry and I forgave him. Now, he'll still think I'm upset with him, and that might make him not want to come back."

Midnight neighed softly as if to say, *it will be okay.*

"Thank you, Midnight. I needed that. I hope it will be okay. I hope he doesn't give up on me." She leaned her forehead against his head, her nose pressed into his muzzle, and stood there for who knows how many minutes until a chill broke out across her skin. She hadn't realized she was cold, but it made sense with the storm cooling off the air and her bare feet in the wet grass. "I should probably go." She kissed his muzzle before pulling away and gazing into his violet gaze one more time. "Good night, Midnight. Thanks for visiting me." She waved her fingers at him before turning away and heading back toward the house.

CHAPTER 6

THE NEXT DAY the sun was shining, and it seemed all the plants were rejoicing in the warmth, renewed from the showers the day before. Ayanna ate breakfast with Grace before heading off for a swim. Even though she was almost positive Corydon wouldn't be there since it wasn't their meeting day, she still had a sliver of hope. She walked along the familiar path, tracing the tree trunks as she passed. Her heart soared as she stepped into the clearing around the pond, high on hope, only to crash back down when she saw the boulder and pond were vacant.

She trudged toward the rocks, stripping her clothes along the way and carelessly tossing them toward the rocks, along with her towel and bag. When she was down to her swimsuit she stepped into the cool water and swam as far and as hard as she could, doing laps within the constraints of the pond. It wasn't much, but it was enough to help her release some of her pent-up frustration. When she had worn herself out, she let herself relax and float on her back, replaying in her mind the day they had met and all the days leading up to the present. She savored them like the last piece of chocolate birthday cake.

When she was finished, she grabbed her towel and lay out on the rocks, letting the sun's rays warm her and dry her off. After half an hour or so, she drifted off and dreamed about him.

The sun was much lower in the sky when she awoke. She grabbed her shorts and socks off the rocks, lacing up her shoes once they were on. Finally, she picked up her shirt just as a flash of blue and manila tumbling off the rock caught her eye. She bent over the side and gasped. There was an aqua blue flower, the same shade Corydon had once used to describe her eyes, and tied to it was a rolled-up piece of yellowed paper. She picked them both up delicately, bringing the flower to her nose to inhale its scent. This one smelled like a delicious men's cologne. Her knees had gone wobbly, so she leaned against the boulder and set the flower to her left. The paper was rolled like a scroll and tied with a blue ribbon. She traced her finger along the material; it didn't feel like the paper she was used to and looked as if it may be parchment or something handmade. She gripped the blue ribbon between her fingers, and it was smooth, soft like silk. She pulled gently on the knot and the ribbon unraveled in her lap, the scroll unfurling.

"How?" she whispered aloud. If he'd left it there the day before, it must've been magic because there was no way it would've stayed dry. The only other option was that he'd left it for her that morning, or late the previous night after the rain had stopped. Her heart fluttered as she unrolled the parchment and held either end, eager to see what was inside. His handwriting was elegant and masculine. She held her breath as she read.

My dearest Ayanna,

I hope this letter finds you. It may be silly of me to leave this note, not knowing if you will return to find it, but I have to hope. I have to hope that it was the rain that kept you away and not your feelings for me. I have to hope that you can find it in your heart to care for me even knowing exactly what I am. I have to hope I will get to hold you in my arms and taste those sweet lips again. I have to hope, because without hope I have nothing, and without you I am completely lost. You are my beacon through the darkness.

I didn't know what living was until I met you. I had never felt such emotions or dreamed of such happiness in my future before knowing you. You've taught me humans have more value than I could have imagined, and you've made me laugh at a time when my life has been seriousness and rules and regulations. Even if you decide to never see me again, I will forever cherish every moment we spent together. For now, I will continue to hope that I will soon rest my eyes upon your beautiful face once more.

Until then, all my love,

Corydon

She read the letter countless times, pulling his words around her like a downy blanket. She lifted the parchment to her nose and breathed deeply; the paper smelled like him. Then she rolled it back up and retied it with the ribbon before gently placing it in her backpack. She searched for something to leave him in return and sighed with relief when she found a scrap of paper and some tinted lip gloss. She swiped the gloss over her lips then pressed a kiss to the center of the paper. She folded it carefully into an origami heart and placed it where her shirt had been on the rock. Then she found a small rock to place on top to keep it from blowing away in a breeze. She hoped if he returned before they were next supposed to meet, he would know she had been there, hoping to see him.

That night she was so drained from being out in the sun all day, she was out for the count the minute her head hit the pillow.

The next day when she went back to the pond, she noticed fresh horse tracks in the clearing around the cottage and was sad to know she had missed Midnight's visit. Her disappointment only grew when she found the pond empty. The only thing that lifted her spirits was seeing that her heart was gone. She searched all around the rocks and even in the water to make sure it hadn't gotten blown away by the wind or something, but it wasn't there. She hoped it had made its way to Corydon somehow. She lazed around the pond for a few hours before growing bored and hiking her way back to Grace's.

The next few days passed in a similar manner. Some

days she went to the pond, others she spent at home with Grace. Once or twice she saw fresh horse tracks around the tall oak but never caught sight of Midnight before she went to bed.

The morning before she was supposed to meet Corydon again she went to gather blackberries near the house to make a pie. She started toward the back of her house, working her way around the clearing just inside the wood. When her basket was full, she approached the tall oak and was delighted to find a brilliant pink flower, the likes of which she had never seen before. At first, she thought it might be a dahlia, but the petals were too wide and delicate, more like a rose. The pink was a shade so vibrant she was sure the flower had come from Fae, and she lifted it to her nose to inhale its sweet scent. It was as if the sweetest raspberries were captured in the blossom. She inhaled again and smiled widely, knowing exactly who had left it there for her. She gingerly placed it in her basket on top of the blackberries then ambled back to the cottage with her mind in the clouds.

"Ayanna?"

She blinked her eyes and gazed up into Aunt Grace's concerned face. She couldn't remember how or when she had made it into the kitchen, but a quick glance behind Grace told her she had somehow done it.

"Are you feeling okay, sweetheart?" Grace's eyebrows scrunched in concern, her mouth folding into a crease as she pushed Ayanna's bangs out of the way and felt her forehead with the back of her hand.

Ayanna didn't understand her concern. Everything felt amazing. It was as if she was feeling alive for the very first time and her whole being was bursting with sunshine and happiness. She blinked, trying to concentrate on Grace while her feelings begged her to get lost in the moment and every sensation she was suddenly experiencing. She smiled. "Oh yes, I feel wonderful. It's a beautiful day outside, have you noticed?"

Ayanna walked around Grace and placed her basket on the kitchen table. She hummed as she strolled through the kitchen, grabbing a glass and filling it with ice-cold water from a jug in the fridge. She pressed the glass to her lips and took a sip. The water was delicious and refreshing, and it had a sweet taste she had never noticed before. She closed her eyes, savoring every drop as she drained the glass.

"Did you put something in the water to make it taste this sweet? It's delicious," she commented, opening her eyes and placing her glass on the counter.

Grace was staring at her in the most peculiar manner. "The water is the same as always dear, straight from the tap… Are you sure you're feeling okay?"

"Okay? I feel better than okay! I feel magnificent!" She threw her arms wide.

"Did you maybe eat some bad blackberries or some other type of plant while you were out there?"

"Don't be silly! Of course I didn't. The blackberries are fine. You can try one for yourself." Ayanna walked toward the table and grabbed her basket, lifting it to Grace in offering.

Grace peered into the basket, but instead of retrieving a blackberry to eat, she lifted the exotic pink flower. "Where did you get this?" She pinched the stem with her pointer finger and her thumb and held it away from her, tilting it back and forth, studying it meticulously.

"Oh…I found it. Isn't it just gorgeous? And its scent!

It's like raspberries in flower form. You should smell it. It's amazing!"

Grace's eyes widened then she placed the flower in a Ziploc bag and sealed it shut.

"Wait…that's my flower!" Ayanna protested.

"Not anymore, sweetheart. You don't know what you're messing with there."

"What are you talking about? It's a flower."

"Have you ever seen a flower like that before?" Ayanna shook her head. "That's because it's from Fae. I'm not sure exactly what magic it contains, but I have a feeling it's probably responsible for how you're feeling right now. Come dear, let's get you to lie down for a bit." Grace picked up Ayanna's glass and refilled it then led her upstairs to her room.

"But I'm not tired," Ayanna whined.

"I know, honey, but I really think it would be for the best." She lightly shoved her toward the bed, and when Ayanna sat down, Grace helped her remove her shoes.

"Oooo, it feels like I'm lying on a cloud."

Grace's eyes sparkled with amusement. "I'm sure it does, sweetheart."

"Grace? How can a flower make me feel like this just from one little smell?" Ayanna held her fingers up, leaving just a tiny bit of space between her forefinger and thumb.

Grace smirked at the gesture and took a few moments to decide the best way to explain it. "Do you remember when we watched *The Wizard of Oz*?" Ayanna nodded. "And do you remember the scene with the poppies?"

"How the flowers made everyone feel sleepy?"

"Exactly! I think it's probably like that, although I'm

not sure because I haven't encountered that type of flower before. I'll have to leave a message for Enora and see if she can come by to take a look. In the meantime, missy, you are not to pick up or smell any strange flowers. I'm serious—we don't know how all their plants affect humans, so let's play it safe for now. Deal?"

"Sir, yes sir." Ayanna put her first two fingers to her forehead in a saluting motion while Grace rolled her eyes.

"We'll talk about this more when you're feeling more like yourself. For now, I want you to drink more water and try to sleep it off, even though you may not feel like sleeping, okay?"

"Okay." She sighed, snuggling farther into the blankets. Grace made sure she took another giant drink of water before leaving the room to get a message to Enora. Ayanna wondered how that worked. Did they have a pick-up spot for messages sort of like she and Corydon had? Or was there any easier way to get your messages to Fae? Thinking of Fae made her thoughts wander to Corydon, centering on him and seeing him again as she drifted away.

Ayanna awoke several hours later with a pounding headache. She groaned as she rolled over, blinking her eyes open slowly. The room seemed too bright even though the sun was setting outside.

"Oh, thank goodness!" Grace exclaimed, reaching over to smooth Ayanna's hair out of her eyes. "I thought… well, I was worried. The way you slept…"

"You thought I'd pull a Sleeping Beauty on you and not wake up?" Ayanna surmised from piecing together Grace's statements.

"I guess that's one way of putting it."

"I'm okay. I feel like crap, but I'm okay." She grasped Grace's hand and gave it a reassuring squeeze.

"What do you remember?" Grace asked.

Ayanna's mind raced, recalling the events of the morning. "Can I get a glass of water first?"

"Sure, sweetheart." Grace left the room to get the water she'd requested while Ayanna tried to piece together what to tell her. She couldn't let her know about Corydon, not until she absolutely had to. Grace would forbid her from seeing him again, especially after this. The incident with that flower would only strengthen Grace's argument for her to avoid all Fae. Then of course there were the other questions swimming through her head. Had Corydon known the affect the flower would have on her? How could he not with as many years of experience as he had? There was also the niggling doubt that came with him being Unseelie; he might have known what would happen and still left it for her, but why?

Grace returned with her water, interrupting her thoughts. She sat up, propping herself against her pillows, and sipped the water. Her headache seemed to lesson. She debated asking Grace for some Tylenol but decided she would just grab some on her own later. Grace waited patiently for her to speak.

"I was out picking blackberries, just like I said I was going to. I hadn't gone very far from the house and I found that flower lying on the ground. It was beautiful and vibrant, so unlike anything I've ever seen before. So, I picked it up to study it closely. Honestly, Aunt Grace, it never even occurred to me that it could have been from Fae." She was lying, but she met Grace's gaze apologetically. She was sorry for the worry she'd caused her.

"It's okay darling. We're just going to have to be more careful. I'm not sure why it was there or how it got there, but I will find out."

Ayanna fought the urge to flinch. She hoped Grace never found out how and why it was there. "Anyway, I did what most normal people do when they encounter a beautiful flower—I smelled it. It smells wonderful, by the way, like raspberries and something floral, maybe honeysuckle. Shortly after smelling the flower, I felt magnificent, as if I were truly alive for the first time, and I came home. You know the rest from there."

"That I do, dear. I'm so relieved you're okay. Please promise me if you encounter any plants you are not familiar with, you will not touch them in the future."

This was definitely one thing she didn't have to lie about. "I promise. I won't touch anything I'm not familiar with. I'll be more careful, Aunt Grace. Thank you for taking care of me."

Grace leaned over and kissed Ayanna on the forehead. "I'm going to go start on dinner now that you're up. Take your time coming downstairs. I love you."

"I love you too."

With that Grace left the room. Ayanna sat there for a few more moments, her head filling with questions, fears, and doubts, the ache returning with a vengeance. She stumbled from the bed and into the bathroom, grabbing a couple Tylenol from the medicine cabinet. She splashed water on her face and grabbed her water, drinking down the pills before ambling downstairs. She could hear Grace cooking in the kitchen but didn't feel up to sitting in there and keeping her company, so she plopped herself on the couch and turned the TV on, hoping for a distraction.

The evening passed rather quietly, both of them lost

in their own thoughts. Ayanna was curious to ask Grace how she got in touch with Enora, but she didn't want to remind Grace of the serious events that had unfolded that afternoon, so she filled the dinner with mindless comments here and there about summer activities and the time she had left before school started again, which was quickly dwindling. It was hard to believe she only had a few more weeks left. They made plans to go into the city (a three-hour drive away) for the weekend on Saturday morning and stay until Sunday or Monday to purchase new school clothes and supplies.

The discussion of school was a reminder that her time with Corydon would soon be cut short. How would she be able to get away once school started? That was a conversation they would have to have, perhaps not the next day with the more pressing matter of the flower to deal with, but it was an issue that would have to be discussed soon.

She spent the rest of the evening watching TV with Grace and trying to keep her mind off everything. The pounding headache returned so she called it a night and dragged herself up to bed. She had hoped she might see her stallion that night, but she didn't feel like attempting to sneak out of the house. She glanced out of her window into the dark night and was only met with darkness and sparkling stars, no moon in sight. She sighed and climbed into bed. Hopefully Grace would still let her leave the house in the morning and she could get some answers.

CHAPTER 7

THE **NEXT DAY** it took a great deal of coaxing on Ayanna's part to get Grace to agree to let her leave the house, let alone go for a swim. It seemed to help that Grace had been to the pond before and would know exactly where to find her. Ayanna struggled to keep the panic at bay, but if Grace were listening closely, Ayanna was sure she would hear her pounding heart. Aunt Grace interrupting her rendezvous with Corydon would be the worst possible thing to happen. She promised a million times over to not touch any strange plants and keep any eye out for animals or strangers. She also swore she would be back in just a few hours and took a watch with her to make sure.

After what seemed like a decade of promises, she was able to leave. She heaved a sigh of relief, blowing her bangs out of her eyes as she hiked along the path toward the woods. She stopped just before the clearing to fix her hair and apply a fresh coat of lip gloss. She took a deep breath, her heart soaring with the possibility of seeing him.

She stepped around a tree and first caught sight of him sitting on the boulder, weaving something out of grass. She observed him for a few moments, taking in his handsome, sharp profile and his white shimmery hair, which reminded her of snow sparkling in the sunshine. He had the top pulled partially back, a few strands still escaping to frame his face, the rest gathered behind his pointed ears. He was wearing a sleeveless charcoal grey tunic with three black clasps across his chest and black leather pants. The top showed off his toned arms, and at that moment she wanted nothing more than to run her hands across them. She didn't realize the magnetic pull he had on her until she was just a yard away without any recollection of telling her feet to move.

As if he could sense her presence, he lifted his gaze from his hands and stared at her. She read a mixture of relief and hope swirling in his violet eyes. "You came." The disbelief lacing his words made her heart ache for him; to know she'd caused him even an ounce of heartache with the possibility of her rejection filled her with regret.

"I tried to be here sooner, but the rain…"

"I know." He smiled, pushing off the rock and plucking the origami heart from his pants pocket. "I was hoping you would return."

She stepped toward him more quickly, closing the distance between them. "Cor, I'm sor—" He didn't even allow her to finish her apology before his lips crashed down on hers, stealing her breath. He pulled her against him, holding her tightly, as if scared she would slip away from him, but she wasn't going anywhere. She didn't want to be anywhere but in his arms. They remained wrapped around each other for quite some time, sharing a single breath between them, attempting to express their feelings, not quite ready to put them into words. It was the single most beautiful moment in Ayanna's life.

When they finally came up for air, she took his hand and led him toward the boulder, knowing their time was short and there was a lot to be said.

"Corydon, I want you to know that…"

"I know." His eyes softened with understanding.

"But please let me say it," she continued. "I'm sorry. Being Unseelie doesn't change who you are, and I realize that now. I think the information just took me by surprise, but I want you to know I would have come last week if it weren't for the rain. I had made up my mind to see you again." She rubbed her thumb across his fingers as she spoke, enjoying the feel of his skin.

He squeezed her hand in return. "You have no idea how happy you've made me."

She scooted closer to him and rested her head on his shoulder. He lightly pressed a kiss to the top of her head in return and squeezed her hand again. They sat together for a few moments, just soaking in each other's presence before the reality of their situation tugged on her conscience. As much as she hated to ruin the moment and their beautiful reunion, she knew she needed him to give her the whole truth, starting with the flower that had made her high. She needed to have all the facts before she could let herself be swept away by him again. "Can I ask you something?" She was afraid to meet his gaze, so she stared down at their hands.

"Of course. You can ask me anything."

"Did you leave me a pink flower?"

He smiled shyly. "Depends…did you like it?"

She frowned, unsure of what to make of his remark. It was obvious he'd left it, but did he know about the side effects? She lifted her head and scooted away from him. As much as it pained her, she needed the distance to resurrect her guard. If he'd known what he was doing by giving her that flower, she shuddered to think it, but it would confirm some of what Grace had been saying about Unseelie being manipulative.

She decided to try to switch topics, throwing him off balance to discover the truth. His brow furrowed at her sudden distance. "Did you know certain herbs and flowers can have side effects on people?" she asked unemotionally, her gaze seeking the truth in his eyes. When she was only met with confusion, she pressed on. "Like, some plants are poisonous, and others can make you feel high if consumed." She knew he still couldn't tell where she was headed, but she needed to know the truth. Had he given the flower to her knowing the effect it would have on her? "Do you have plants like that in Fae, Corydon?"

His eyebrows pulled down farther, his frown deepening. "Yes, of course. All plants can be harmful or helpful. What are you getting at, Ayanna?" His eyes narrowed, his body stiffening at her unspoken accusation and use of his full name, reminding her of how volatile his emotions could be.

She inched farther away, trepidation, irritation, and the possibility of betrayal simmering under her skin, souring her elation from their reunion. "What effects do those raspberry pink flowers have on humans?" She raised her chin, daring him to deny it and then stood to face him, unable to sit still with her body buzzing. She clutched her shaking hands into fists to fight the emotions swirling within her. She wanted to believe he was innocent, that they could go back to their happy reunion. This was it, the moment of truth. His answer, his reaction could end everything and render her heartbroken.

She studied him closely for any indication of guilt, observing the transformation in his face as her words and meaning sank in. His forehead scrunched before releasing and his glare widened with realization. His shoulders slumped forward, and he stared at his feet, unable to meet her gaze. His monotone voice whispered, "I understand if you never want to see me again."

She closed her eyes, sighing in relief. His body spoke the truth: he hadn't considered or remembered the effect the flower would have on her when he left it. She should've been smiling, but his resignation in the matter—that he would so easily let her go as if he thought of her as someone who would eventually find a reason to leave him—broke her heart a little. She knew how much power he held over her heart, but it wasn't until that moment that she realized how much she held over his. It melted all her remaining uncertainty about them away.

She knelt before him, tilting his chin up with her finger until his wet eyes met hers. "Did you mean to do it?"

"Does it matter?"

She slid her hand to cup his chin, already reading the answer in his body language, her own sighing in relief, letting her temporary guard crumble to the ground. "Of course it matters, Cor."

He brightened at her use of his nickname. "No…I didn't remember the effect the zahra has on humans when I left it for you, honest. I just saw it, and its beauty reminded me of you so I left it as a gift. I didn't think… I'm so sorry, Ayanna—so sorry. Are you okay?"

She dropped her hands from his face, using them while she talked. "Yes, I'm okay now. It was an interesting day, I will say that. It wasn't really harmful, just made me feel incredibly good, and then not so good afterward, like what

I imagine a hangover would feel like after a night of drinking too much wine. Does that make sense?" She wasn't sure if he understood the concept of being drunk or hungover.

Corydon laughed. "We have wine in Fae too. We call it ambrosia, and it's much stronger than human wine, so trust me when I say I completely know how that must have felt." His cheeks flushed then his face froze and he grabbed one of her hands, holding it tightly. "Do you forgive me? Will you still see me again?" His questions ran together with panic.

She smiled reassuringly. "Yes, I forgive you, and yes, I'll still see you." He tugged her forward until she fell into him in a tight embrace. She pulled back after a minute. "Although, in the future, please reference your gifts with their effects on humans." He agreed before crashing his lips against hers.

They eventually moved to lie in the grass before Ayanna pulled away. "I can't stay long," she explained, sitting up. "Aunt Grace is worried about me and is being extra cautious after yesterday. I think she may be onto the fact that a Fae has been near the house." Corydon pulled himself up and opened his mouth, but she held up her fingers, placing them against his lips. "Don't worry, I didn't tell her about you. She wouldn't understand, but there's something else I need to talk to you about before I leave, and you're probably not going to like it."

He pressed a light kiss to the fingers resting against his lips in silent encouragement, and then she brought them down to hold his other hand.

"I start school soon…sooner than I'd like. When I do, well, I won't be able to meet with you during the week, and I'm not sure if I'll be able to get away every weekend.

I'll have homework and chores and things to do with Aunt Grace that will now have to be done during the weekend instead of during the week."

Corydon bit his lower lip. "How long do we have?"

"Two more weeks."

His expression stiffened in resolve. "Then we will make the most of the time we have left together, and if that's all I can have of you, I will cherish every second."

His words made it sound like their relationship had an expiration date, but that wasn't what she'd meant at all. Still, if she truly thought about it, she wasn't even sure what their relationship was. She knew what it was to her, what he meant to her, but she had no clue how he felt. She sighed. *I guess this is as good a time as any to find out.*

"What am I to you, Cor?" He quirked an eyebrow, unsure of what she was asking. "Am I your friend? More than your friend?" she hinted, reluctant to throw the term girlfriend out there.

"Of course you are my friend. You're my best friend."

Her face fell instantly and her gaze slid to their joined hands, not wanting him to see how much his words hurt her.

He squeezed her hands. "Look at me, Ayanna." She flicked her eyes up, his a glittering lavender. "You are my best friend, but you're also much more than that. You… you're…" He paused to take a deep breath and release it, his last words coming out barely above a whisper. "You're my heart."

That was all she needed. She didn't need a label, she just needed to know he felt the same way. She kissed him passionately then rested her forehead against his. "Even though we only have a few weeks left of free time, it does not mean this will be over. I still want to see you. I can't imagine not seeing you, spending time with you, feeling you in my arms. I just wanted to let you know we may not be able to see each other as frequently as we would both like. Of course, it will seem longer for me, but still."

"Every day away from you is too long," he said breathlessly, his eyes shimmering with devotion. "But I am with you on this. We will figure this out together. I can't imagine not spending time with you either, but we will make it work. I'm not giving you up." He pressed a rather chaste kiss to her lips.

She hugged him tightly before bidding him goodbye, aware that she needed to return home before Aunt Grace came looking for her. She cherished their final embrace and kiss then ran off back toward the house.

Grace was visibly relieved when Ayanna walked through the door.

"Are you feeling okay, dear? You look a little flushed."

Ayanna's cheeks heated with Grace's words. "I'm great, just a little hot from the hike back. I told you this morning, I feel good. I think whatever it was yesterday is all done with now. Oh, and I didn't see or touch any strange plants along the way."

"Good. I'm glad to hear that."

They spent the rest of the evening as they had spent many others and went into town the next day. They did all of Ayanna's back-to-school shopping, picked out some new clothes at the mall, ate at a delicious Italian restaurant, and went to the movies. All the things Ayanna missed about the big city, Grace tried to fit into their one weekend. It was rather endearing.

The next two weeks passed in a whirlwind of school registration, senior orientation, completing her summer reading assignments, devouring as much information about Fae as she could through Grace's books, and helping Grace around the house. One of the afternoons Grace sent her out to pick berries for a pie, and Ayanna returned to find that Enora, Grace's Fae friend, had been by. She wasn't sure what to make of the fact that Grace had intentionally sent her away knowing Enora would be coming to the house. She tried to pretend her disappointment was merely because she was curious about Fae in general, which was definitely part of it, but she also wanted to see what other Fae looked like compared to Corydon.

She met with him on their normal meeting day, and they spent time swimming, talking, and just enjoying each other's company, wrapped in each other's arms, where the world seemed a simpler place. When she was with him, it was almost as if she could ignore the outside world, as if they existed in their own little bubble. The last weekend before school started was spent with many reassurances of meeting as often as they could, and agreeing on how they could let each other know if there was going to be an issue (leaving a note at the boulder or the tall oak tree). There was no denying the fact that she was head over heels in love with him, and while she was sure he felt the same since he had confessed to her being his heart, she had trouble saying the words aloud to him. It was terrifying to make herself that vulnerable to another being. For her, loving someone was mixed with the grief of losing them, and she wasn't quite ready to face the fact that some day she might lose him too, probably not to death, but surely he would tire of her eventually. Her newness would fade and her quirky human traits would start to annoy him, so she kept those words inside, afraid to give him that last little piece.

Chapter 8

When Ayanna had arrived at school in the spring of the previous year, she had caused quite a stir, being the new girl in a tiny town (and an even tinier school). There were probably only about twenty students in her class, and every one of them had initially seemed curious about her. Of course, the glamor of being new quickly faded when they realized she was withdrawn and reserved for the most part. She was lost in a world of her own grief and none of them could break through. A few boys showed interest but gave up after her quick dismissals. So, it was no surprise that when she returned to school for senior year, her classmates mostly ignored her.

The student body still saw her as an oddity, and living out in the woods with Aunt Grace didn't help her case. She overheard the whispers sometimes, but for them to hurt, she would have had to care what they thought about her, and frankly, she didn't. Now that she had Corydon, she felt like she didn't need any friends. Besides, if she got any friends, they wouldn't understand her relationship with

Corydon. It wasn't like she was a bitch or anyone was rude to her; they all politely tolerated her standoffish manner. Of course, this made Aunt Grace worry, but Ayanna reassured her that she was friendly enough at school and that Aunt Grace was all she needed for the time being, which made her aunt give her a sad little smile and a giant hug.

August faded into September, which bled into October. There were only a few times she was unable to meet Corydon. On those days, she would find a letter at the base of the tall oak tree, usually accompanied by a flower (never one that caused the same side effects as the zahra), which she sometimes smuggled into the house but usually left out in the woods for fear of discovery by Aunt Grace. She cherished every one of his letters, stowing them in an old aluminum tin with a faded blue floral design that used to belong to her mother, and she found herself rereading them quite frequently. He had such a way with words, and it was like her very own letters from Mr. Darcy.

The more time she spent with him, the harder it was to keep him a secret. She thought about confessing to Grace that she had met someone, and she thought Grace might have her suspicions, but she was pretty sure Grace would want to meet any boy she was involved with, and that couldn't happen.

There were several nights her midnight stallion came to visit her, usually around the times she wasn't able to see Corydon, and he helped relieve some of the ache. She would confess everything to her equine companion as if he were her best friend, and while he was incapable of speaking back, there was something in his eyes that told her he understood. Sometimes he would nudge her for more affection or huff in irritation, especially if she talked about school and how the kids there mostly ignored her. His favorite thing was to lean his muzzle against her neck and breathe in deeply, which she found endearing. He was almost like a giant puppy.

On the last weekend of October, the weather turned quite chilly. She was sitting between Corydon's legs, leaning against him as he leaned against the boulder, and she was thinking about Halloween. It amused her to no end to think about how many children would be dressed up as fairies, knowing none of them would have it right. She shook with silent laughter and Corydon poked her. "Tell me, I want to laugh too," he teased.

"Well, we have this holiday at the end of the month where the children all dress up in costumes as different things like superheroes, witches, zombies, vampires…and, well, some of them dress up as fairies. I was laughing because now that I know a real Fae, I know how wrong they are."

"They dress up as fairies?" His nose scrunched and she laughed, nodding her head. "What do they wear?"

"Um, well most of them wear glitter, and these frilly layered skirts made from a sheer fabric…and wings, sometimes with a wand." She turned toward him to see his reaction, which was quite comical, so much so that she laughed harder. His face was scrunched up in complete and utter disgust.

"Wings? They think we have *wings*?" He looked as if the idea of having wings was the most appalling thing he had ever heard. "Where would they get such an idea?"

"Stories or Disney, I suppose…who knows." She shrugged, still amused by his reaction.

He paused, lost in his own thoughts for a few moments. "You aren't going to dress like that, are you?" His eyes narrowed slightly, and she burst out laughing again.

"No, definitely not!"

"Good." He nodded, seeming appeased by her answer.

November came and brought snow with it. Her reasons for being in the woods were no longer valid without berries to pick or good temperatures to swim in. The snow made it difficult to navigate out there at times, and she could see the frown lines every time she told Grace she was going for a hike, but she wouldn't give up her time with Corydon for anything. The cold faded away next to his abnormally hot body. He seemed to almost radiate heat, which became more apparent in the colder temperatures. He made her feel alive, and they would spend hours sitting, kissing, and talking, sharing stories of their lives and what had been going on since they last met. He seemed just as fascinated to learn about her day-to-day life as she was to hear stories about Fae. Once she made the mistake of telling him she wanted to go there.

He froze. "You can't," he ordered abruptly. She was always taken aback by the shifts in his moods, especially if she ever brought up his parents. His father was a huge sore spot.

She pulled away, putting distance between them. "Is it not possible?" From what she had read in her books, there were many occasions were humans stumbled into Fae unknowingly.

"It's not safe—not for you, not there, not ever." His face was set in stone, but his eyes held regret and anxiety within them. She dropped the subject, eager to think of better things.

When she was alone that night, she did what every typical teenage girl does: analyzed their conversation, his exact wording and tone. The realization that this sneaking around was what their relationship would be until she left for college made her stomach sink. Thanks to Grace's encouragement, she had already applied to several colleges and received letters of acceptance, but she was still waiting to make a final decision. She was leaning more toward staying close by, but even the closest college was too far to commute and still live at Grace's house. She could come back on the occasional weekend or over breaks, but was it worth it? Was this something she wanted to pursue when she couldn't even say for sure if there was a future for them?

Usually when that kind of thought invaded her mind, she shoved it out quickly and forcefully, telling herself to enjoy the moments they had and she could face the heartache of leaving him for college later. She was already in too deep, so breaking up now wasn't an option she was willing to consider. She knew in the long run, it wouldn't save her any pain.

She saw even less of Corydon in December and January due to the snow. Grace bought her a pair of ice skates for Christmas, which were a great excuse to go to the pond, but even so, it was cold and the weather did not always cooperate. The moments they spent together, he drank her in as much as he could, constantly touching her, kissing her, professing his adoration and devotion, but never quite using that four-letter word she longed to hear. Instead he seemed to show her his emotions with every caress, press of his lips, and tangle of tongues.

She savored their moments together and became more depressed the longer she went without seeing him. She worried he may find someone else in her absence, especially since they had barely gone further than making out. She wasn't naïve; she knew what most kids her age were doing, and even though she felt that she loved him, she couldn't bring herself to cross that line with him until she could say the words.

During their time apart, her major reassurance that he was just as smitten as she was were the letters he left for her. They would have made any girl's heart melt. Sometimes he even wrote her love poems, which practically made her swoon. She kept every single one in the tin under her bed.

One time he left her a gift, a dainty silver chain with an almost heart-shaped disk filled with tiny dark blue crystals that reminded her of the night sky. It was beautiful. She wore it every day, and when Grace asked her about it, she claimed a boy at school had given it to her as Christmas gift. Of course, the next time she saw him, she made sure to let him know how much she loved the necklace. His eyes sparked with pleasure, almost glowing when he first saw his necklace around her neck, and he smiled widely. He told her he loved seeing something of his on her, said it made him feel closer to her when he wasn't there, knowing his necklace would be close to her heart. She melted a little with that confession, eager to wear it always.

During those weeks they were unable to meet, Midnight helped keep her sane. She saw him almost every week during those frigid months, sometimes more than once a week. It seemed he enjoyed the cold and she would stay out with him, talking and stroking his fur until her fingers were numb. She knew their time together would come to an end sooner than she wanted to admit.

There were a few rocky days—her father's birthday, Christmas, her mother's birthday, and Valentine's Day. Grace always did her best to cheer Ayanna up, which was thoughtful and kind, but those were the days she felt Corydon's absence the most. She finally felt like she had someone to lean on, but he wasn't there when she needed him. She wrote him letters and left them by the tree or the rock, depending on how far out she could hike that day, sometimes with a trinket she made him—a small plastic container of Christmas cookies, another one of her scrunchies, a bracelet she braided for him, a Valentine's Day card. The little things let him know she was thinking about him.

February came and went in the same manner. The beginnings of spring had her itching to be outside and spend time with him. The snow was starting to melt, and the days had become warmer, enough that she could hike to the pond every time they were supposed to meet. It had probably been about a month since she saw him last and she was eager to lay her eyes and hands on him again, but he was a no-show.

Two more weeks went by without him, but this time there were no notes, and the letters she left for him remained there untouched. She began to panic. What if something had happened to him? What if he was hurt? Had he found someone else? Was he tired of her and her human quirks already? Was the time apart too long for them to recover? It was a constant barrage of questions that remained unanswered, churning her stomach and leaving her home sick a few days from school. Grace became concerned at Ayanna's shift in mood and illness but figured it was her way of dealing with the anniversary of her parent's deaths.

Ayanna was relieved that Grace seemed to understand her mood, although when reminded of the significance of the date, it only pulled her a little deeper. Had it really been a year without them? Guilt settled in her stomach, heavy as a stone. How could she have forgotten the date? How had she let herself get so wrapped up in Corydon that she forgot about them? That night she couldn't sleep, her mind constantly playing the night of her parents' accident on repeat. She got out of bed to stare down at the window and was relieved to see her stallion grazing in the clearing. She watched him root around and chew the fresh grass, occasionally lifting his head, almost as if looking for her at the window.

She quietly tiptoed downstairs, slipping on some purple rain boots Grace had bought for her. Once she got beyond the porch, she raced toward the horse. He lifted his head and whinnied. As she reached him, she slowed as to not startle him, and when he was within reach, she threw her arms around his neck, burying her face into his mane and inhaling his woodsy animal scent. He smelled almost magical and she wondered briefly if perhaps he was a creature of Fae, but almost as quickly, she dismissed the thought.

"Hey boy, I've missed you." She pulled back to stroke his face, and he nuzzled into her hand, making her giggle. "I know, you've missed me too. Where have you been,

Midnight? Did you get yourself a girlfriend who kept you away?" He huffed, pawing the ground with his left hoof, indicating that he found her question to be ridiculous, or at least that was what she interpreted his action to mean.

"Okay, so you're single then?" He snorted and nudged her side with his nose, and she released a full-on belly laugh at that one. "Oh, I have missed you, buddy."

She leaned into him, stroking his muzzle in an affectionate snuggle. They remained like that for several moments, just soaking in each other's warmth and taking comfort. He pulled back first, stepping backward gently. She wiped away a few tears she hadn't realized had fallen. He stared at her, studying the movement, and she wondered if the presence of the tears was what had caused him to pull away.

"I'm sorry," she mumbled as she sniffed. "I hadn't realized how much I needed that until you were here. It's been a hard few days for me, you see." Then she began to talk. She told the horse about her parents' death and then moved on to how she hadn't seen Corydon in ages and how she was worried he didn't want to see her again. She released everything that had been weighing so heavily on her heart.

Midnight stepped closer, pushing into her and offering her what comfort he could while she spilled all the things that haunted her. His eyes held such compassion she could have sworn he understood her words, or perhaps he just sensed her emotions. Either way, she was going to soak up everything he offered. It was easier to let him help heal her than to tell Grace about Corydon, and she was so grateful he was there that night. She gave him one last hug before bidding him good night, feeling as if the sun was going to rise soon, and she turned back to the house, sneaking up the stairs and crawling into bed, no longer feeling like she was drowning in her sorrow. She felt like she could swim again.

She returned to school the next day, much to Grace's relief, and life continued.

March came and went without word from Corydon. She studied, finding things to distract her from focusing on his lack of communication. Eventually she decided enough was enough. Her senior year was almost over and she had spent it pining over him, never realizing they were star-crossed lovers not meant to be in her reality. She decided the only thing she could do now was to let him go, so she wrote him a goodbye letter. She poured her heart into it, revealing all her fears about their doomed relationship and how it was better if things ended this way. By the end, she had almost convinced herself that giving up on him and what they had was for the best.

That weekend she hiked out to their spot to leave the note for him, one final visit before she tried to make herself forget her feelings for him, to make herself focus on the future. Despite telling her stupid heart to stop feeling, it still leapt as she entered the clearing around the pond, her traitorous eyes desperately searching for him. Her heart sank when they came up empty. She sat for quite some time on one of the large boulders, dipping her toes into the water, allowing herself to bask in memories of him and shed tears for her breaking heart. She clutched the letter in her hand as sobs wracked her body.

She was so lost in her own despair that she didn't hear him approach, and she jumped when his arms wrapped around her, drawing her into his chest.

"Shhh…I've got you," his familiar voice soothed in her ear. "I've got you, sweetheart." She dropped the letter as she spun and smacked against his chest, shoving him hard, but he didn't budge.

"Where have you been?!" she yelled, pounding against him. "Why did you leave? Why haven't you written?!"

Corydon pulled her to him so she could no longer pound against him, her arms trapped between them. He cupped the back of her head and whispered, "Shhhhh…" over and over again. "I'm so sorry, Ayanna. I never meant to hurt you."

She pulled back and could see the apology in his eyes. However sincere he was, it didn't make up for the fact that he had been missing for so long.

She shook off his hold and took a step back. She wiped her hands roughly across her face, mad that she had let him see her so broken. She put her hands on her hips to keep them from reaching toward him. "Yeah, well, you did," she snapped.

He winced at her tone. "Will you let me explain, at least?" She shrugged as if his explanation didn't matter to her one way or another, so he took the opportunity to continue. He began pacing back and forth in front of her. "I've tried to come so many times since I found out. I've needed to see you, to wrap my arms around you, to take comfort in you, but they've watched my every move. It's just…" He paused, running his fingers through his hair, his shoulders slumping forward. He took a deep breath. "My dad died, and they think he was…they're pretty sure he was poisoned…by my brother's wife."

Ayanna gasped. Every explanation she could have thought of would not have prepared her for that. She rushed toward him and threw her arms around him, gathering him against her chest, offering the comfort he so desperately needed. He stayed there wrapped in her embrace for several moments. "That's just awful, Cor. I'm so sorry, I truly am. I know…" She swallowed hard, keeping the memories of her own grief at bay. "I know how hard it is to lose a parent."

He pulled back a bit but entwined his fingers with hers, needing her to anchor him. "The thing is…my dad was known for being cold and oftentimes cruel, even to his own children, but I think that's what he had to be in his position…which I guess is my position now. I inherited his title when he died, so while I should be grieving his death, I feel angrier than anything else. I don't want his job. Hell, give it to my brother for all I care, but that's not the way things work, especially not since Rodric's wife was the one who poisoned him."

She hoped he would elaborate as to what position he'd inherited but he didn't, and really, she was a little afraid to ask. She squeezed his hand, offering up what she couldn't say.

"So, I haven't been able to sneak away. They've been watching me constantly, and now with these new responsibilities, I just…I… *Ugh!*" He released her hand and stood. "I wish it didn't have to be this way, but I can't now. It's impossible and I was selfish to think I could have… This is just so hard. Please know, Ayanna, that I never went into this wanting to hurt you. I never even thought I could fall in love with a human, but I did. I fell in love with you so hard, and I will never regret that. I can only regret what I know I have to do, for you, for me, for both of us."

Her heart stuck in her throat, knowing what he was about to do before he said the words. She quickly threw her arms around him and pressed her lips to his, wanting one last kiss, one last memory of passion before he threw it all away, as she knew he would. He kissed her back as if she was the air he breathed. "I love you too," she whispered against his lips. He took the opportunity to kiss her one last time, and she knew he was saying goodbye.

He pulled away gently. "We can't do this. I can't see you anymore. It would only put you in danger, and I'm not willing to allow that, so I'm letting you go. Please don't fight me on this."

She had already accepted the loss of their relationship when she brought her Dear John letter with her, so it didn't hurt quite as much as she had expected to hear the words from his mouth. "I understand." She really didn't want to fight with him; knowing he was ready to throw in the towel and he wouldn't fight for their love was enough.

She cupped his face and ran her finger across his cheek, his dark purple gaze meeting her blue one. "Goodbye, Corydon." She dropped her hand and turned, running for the woods, afraid she wouldn't be able to follow through if she slowed or hesitated. She ran through the woods, pushing through her pain. She only stopped when she came upon the tall oak tree at the edge of the clearing. She leaned against the trunk, attempting to catch her breath and slow the tears that were streaming down her face. While she knew the end of their relationship was inevitable, it didn't take away the pain. She slid to the ground and sat there replaying their conversation until the sky began to darken then she pulled herself up and stumbled into the house. She called out to Aunt Grace that she didn't feel well as she climbed the stairs and collapsed on her bed.

Chapter 9

THE **WORLD AROUND** her sprang anew with life, and the woods rejuvenated with the birth of spring. Ayanna's life slowly returned to the way it had been before she met Corydon. Grace made an effort to spend as much time as she could creating special memories together before her senior year ended. It was sweet and endearing, and Ayanna found her heart beginning to heal. She decided on a local liberal arts college that was close enough that she could still drive back to see Grace on the weekends and over holiday breaks. She still wasn't sure what she wanted to study, but she knew she had time to figure that out. Graduation was a small event at her school, and the normally joyous milestone was tinged with grief as she crossed the stage. Grace cheered as widely and loudly as she could to make up for the fact that Ayanna's parents weren't there to cheer her on, so Ayanna smiled, trying to play off her watering eyes for happiness, but of course Grace saw right through her. Since the town was so small, the tradition was just to have a barbeque in the square around the gazebo to celebrate all the graduating seniors. It wasn't that hard to fade into the background at the event, just like she had at school. No one seemed to take much interest in her except Grace, and they snuck away early on.

"I'm sorry they couldn't be here today," Grace finally said, squeezing Ayanna's knee in the front seat of her truck. "They would be so proud of you…they are proud of you. Now, I know we haven't had much discussion of our beliefs about the afterlife, and I never really offered to take you to church, nor did you ask, but that doesn't mean I'm not a spiritual person, and I do believe they are in heaven watching over you. They saw you walk that stage today. I'm sure your mother shed a few tears, probably not as much as your father, as you were the light of that man's life. I know he loved my sister dearly, but with you, it was like a whole different kind of love. His world revolved around you."

Ayanna wiped away a few stray tears. She was a daddy's girl through and through. She could almost imagine his loud booming cheering above the crowd, how he probably would have elbowed the parents next to him yelling, "That's my girl!" He had always been her biggest fan. The bittersweet mixture of emotions swirled within her.

"Thank you, Aunt Grace." The rest of the drive was spent in a comfortable silence. Her aunt always seemed to understand Ayanna's emotions, giving her exactly what she needed instinctually. That silence, the time to allow herself to think about her parents and how proud they would be while at the same time grieving the memories she would never experience with them was exactly what she needed.

When they returned to the house, Grace suggested a rom-com movie marathon, but Ayanna's heart just wasn't in it. She politely declined and hugged Grace fiercely, trying to convey all her gratitude and love for the only family she had left.

Grace returned her embrace and rubbed a soothing hand across her back. "I love you too," she whispered.

"I think I'm going to go for a walk. Is that okay?"

"Of course, sweetheart, whatever you need. How about I make your favorite pasta dish for dinner tonight to celebrate?"

Ayanna smiled, but it didn't quite reach her eyes. "I would love that."

She changed her shoes from sandals to sneakers but left her sundress on; it would be stupid to wander around in the woods with dress shoes on. She grabbed a notepad and a pen, shoving them into an army green messenger bag, figuring it may help to write down her feelings. She took a quick glance at herself in the mirror, fingering the necklace she never had the guts to take off, its blue crystals sparkling. She threw the bag over her shoulder and called out to Grace as she stepped out the door. "I'll be back before dinner. I love you!" Then she closed the door behind her and started to walk.

She wasn't sure where she wanted to go and just let her feet carry her somewhere else. She stopped from time to time to write whatever thoughts or emotions were going through her head in her notebook or to pick a handful of blackberries to eat straight from the bushes. It took a little longer to find ones that were plump and dark enough to eat as it wasn't quite berry season yet, but she savored each bite she was able to find. She'd miss this when she left for college; even coming home on weekends wouldn't be the same. Besides, she wasn't sure how much she would be able to come home with her classes. She'd just have to wait and see.

She was so lost in her own head that she tripped over a

tree root, and only then did she realize her stupid subconscious had brought her to the pond. She sighed. It was the first time she had set foot near their spot since they broke up. Putting space between them had been the only thing to keep her from thinking about what could have been. That was one aspect of college she was looking forward to—meeting new people. Living in a tiny town had not afforded her the opportunity to meet anyone who sparked her interest until she laid eyes on Corydon. College held the hope of meeting someone she could fall in love with, someone human.

She sat down on one of the boulders and unlaced her sneakers, letting her toes dip into the water. She swung her feet back and forth, writing her thoughts and feelings down in her notebook. Somehow her notes turned into a letter to Corydon, telling him what her plans for the future were, like a final goodbye and *have a nice life* kind of note. She didn't think she could bear to come back and swim when the water was warm enough anyway, and even if he never found it, it was a final piece of closure for her.

She laced her shoes back on her feet and stood. She tore the letter from her notebook, folded it into an origami heart, and pressed one final kiss to the paper. Then she set it on the boulder and found a small rock to place on top to anchor it down. She retrieved her bag and tucked the strap over her shoulder, turning to start the walk home.

As she neared the edge of the clearing around the pond, a movement off to the right caught her eye. An imposing figure stepped out of the woods. He lacked Corydon's lithe yet toned build, instead reminding her more of a body builder. He was wearing a sleeveless black shirt with black pants and boots, and his chiseled jaw was accented by a well-groomed, short, black goatee. He smiled wickedly revealing a mouth full of sharp teeth. Her flight-or-fight instinct kicked in, and she fought the urge to run like skittish prey. She could tell he would just love to chase her, and what chance did she stand against Fae?

"Hello there," he leered in a gravelly voice.

"Um, hello. I was just leaving—have to get home to my family." She licked her lips, her heart in her throat, her legs itching to run.

As he stalked closer, she noted that his dark hair was pulled partially back, revealing the pointed tips of his ears, confirming what she already knew in her gut.

"Oh shit," she whispered before she broke into a run. She didn't get very far before her legs froze as if she was cemented in place. Her momentum tipped her forward and she braced herself as best as she could for the impact. Her right palm struck a rock while her left arm screamed in agony.

"Tsk, tsk, little mouse. Why were you trying to run?"

Her pulse thudded erratically. The lower half of her body was paralyzed. She attempted to crawl by using her arms and hands to drag herself forward, but the pain in her left arm caused her to cry out, and she feared it was broken.

"I asked you a question, mouse." The Fae sneered, his feet stopping right in her line of vision.

"Please, sir, I just want to go home," she begged, but she knew it was no use. It must've been his magic holding her in place.

"Now, now, where's the fun in that?" His hands gripped her shoulders tightly as he hauled her to her feet. He looked her over from the top of her head to the tips of her toes, a predatory gleam lighting his eyes. He smiled, running his tongue across his pointed teeth. "Nope. I think I will keep you for a while."

She tried to thrash her upper body against his grip, her arm throbbing, but after a few moments she found herself completely frozen in place.

He laughed as she struggled to catch her breath against the growing panic. "Oh, I think we'll have a lot of fun together. Come on now."

His eyes flashed pale seafoam green, and her legs started walking without her permission. She was a prisoner in her body, and the feeling of absolute helplessness against his magic shook her to the core. She was his own personal puppet. The thought of what he could do to her made her shudder internally.

"P-Please let me go. I won't tell anyone, I swear."

He scoffed, ignoring her pleas. She continued to beg. She debated mentioning Corydon's name, but she wasn't sure if that would make things better or worse. She glanced toward him and noticed he was thumbing through her notebook. He must have picked it up as she was attempting to flee. She deflated; he'd find out about Corydon soon enough on his own if he continued reading.

Ah hell, here goes nothing. "My boyfriend will be furious if you hurt me." The Fae rolled his eyes, obviously believing the boyfriend to be a puny little human, so she continued. "He's like you, you know, and when he gets angry…"

"What do you mean he's like me?" he demanded.

"He's Fae…unless I'm wrong about your magical powers." She froze in the same second his steps faltered.

"You're lying." He stepped around her to look into her eyes, but the sunlight caught her necklace, drawing his attention there. He snarled, "Stupid little mouse, that boy is not your boyfriend. You're his pet."

"I'm not anyone's *pet*, and I'm not lying, I swear. Perhaps you know him—his name is Corydon."

The man's eyes widened with recognition, and then he released a booming laugh. "Corydon, you say?" He spoke as if she were a complete imbecile for suggesting such a thing. Even more worrisome was that he smiled widely. "Well, what do you know—I do know your 'boyfriend'. How about I take you to him?"

She inhaled sharply, remembering Corydon's desire to never see her in the Fae realm. "Um, no…that's okay. He isn't expecting me."

"I'm sure he's not," he mumbled amusedly under his breath before he continued. "Let's surprise him. I'm sure he will *love* to see his pet again." The way he emphasized the word love made her pause. She knew Corydon wouldn't be pleased to see her in Fae, but surely he would help in whatever way he could. It wasn't that long ago that he was professing his love to her.

"Why do you keep calling me a pet? I'm no one's pet," she protested.

He pointed a finger at the stone draped around her neck. "Your claiming necklace seems to say otherwise."

"Claiming necklace?" What the heck is he talking about?

"That pretty little bauble around your neck. I haven't seen one in quite some time, but it's what some of the Fae like to use when they claim a human, means the human belongs to them and no other Fae are supposed to mess with the human, although most of our folk prefer a collar over a dainty little necklace." He snorted as if the idea of giving a human a necklace was an outrageous idea.

"I'm not his pet. He's my boyfriend."

"Sure you are, little mouse," he shot back with a snigger.

"You know, if you aren't supposed to harm a claimed human, maybe you should let me go." She hoped he wouldn't notice the tremor in her voice.

"Oh, but this is just too good. Sleep now."

She yawned loudly, her limbs finally back in her control. She cradled her injured arm against her chest. "But I'm not…" she yawned again, her eyes drooping.

"Shhhh…sleep." He pressed a finger against her lips briefly.

She swayed on her feet, fighting the exhaustion. Her adrenaline was now the only thing keeping her awake. He grabbed her shoulders and commanded her to sleep once more. This time her body obeyed and she drifted into unconsciousness.

Chapter 10

"Wake up, little mouse," her capturer whispered, giving her a slight shake.

She drew in a deep, fortifying breath. She was slumped over the front of a horse. She tested her limbs, wiggling her fingers, and she nearly sighed with relief when they brushed across the horse's mane. She wasn't sure how long she'd been unconscious, but her eyes told her she was far from home. She could see a well-trodden dirt path underneath the horse's feet.

"Sit up," he growled, and her body moved accordingly.

It was probably for the best, as she thought she might slip off the horse if she had attempted to rise on her own. Unfortunately, the movement sent a sharp pain through her broken arm and she hissed. The Fae behind her chuckled, seemingly amused by her pain. She shouldn't have been surprised; with what Grace had told her as well as what she had been able to glean from the books in her library, Unseelie Fae tended to take pleasure in tormenting humans.

"Aw, does the little mouse need a healer?" he teased.

She straightened her spine, unable to cradle her arm the way she wanted to as she needed her free hand to grip the horse. She was disappointed to discover that her legs were well and truly locked around the sides of the horse; she wouldn't be moving them until he released his hold over her. She bit back the retort on the tip of her tongue, knowing insulting him would get her nowhere. Let him think her a passive little mouse until the time came for her to strike. He may have control of her body, but he did not have control of her mind. She took the time to study her new surroundings, and she could see that they were passing through a village. She felt as if she was riding through the set of the movie *Braveheart* with all the small thatched roof cottages. *Seems the Fae are fans of the middle ages.* She briefly wondered if they had electricity or indoor plumbing. There were Fae milling about here and there, all of them more gorgeous than any model on the cover of a magazine. Their hair varied in shades from natural colors to lavender and deep blue, and while most wore theirs long, some trimmed it short, and others pulled back to show off their pointed ears. Their wardrobe was very eclectic. Many of the men wore leather pants with some sort of tunics, while others preferred tight short-sleeved shirts. The women mostly wore dresses, although those varied in length, color, and design from something she would expect to see at a Renaissance festival to some very scandalous attire that belonged more in a nightclub than walking around town in the middle of the day.

What struck her the most were their eyes, so striking as they glowed. She was sure any shade you could think of was represented, and they all followed her curiously.

"Where are you taking me?" she asked, hoping it wouldn't be his home.

"To see your 'boyfriend', as I said before. I mean, if he

is your boyfriend, he will be happy to see you, won't he?"

"No," she whispered.

"Speak up, little mouse."

"No, I don't think he will be happy to see me. I think if anything, he'll be angry with you for bringing me here."

"Is that so?" He ran a hand across her shoulder, causing her to shudder with revulsion. He laughed loudly, taking pleasure in the fact that he made her uncomfortable—either that or finding her words to be humorous; she wasn't sure which.

"I believe so," she murmured quietly, but honestly, she had no clue what was about to happen and it terrified her. *God, I'm such an idiot. I should have never gone back to the pond*, she thought, reproaching herself.

It wasn't long before they neared a stone castle. She tried to take deep even breaths to calm her nerves and ignore the pain her arm was causing. They approached a guarded entrance to a courtyard where two men stood watch, their hands on the hilts of their swords, which were sheathed at their sides. "Speak your business," one commanded.

Her capturer smiled. "I have a gift for the king."

Her eyes widened; this was definitely not where she wanted to be. She didn't want to get Corydon in trouble with his king. She tried to open her mouth to protest but found her mouth would not cooperate.

"Quiet, little mouse," he warned softly in her ear.

The guards allowed him to pass. He dismounted his horse just beyond the gate, inside a courtyard, and then lifted her off the horse as if she weighed nothing.

"Follow me and do not speak unless you are spoken

to," he ordered.

She heaved a sigh of relief finding her mouth was back under her control. She cradled her left arm against her body with her right hand. Only then did she notice how scraped her palms were. She glanced down and saw her knees were also torn open, a solid trickle of dried blood running down her leg. She looked a mess. She followed the Fae unconsciously into the castle. It appeared more ornate and slightly more modern inside, more Victorian than Medieval. It was luxurious, almost like stepping into Prince Charming's castle from *Cinderella*.

They were greeted inside by another guard and led to a room off to the side of the main entrance. The guard opened two double doors just as a teenage boy with long golden brown hair ran out. He stopped immediately when he caught sight of her, his eyes flashing from light green to emerald as he bit his bottom lip in a nervous gesture. She stared at him curiously as she followed behind her kidnapper, almost twisting her head to glance back as they stepped through the door. The boy gave her a small pitying smile before the doors closed in front of him.

She turned back to see several curious Fae watching her. She scanned the small crowd for any sign of familiar silver blond hair and violet eyes, but came up emptyhanded. She cast her eyes downward, unable to fight the disappointment of realizing perhaps no one would be there to save her.

"Your Majesty, I have brought you a gift," her capturer called as they approached a dais with a throne. She couldn't see around his hulking figure to view just who sat atop the throne, but she didn't have to wait long as he grabbed her rather forcefully and shoved her to her knees in front of him. She yelped as one of the newly formed scabs on her knee ripped open.

Slowly, she brought her eyes up, planning to plead for mercy. In front of her there was not one but two thrones on the dais. On the smaller of the two sat a man who studied her intensely. He had shimmering white hair, long like Corydon's. In fact, he very much resembled Corydon, only he looked a few years older and his eyes were a bright aquamarine.

A familiar voice shook her from her perusal, quickly swinging her gaze toward its owner, and what she saw stirred a bittersweet blend of hope, disbelief, and betrayal. "What is the meaning of this?" Corydon growled. His hands clutched the ends of his chair and his eyes swirled from plum to lavender. She gasped.

The man behind her was clearly enjoying being the center of attention and bringing discomfort to his king, which she found odd, but then she remembered what Corydon had told her, how recently his father had died and he'd had to take over. She wanted to laugh and cry at the same time as all the odd things he'd done, the tiny snippets he'd revealed, and what he'd not said about his family all fell into place. Of course, it made perfect sense, but that didn't keep it from hurting any less or feeling any less like a little bit of a betrayal on his part by not sharing that part of himself.

"Well, sire, she said you were her boyfriend, so I thought I'd return her to you."

The crowd tittered, as if he had said something positively ludicrous. Her gaze didn't leave Corydon for one second. She could see the anger that vibrated off his body, and she worried exactly who it was aimed toward. Her wide eyes slowly narrowed; she would not beg this king for mercy. In fact, he should have been begging her for forgiveness. Her lips pressed tightly together, reining in her betrayal-fueled anger. The man she assumed was his brother leaned over and spoke in his ear, but she was too far away to hear what he said.

Corydon then turned and addressed the crowd. "Leave us, now!" The command was said with such force that she dared anyone to disobey it. The laughter immediately ceased as everyone scampered from the room, leaving her, her kidnapper, Corydon, his brother, and a guard at each door in the room.

"Is she injured?" he roared.

"What does it matter, Your Majesty?" the Fae shrugged.

Corydon motioned to stand, but his brother placed a firm grip on his knee, keeping him on the throne. "I think what my brother means to say is thank you for the lovely gift."

"That is not what I meant at all, Rodric, and you know it. Her necklace should have warned any Fae from harming her," Corydon grumbled quietly.

"Corydon." His voice pleaded and commanded at the same time. It was easy for her to see that Rodric thought himself to be the one truly in charge and was merely humoring Corydon because of their strange traditions. She noticed Rodric's grip on Corydon's knee tighten.

"Thank you for your gift, although in the future I would appreciate my gifts to be in the form of information about Lachlan's plans, jewels, or hunted game." Corydon's voice took on a cold tone of indifference, but she could still hear a tinge of barely restrained rage.

Rodric coughed.

"Oh, and please stay to join us for a feast this evening."

"Will my gift be the centerpiece?" her capturer asked.

After a few harsh whispers from Rodric, the king actually did stand. Stepping down from his throne and the dais, he approached her. She stared at his feet, unable to meet his gaze again. This time she couldn't help the tears that slipped down her cheeks. He pressed his thumb under her chin and tilted her face toward him. The cold mask of indifference she had seen once before was visible on his features as his eyes glanced over her, studying her as if she were a prized heifer instead of a girl he'd once loved.

"Perhaps if you had been gentler with her, if you had recognized what she wore around her neck… As it is, it will take a while for her to be presentable." He dropped his fingers and wiped them against his pants. He turned around, his back toward them. "That will be all. You are dismissed." He pointed toward a guard at the door nearest to his throne. "You, fetch Alvina." He turned to the other guard, issuing a similar command, except this time for a healer. He said nothing more and refused to face her. She wasn't sure what she'd done to cause such coldness in him, but it broke her heart all over again. She hunched over, a broken pathetic girl, and let the tears overtake her. To anyone else it may have appeared that she were a terrified human, worried for her life.

Sometime later—it could have been only a few minutes, but it felt like a lifetime to her—a door opened. A woman tried to pull her up by her shoulders, causing her to cry out in pain.

"Stop!" Corydon ordered immediately, and the hands dropped. "I will take her."

"Come on, Corydon. It isn't proper. Think about what the others will say," Rodric stated.

"And what should I do? Just let her scream in pain?"

"Yes, that's exactly what you should do. That's exactly what Father would have done, what any Unseelie King would do, and in fact, some would even feed off her pain, rejoice in it." She could tell Rodric wasn't saying these things to be mean, but rather to explain to his brother how a person in his position should act. However, Corydon wasn't hearing any of it.

"Let them talk."

Rodric sighed. Strong arms gently lifted her, careful not to jostle her arm. "At least let one of the guards carry her," Rodric pleaded.

"No!" Corydon held her uninjured side against him with her legs swinging over one arm and the other supporting her back, and then he hissed as he noticed her bleeding knee. "Are you okay, Ayanna?" he whispered. She met his violet gaze, his eyes laced with concern.

She shook her head but did not speak. It was too much. She closed her eyes, gritting her teeth against the discomfort caused by every step, trying not to cry out again. He carried her for some time before gently depositing her on a soft bed.

"I've got it from here, Your Majesty," the woman claimed.

"Thank you, Alvina. Please let me know once the healer has arrived." He sighed longingly as he gave her one last glance before leaving and closing the door behind him.

"I don't know what it is about you, my dear, but no good can come from this." The woman frowned. "I would suggest you take this off and hide it. It will cause more harm than good here." She tapped a finger against Ayanna's necklace.

She tried to protest. "I don't…"

"I know you don't understand—you humans never do. You are such selfish, careless things." Alvina shook her head. "Rest now, and the healer will be with us soon."

She worried the woman may force her to rest as the other Fae had, but she didn't. Instead she turned her attention to fixing a temporary bandage around her knee, probably to keep any blood away from the sheets she was now lying upon. Ayanna closed her eyes, attempting to process everything that had happened in the last twenty-four hours. The tears silently slipped out of their own accord, but she willed them to stop, afraid to cry in front of others. She didn't want any of them to take any joy or "feed" on her discomfort and despair. When the tears stopped, she let the emotional exhaustion pull her under.

A hand caressed her forehead, chanting words in a language she didn't understand. The gentle touch then moved down to her shoulder and left arm, and she whimpered.

"Shhh, now, it's okay. I'm here to fix you right up," a warm feminine voice soothed.

She blinked her eyes open to see a beautiful woman bent over her. Her eyes were closed in concentration as she whispered the strange words. Ayanna looked down at her left arm where the woman's hand rested and saw it glowed under her touch. Her first instinct was to flinch away, but the contact felt warm and comforting. She glanced back up at the woman, observing her long moss green hair, sharp pointed features, and of course, her beauty. Most girls would pay good money for cheekbones like hers. The language she was speaking sounded beautiful, and unlike any Ayanna had heard before. The woman finished and opened her eyes, which were a bright, glowing silver.

"There, doesn't that feel better now?" The woman gestured toward Ayanna's left arm.

Ayanna gently moved it, anticipating pain, but it never came. It felt as good as new. "Yes, thank you."

"You're welcome, child. Now, as to the scratches and your knees, I did the best I could, but I used most of my magic fixing your arm. It was shattered in several places."

She looked down at her knees, which still looked raw but glistened as if covered by antibiotic ointment. She guessed the woman read her puzzled expression because she continued to explain.

"I applied a salve to your knees, but it will take a little time for them to fully mend. Try not to wipe it off until morning, and that should do the trick. I'll leave the tin in case you need a second application later. Of course, you may still be a little sore, so take it easy. I wish there was something I could to do to fix that"—she moved her hand to rest it over Ayanna's broken heart—"but I'm afraid I can't."

"How did you know?" she whispered.

The woman smiled sadly. "I can feel it. I can feel what you are feeling. I feel where your pain is and that helps guide me as a healer to find what I need to fix. Unfortunately, there are some wounds only time can heal, not magic."

She took the woman's hand off her chest and squeezed it. "Thank you..."

"Enora." The kind Fae smiled as Ayanna's jaw dropped.

"You're...you...you know my aunt."

Enora quirked her head to the side, and as she seemed to put the pieces of a puzzle together, her lips tugged down. "Oh, no. This is not good at all." She shook her head before stilling and meeting Ayanna's gaze full on. "Ayanna?"

She nodded in reply. "Can you…could you please let Aunt Grace know I'm okay? I didn't mean for this to happen, and I'm so sorry."

"Of course. I will reassure her to the best of my abilities, but you must listen to me closely." She moved closer, her mouth merely a breath away as she whispered urgently. "You must watch your every move here. You are not safe, no matter what you may think. If you find the opportunity, run and never come back."

"I understand." She swallowed thickly.

"I don't think you truly do. You are in a serious situation. Even if the young king does care for you, he rules at the whim of his people, and they are not kind people."

"You say that as if you are not one of them."

"I am. Unseelie is not something you choose to be, rather it's in your blood. I'm just different. I think it comes with being a healer and understanding other creatures at a deeper level. I just can't find it within myself to harm. The others, however, they won't hesitate—in fact, most of them enjoy it. Never let yourself be alone with one of them if you can help it, and never trust them completely, even the one who caused that pain." She pointed to Ayanna's heart. "Remember that he caused it and he will again, even if he doesn't mean to. It's in our nature." She opened her mouth to say more, but they heard heavy footfalls and shouting approaching outside the door. Enora put a finger to her mouth as they both stilled to listen.

"The queen's quarters?! What the hell are you thinking?" yelled a male voice.

"I will not listen to any more, brother. I am the one in charge here, or did you forget that?" She could hear the anger surging through Corydon's words.

She did not hear his brother's quieter reply.

"She is here and she will be staying until I want her to leave. I don't care what the others think, and I don't need to listen to their opinions. I am their king! I'll make sure they do not question me."

"I don't think you're thinking this through fully, Corydon."

"I don't think *you* understand. I never wanted her here. I fought to keep her away, but now that she is here, I'm not letting her go. I love her!"

Ayanna drew in a sharp breath and Enora swung her head toward her, studying her with new eyes. "Well, *that* is certainly interesting," she whispered.

The men paused before Rodric said something more that they couldn't make out through the door.

"We will not discuss this later. What I say goes. If you can't follow that, perhaps you should leave."

More words were spoken but not heard by the eavesdroppers before someone not so quietly stormed away. There was a swift knock at the door, and a second later the king stepped through, closing it behind him.

"Ah, Enora, I'm so glad you could make it. I was relieved to hear you were home from your travels. Our patient required a more…delicate touch than the normal court healers provide."

"It was my pleasure, sire." She curtseyed gracefully in reply, holding the lengths of her flowing forest green skirt to the sides. The skirt looked much like something her aunt would wear, which caused Ayanna to smile briefly.

"And how is our patient?" Corydon's violet eyes studied her from head to toe.

"She's much improved. I was able to mend the bone in her left arm, and the salve is working on her cuts. She should be good as new by morning, but I'll leave a tin of salve with her just in case." Enora smiled, placing a small bronze container on the bedside table.

Ayanna pulled herself up to a sitting position now that she could use her arm. She was tiring of hearing them talk about her as if she wasn't sitting right there.

"Your Majesty, if I could have a quick word with her in private before I take my leave, I'd greatly appreciate it." The king looked offended by her request, so Enora quickly supplied an excuse. "I have matters of a feminine nature to discuss with her."

A blush deepened his cheeks and neck and he glanced down at the floor. "Of course, but only a moment," he stammered before walking out of the room and closing the door behind him.

Enora chuckled softly. "It never fails—mention the mysterious workings of a woman and a guy will turn tail and run." She looked at Ayanna and took her hand in her own. "I must leave you now, my child. I'll pass along your messages to your aunt as soon as I am able, but I need you to promise me to be careful." She whispered as softly as she could, aware that their conversation was being listened to through the door. "While his words may mend what is broken, history will only repeat itself in the end." She frowned. "I know you don't understand now, but there will come a day when you do, and I will be here to help you. *When* you should need me..." She slipped a small rock from her pocket. It looked like any other smooth, grey river pebble, but when she pressed it into Ayanna's palm, a silver shimmer rippled over its surface. "All you have to do is place this in your palm and urge your heart to reach for me, and I will come as soon as I can."

"Thank you, Enora. I'll keep this somewhere safe," she promised, tucking the rock under her pillow for the time being.

Enora hugged her and placed a kiss to her the top of her head. "Guard it along with your heart." Then she opened the door. "A word, please, Your Majesty," she requested before closing the door behind her. Ayanna could hear her talking to Corydon in the hallway, but this time it seemed they both were aware she was listening from inside the room because she heard their footsteps pull them a little away from the door. She could only hear the murmur of their voices and was unable to discern any words, so she gave up and took in the bedroom around her.

It was large and spacious, more the size of the living room back at the cottage than any bedroom she had been in. She rested on a soft queen-sized bed carved out of dark wood, complete with a short white canopy overhead. The pillows and the mattress were softer than anything she had ever felt. She imagined it must be what sleeping on a cloud would feel like. There was an end table, dresser, armoire, desk, chair, and vanity, all of matching dark wood with ornate floral designs carved into them. There were traces of gold and green in the designs, and it looked like pictures she had once seen of the furniture in the palace of Versailles, so rich and antique.

A knock at the door startled her out of her thoughts. Corydon entered, looking even more handsome than when she had last seen him months ago. His Fae features seemed sharpened and more pronounced, his beauty almost painful to look at because it made her yearn for things she knew weren't possible. He approached her bed hesitantly. "Are you feeling better?" He pulled the chair next to her bed and sat down.

"Yes, thank you." There was an awkward formality between them, as if she didn't know how to treat him now that his identity had been revealed. *Was any of what we had real?*

"Do you want to tell me how you came to be in a Fae's possession?" He gripped the chair tightly, his knuckles paling with the effort.

"I was not in his possession!" she argued.

He huffed dismissively. "My eyes and the rest of the court would say otherwise."

She crossed her arms over her chest, irritated that he was accusing her of something when he was the one who had lied to her. "Fine, you want to hear what happened, I'll tell you. I went to our spot one last time, to say goodbye. I was going to leave you a note, though I doubt you would have received it, *Your Majesty*." She sneered his moniker, her voice thick with her own accusations. "I was leaving when he came after me. I tried to get away, but he was too fast. He used his mind control juju to make my legs stop working so I fell. That's how I broke my arm and scraped my knees."

"Mind control juju?" His lips quirked up at the corners.

"Yes, mind control juju! I don't know what to call it, all I know is one moment I was in control of my body and the next it was at his beck and call, following his every command. He made me stop, so I fell. He made me walk back to his horse and when I proved difficult, he decided the easier way to transport me would be to make me sleep.

"I woke up later, thrown over his horse in a strange place. He said he was taking me to see my boyfriend, and much to my surprise he took me to the king, who turned out to be my no-good, lying ex."

He flinched at the venom in her words, his grip once

more tightening around the chair. "And why did he think I was your boyfriend?"

A lance through the heart.

She hissed in a breath. *Is he really so callous?* "Maybe because of your stupid 'claiming' necklace. Thanks for that, by the way, but I am no one's *pet*. You know what, I don't have to tell you shit. Just take me home, and I can guarantee you'll never see me again." She reached around to unclasp the necklace and shoved it at him.

"If only it were that simple, but it's not. I told you how dangerous it was to see me. I warned you what might happen when I ended things. I thought I was protecting you, but obviously, you are determined not to heed my warnings." He refused to acknowledge that she was holding the necklace out to him.

"Screw…you…Cor!" She threw the necklace at him, watching as it slid down his chest and hit the floor. "I did not bring myself here—in fact, I tried to run away. If I had it my way, I'd be back at home with Aunt Grace, not here with someone I thought I knew."

Her words struck him and he released his grip on the chair, rubbing the heel of his hand into his chest over his heart. "Yes, well, I can see we both have made some mistakes."

"You mean you lying to me and never telling me who you were? What the hell was I supposed to do when that psycho decided to kidnap me? He was going to do it no matter what. I only used what I had in my arsenal, hoping somehow it would make him think twice or bring me to you, so you could help me get out of this mess. Had I known who you were, perhaps things would've turned out differently, but you never provided me that opportunity, did you? I thought you said you would be honest with me?! God, were you *ever* honest with me?" Her voice rose to a yell with each question, her anger fueled by betrayal.

He stood abruptly, shoving the chair into the wall with the force. "Of course I was honest with you!" he yelled back, then he stopped himself. "You're the only one who truly knows who I am," he admitted softly, walking around the room as if it would help him gather his thoughts. "I am not this"—he motioned to the fancy clothing and his crown—"no matter how hard I'm trying to be, but it's not like I had a choice. I would gladly hand over the fucking throne to Rodric if it were possible, but no, because of some stupid genetic luck I was born with the royal-colored eyes instead of him so am stuck with this responsibility, and then his wife had to go and kill off my dad so I was thrust into the position much sooner than I ever thought I would be. I've never had any say in the matter. The only piece of my life I ever felt some control over was my time with you. It was only then that I felt like I could finally be myself, but I had to give that up too when he died because you are so fragile."

"I am not fragile," she protested, though she knew what he was trying to say. Her heart softened at his confession, understanding why he didn't want her to know about that part of him.

"But you are. You couldn't fight off that Fae and he could have done much worse, if you really think about it. Any of them can, and they may try now that you are here. Sure, our people are known for having romantic relations with humans from time to time, but none of them truly last, not with the difference in our aging rate. Most Unseelie see humans more as playthings, here for their amusement, and I will not let you become one."

"So, send me back."

"It's not that easy." He sighed. He approached her bed cautiously, and she scooted over, allowing him to sit next to her. He sat at the edge of the bed, facing her and tucking one leg underneath himself. "I wasn't very good at hiding my emotions when I saw you again, and too many have seen through me." He cupped her face, running his thumb across her cheek. He brought her head toward him and kissed her forehead. "If I let you go now, I'm afraid someone will use you against me. They'll seek to harm you as a means to getting to me, so I cannot let you go."

"What do you mean you can't let me go?" She pulled her head back so she could look into his eyes.

"You'll have to stay here where I can keep you safe."

"So, I'm your prisoner now?"

"No. You are not locked up, are you?"

"But I'm not allowed to leave?"

He nodded his head.

"I'm pretty sure that still makes me your prisoner. A gilded cage is still a cage," she argued. "I had plans. I'm supposed to leave soon for college. What about Aunt Grace? She's probably already called the police and filed a missing person report."

"You can write her a letter and I'll have it delivered immediately," he offered as if that one positive would cancel out all the negative. He grabbed her hand. "I'm sorry you seem to find staying with me such a distasteful idea, Ayanna. I wish I could let you go, but it's just not possible—although, if I'm perfectly honest, I'm not sorry you're here and I get to spend time with you again. I've missed you so much."

He leaned in to kiss her, but she was too angry to fall back into his arms, so she turned her face toward the only windows in the room and his lips fell against her cheek.

He sighed, his eyes pleading with her to understand where he was coming from. "I'll try to make it up to you. I have a tutor here, one of the best, and I'll have him teach you so you can continue your education. If there's anything you want apart from going home, all you have to do is ask it and I will try my best. However, for the time being, I'd like you to stay in this room. I have matters to attend to as king, and I have to figure out how best to address my people about you, who you are and what you mean to me. I will have Alvina bring you dinner and will check on you once more before I go to bed. Get some rest." He kissed her cheek and stood up, bending to pick up her necklace off the floor and placing it on the vanity before leaving.

She heaved a dramatic sigh, throwing herself back against the bed. What the hell am I going to do now? And how am I ever going to get out of this mess?

True to his word, the older woman from earlier brought her dinner. She wondered how old she had to be in human years to already look aged as a Fae—probably centuries— but didn't dare ask her. You never ask a woman about her age. The woman dealt with her as if she were an irritating child keeping her from her real job, and she thought perhaps in some way that was true. One thing was certain: this woman was not going to be her friend any time soon, so she would just have to deal with her much like a kid deals with an adult she doesn't particularly like. She tried to be as polite and sweet as possible, all the while keeping her defenses up and anticipating any little attack. After depositing a tray of food and drink at the desk, the woman left.

She remembered what she had read about Fae food and drink and how it could affect humans. If she weren't so hungry, she could've resisted, but she doubted Corydon would intentionally poison her. Then she remembered the zahra flower and how he had unintentionally done something similar. She studied the food carefully; it seemed harmless enough. The drink, however, was the color of red wine and smelled sickeningly sweet. She took the glass to the bathroom where she poured the beverage down the drain, rinsed the glass, and filled it with water instead. She was more than relieved that while the exterior of the castle had appeared medieval, they seemed to have some modern amenities, like indoor plumbing. She still wasn't sure whether the lights ran on electricity or some sort of magic, though.

The meal was delicious, what looked like a steak with some mashed potatoes and some sort of bread pudding. It was heavenly. There was a strange purple vegetable as well, but she was too wary to try it so she left it as the only untouched portion of her plate. The rest she practically licked clean. When she was finished, she stacked her dishes on the tray and went to place them outside the door but found it was locked. She pounded against it and stepped back when it opened.

A man stood in her doorway. He was tall but lean and looked like one of the guards she had passed as they entered the castle gates. His skin was dark chocolate, but his eyes startled her with their bright gold hue. "What can I help you with, miss?" he asked, studying her with morbid curiosity.

"Um, I just…" She couldn't stand the weight of his golden gaze and thrust the tray out in front of her. "I'm done with this and didn't know what to do with it."

"Just leave it for one of the servants, miss. They'll

come get it later."

"Okay…thank you."

He studied her for a moment more before rolling his eyes and closing the door. She heard the click of the lock falling into place. *Dammit.* She really didn't want to be locked in. She normally wasn't a claustrophobic person, but it seemed like this might push her there. She walked toward the window, seizing the opportunity to take stock of everything at her disposal. She checked the latches of the window and was relieved when it opened, allowing her to breath in fresh air. She leaned out into the night and looked down. She was on the second floor, and there was no way for her to climb down. *What did I expect, a trellis to scale for easy escape?* She shook her head and searched the armoire and all the dresser and desk drawers, finding them equally empty save for the desk, which held an old-fashioned quill, a bottle of ink, and parchment. She expected Corydon had left it there for her to write her letter. She next explored the bathroom, disappointed to not find anything of use to her unless she wished to wash up or attempt to build a rope out of towels, but she doubted she had a sufficient amount to make it long enough to rappel down from her window. She tucked the rock from Enora into one of the towels on the bottom of the stack, afraid if a servant changed the bedding, they would discover it under her pillow.

She thought she should probably clean herself up, noting the dried blood on her leg, but decided to do so after she wrote a letter to Grace. She didn't know what to write as she was pretty sure Enora was probably already telling Grace the gist, but she didn't want her to worry and knew she had to write something.

Dear Aunt Grace,

~~I'm so sorry I didn't come home today. I meant to, really. unfortunately a Fae found me by the pond as I was on my way home. He put me to sleep and took me to his strange lands.~~

She scribbled out what she'd written and crumpled that piece of parchment into a ball before grabbing a fresh one.

Dear Aunt Grace,

Please don't worry about me. I am safe. I didn't want to leave you, but I had no control over it. Please don't try to find me. I will find my way back to you when I can. In the meantime, rest assured that while I may be stuck in Fae for now, I have been guaranteed safety and I trust he will honor that. I love you and hope to see you soon.

With love,
Ayanna

She hoped her note and Enora's reassurance of her safety would work. The last thing she needed to worry about was Aunt Grace getting captured as she tried to come look for her. When she finished the note, she drew a bath, filling the large tub with water and adding a spoonful of some sweet-smelling salts she found next to the bath. She climbed in, the warm water caressing her skin and soothing her aches. She rested for a while until her skin grew pruney then found some soap and used it to wash her body and hair. She was amazed to see her once bloody knees now only had the appearance of raw pink skin. Enora had done a fantastic job healing her.

She climbed out of the bath, dried herself, and slipped her dress back on, unsure of where to find something clean to wear and not wanting to ask the guard for something so embarrassing. She noticed her tray of dishes was gone. *How odd.* She hadn't heard anyone enter. She climbed into bed, burying herself under covers thinking about the possibility of anyone having been in her room while she was bathing. Her mind spun, attempting to come up with a plan for escape but coming up empty every time.

Eventually there was a knock at the door, and Corydon entered. He noted her wet hair. "I take it you found the bath. Did you get a chance to eat as well?"

"I did." She bit her lower lip. "You don't happen to have something I can sleep in, do you? I don't want to sleep in my dress."

His cheeks flushed with color. "Of course. Give me a moment." He stepped out of the room, returning rather quickly with a large forest green tunic, one she had once seen him wear. He handed it to her.

"Thank you." She climbed out of bed and walked to the bathroom, closing the door behind her while she slipped on his shirt. She brought the fabric to her nose and inhaled deeply, noting that it smelled like him, like a forest after a spring rain. The tunic fell to a few inches above her knees, covering her quite well. The top was loose with a rather deep V she tried to tie closed, but it wouldn't stay that way. Eventually she gave up and stepped out of the bathroom, not wanting to make him wait any longer.

He inhaled sharply as she stepped out. "You always look beautiful, but you in my shirt is a vision that will haunt my dreams for the rest of my life."

It was her turn to blush. "Thank you." She went to climb back under the covers, but his hand on the small of her back made her stop.

"Wait. We need to put more salve on your knees to help them fully heal."

"Of course." She sat on top of the covers, stretching her legs out in front of her and tugging down the tunic, which had crept up her thighs.

"Please allow me." He swallowed hard as he stared at her legs. He untwisted the lid of the tin, and she saw a clear, glittery ointment inside. He dug two fingers into it and brought a small dollop onto her left knee before smoothing it all over her skin with his hand. Her traitorous heart pounded against her ribcage, aching to burst free, his touch sparking electricity throughout her body and straight down to her core. He repeated the same process with her right knee and she fought the urge to shiver under his touch. She noticed his breathing had also increased, his violet eyes shimmering with lust, much as they had after they spent hours kissing on the forest floor by the pond. Finally, he pressed a kiss to the top of each of her knees. "There, all better," he said, his voice low and thick, and he coughed, attempting to clear it.

She fought her hormones and emotions, pulling herself under the covers, figuring that was the safest place for her to be.

"Do you need anything else before I leave you?" he asked, rising and putting some distance between them.

"How long are you going to keep me locked in here?"

He frowned. "I'm not sure yet, but at least until I know someone won't try to harm you."

"Great." She blew out a frustrated breath. "Do you think you could at least bring me some books to read so I'm not sitting here bored, plotting all the possible ways to escape or kill you in your sleep?"

He laughed, dismissing her words as an empty threat. "Yes, I think I can do that. Do you need one tonight or can you wait until tomorrow? If you wait, I will take you to the library where you can pick out your own and meet your tutor. If you want one now, you'll be stuck with whatever I give you."

"I'll wait," she replied.

"Perfect. I will get you after breakfast and escort you to the library tomorrow morning." He leaned over to kiss her again, and while she tried to offer him her cheek once more, he was too fast and stole a brief kiss from her lips. He smiled at her, satisfied with himself. "Good night, Ayanna. Sweet dreams." Then he was gone, leaving her with her fingers pressed against her lips, wondering how she could have so quickly fallen back in love with him, or if it was merely that she had been lying to herself and had never truly stopped.

CHAPTER II

AFTER BREAKFAST WAS delivered the next morning and she had taken her fill, she was surprised to discover that her armoire and dresser had somehow been filled with clothes. *Was it magic or did someone sneak in overnight?* She wasn't sure, but there were tons of options to choose from. She frowned as she sifted through the clothes, a little disappointed to discover that apparently, most Fae women did not wear pants. Her clothes were all dresses, skirts, undergarments (which were very similar to what humans used, much to her relief), and blouses. There were even quite a few ball gowns included. For the most part they revealed a little more skin than she was used to, which made her blush horribly as she sorted through the rainbow of soft fabrics. She settled on a simple navy blue, lace baby doll dress, finding it to be more on the modest side than others, though a bit short.

She was also surprised to see a small box of colorful ribbons on the vanity. She braided her hair to the side and tied it off with a navy ribbon. Her letter had also disappeared, and she hoped that meant it was on its way to Grace. She debated trying the locked door but didn't want to come face to face with the golden-eyed guard from the previous night. She was relieved to hear a knock at the door and see Corydon step through.

"My lady." He bowed formally, which she found odd and slightly unnerving. "I see you found something suitable to wear." His lips quirked up and his tongue snaked out to wet them, showing just how much he appreciated her outfit. She would've blushed if she hadn't already been irritated by his bizarre behavior; instead, she rolled her eyes. "And your knees look much improved." Sure enough, her knees looked as if there had never been an injury. That salve was amazing.

"Um, thanks, I guess—although I'd prefer some pants if you have them."

A small gasp echoed in the room as a female servant entered to retrieve her tray. They both turned to look at her. "F-Forgive me, sire. I did not mean to interrupt." She stared at her feet, wringing her hands until he gave a wave, indicating for her to continue. She fumbled with the tray, almost dropping the dishes in the process. Ayanna stepped forward to help her, but Corydon held up his hand, pushing her back from approaching.

Once the door closed behind the fumbling servant, he narrowed his eyes at her. "You…" He took a deep breath, as if to keep his anger from bursting forward.

She was always wary of his shift in moods. His anger was something she never wished to see again. It made her wonder about just how much he was holding back around her. *How much of his Unseelie nature controls him?*

"Ladies of the court do not wear pants," he stated simply, as if that explanation would explain all.

"But, I'm not—"

"You are now. I made an official declaration this morning that you are to be treated as such. You are important to me, and what's important to the king should be important to the people."

She frowned. The last thing she wanted was special treatment; she knew the resentment it could cause. "But I'm human. Do you normally treat humans this way?" She knew the answer, but she wanted to hear him admit it.

"No." He chewed on the inside of his cheek, and she wondered if he regretted the fact that she had unexpectedly appeared back in his life. "But it does not matter what has been done in the past. I am the king now and I make the decisions. So, if I say you are to be treated as a lady of the court, they will treat you as such."

"I don't need special treatment, Cor."

He suddenly glanced down, unable to meet her eyes. "I know," he whispered, "but it was the only way they might accept you here…with me."

She didn't know what to say, so she just took his hand and squeezed it. He looked so vulnerable in that moment and it made her heart ache, reminding her of the boy in the woods, the one she had met and fallen in love with what felt like ages ago and the day before all the same time.

"So are you going to show me this library of yours, or shall I just sit here and waste away from boredom?" she teased, attempting to lighten the mood.

"Of course." He smiled and held out his arm for her to take, a gesture she had only seen in movies.

When they exited the room, she was relieved to not see the golden-eyed guard. They were in a rather long hallway with only two doors, hers and one directly across the hall, which she found odd. "Where are we?"

"The east wing."

"So, if that's my room, whose room is that?" She pointed from her door to the one across the hall.

"Mine." He swallowed.

"Oh." She thought back to the conversation she'd overheard between him and his brother. If the king's quarters were right across the hall, she was in the suite generally reserved for the queen. *Well, that's a heavy thought.*

He urged her forward, pulling her from her thoughts. She didn't know what to make of that gesture. She still wasn't sure what he wanted or expected from her, and she wasn't about to give up on her hope of returning home. She knew she didn't belong with him no matter how much her heart yearned to be by his side. They were two star-crossed lovers, and fate always had a way of catching up and tragically ripping them apart.

He pulled her across the landing where she looked over to see the stairs leading down to the main entrance she had just walked through the previous day. He pointed out different things as they passed: the dining hall and throne room to the side of the main entrance, the west wing full of guest rooms. He opened the door to the library, which she assumed would be rather quaint based on the door and simple hallway, but she was wrong. It was two stories high, filled with bookshelves and high-vaulted ceilings with an open center. There was an ornately carved spiral staircase off to one side that led to the second landing, while in the center, set under a glass skylight, was a large table that could probably seat about twenty. There were also several oversized cushioned chairs that looked just perfect for curling up in with a good book. She wasn't aware that her jaw had dropped until she heard a chuckle of amusement and felt his finger lift it closed.

"Wow," she said breathlessly, unsure how to describe the beauty before her. He continued to walk her father down and she stared around in awe. Several ornate tapestries caught her eye along with several sparkling chandeliers. It was only then that she noticed a small office tucked off to the side, set apart by a wall full of windows. Inside sat two Fae who looked to be only a few years younger than Corydon, but she knew how looks could be deceiving when it came to their age. One was the brunette she had run into the day before, and the other had short pale blond hair, not quite as pale as Corydon's, but close. She held her breath, hoping Corydon didn't have a son he hadn't told her about. An old man was hunched over between the two, using a map spread across the table to show them different military strategies. The small soldier figurines were a dead giveaway, although upon closer inspection, they appeared to be mini Fae warriors with pointed ears and swords instead of guns.

Corydon cleared his throat and all three of the Fae blinked their eyes up at them curiously.

"Ah, Your Majesty, to what do we owe this honor?" The old man curiously flicked his gaze back and forth between her and the king. The brunette was staring at her as if she were a puzzle he was trying to work out, his brow slightly furrowed. The blond, on the other hand, had his icy blue eyes lasered in on where her hand gripped the king's, his nose scrunched in distaste. She fought the urge to release her grip, not wanting to be intimidated by him.

"This is Ayanna. Ayanna, this is Alfie, our tutor and historian," he introduced them. She released his arm, extending her hand to shake Alfie's.

He grasped her hand in his own and brought it to his

lips, the corners of his eyes crinkling. "Pleased to meet you, milady." His smile was truly genuine and she could see the kindness behind his eyes. His white hair was long and his skin was so full of wrinkles, she wondered how many centuries he must have lived and the wisdom he had to share.

"Pleased to meet you as well."

The king then turned to the younger Fae, pointing to the brunette first. "This is Conall. He's somewhat of a genius with a sword."

"Eh, I'm halfway decent." He laughed jovially and shook her hand.

"Don't let his humility fool you. If I ever get into a fight, he's the guy I want on my side," the king contended.

"Well, it's a good thing he is on your side then." She smiled and turned to the last Fae, who had thankfully schooled his features entirely from when she first observed him.

Corydon walked around the table to stand next to the boy and ruffled his hair affectionately. "And this scoundrel is my nephew, Casimir."

She extended her hand but he gave her a little wave instead. "Hey."

"Oh, is someone being shy?" Corydon teased, elbowing Casimir in the side. "Does the pretty lady intimidate you?"

Casimir's face flamed, but his features were so tight it was hard to tell if it was from embarrassment or anger, or a mixture of both.

"We were just finishing up, sire. It seems Conall here has finished training with the guard and has learned all I have to teach him."

Conall blushed. "Not all, old man. I've still got plenty to learn." She could see the easy affection between teacher and pupil.

"Then I will begin on the royal requirements for Casimir, of course." Alfie smiled and Casimir huffed a breath as he rolled his eyes, clearly not thrilled with the idea.

"Perfect! Since you have a student opening, I have brought you a new one." Corydon smiled. "Ayanna has a lot to learn and I trust you will teach her all she needs to know about our people, as well as furthering her education in any other subject she wishes to study. She was supposed to be going to school in the fall, and although I don't know what they teach at human schools, I'm sure you will be able to help her out."

She frowned at his words and tone. It was clear he thought the education humans received to be trivial. She wondered what Alfie would be able to teach her, but his kind smile put her at ease. "I would be most delighted to assist the lady in any way possible, sire."

"Wonderful. We'll have you start tomorrow. I must be going now, but the lady wanted to select some books to read, so I'm going to leave her in your care. Will you please escort her back to the queen's quarters when she is done?"

"It would be my pleasure." Alfie bowed. The boys stared at them with wide eyes.

Corydon turned and grabbed her hand once more, pulling her into a secluded corner away from prying eyes. "I'm going to leave you with Alfie, but don't worry, he'll be kind to you. I need you to promise me you will not leave this room until he escorts you back to your own. It is not safe for you to wander around the castle…yet. Do you promise?" He cupped her cheek, forcing her eyes to meet his intense gaze.

She nodded.

"Good." Then he pressed his lips to hers, devouring her mouth just as he had done the night before. Once she was completely breathless, he pulled back, his eyes now a few shades darker. "I must go, but I'll eat dinner with you this evening. How about that?" He winked and left her there. She placed a hand on a nearby bookshelf to steady herself.

"You don't belong here," a voice said from the shadows.

She glanced around before spotting icy blue eyes in the darkness.

"Tell me something I don't know," she replied.

"You won't last long—humans never do. He'll tire of you eventually and will toss you to his dogs to play with, so don't get comfortable," he sneered, his upper lip curled back, revealing his sharp teeth in a threatening manner.

Before she could reply, he turned and left. She was so confused from one minute of being kissed senseless and the other of all-too-real threats voicing her own insecurities that she sank into the nearest chair and curled up, resting her head on the side of her arm as she tried to analyze her situation.

A gentle hand shook her awake. "Would you like some lunch and perhaps some tea, milady?" Alfie's kind periwinkle eyes studied her.

"Oh, yes. That would be wonderful. I'm sorry. I didn't mean to fall asleep here."

"I imagine it's been quite an exciting last few days for you." He motioned for her to follow him and led her to the large table where several plates of food, a teapot, and teacups were waiting.

"You have no idea," she mumbled.

"Take a seat. While we eat, we'll talk about what you want to learn from me and what the king has in mind for me to teach you. Then I can show you around the library and you can select a few books to take back to your room. How does that sound?"

"Thank you," she replied. "You are kinder than I expected," she noted as they sat and she began piling food onto her plate.

"Yes, well, I know exactly what it feels like to be an outsider."

She paused with her fork midway to her mouth. "You do?"

He nodded. "I'm not from here, originally. In fact, I don't belong here at all, but returning home is not a possibility."

"So, you're a prisoner too?"

"Just as much as you are, my dear." He smiled sadly. Intrigued, she begged him to tell her his story, and he did. It turned out Alfie was a Seelie Fae and had been captured by Corydon's father more than two centuries ago. He'd questioned him for quite some time, even torturing him for information, and was sadly disappointed when he had nothing of use to tell him. Normally, the Unseelie executed captives, but luckily Alfie was a scholar who had been training to take over the historian's job at the Seelie palace, and the king's own scholar had recently died without training anyone to replace him. His knowledge of both Fae courts made him incredibly valuable, so they kept him. He tried escaping several times, but each attempt only ended up with severe consequences that left him realizing it was in his best interest not to try again. He didn't elaborate on what they did to him, but she thought he might be using his story to warn her against her own attempts.

"Well, enough about me. Tell me about yourself now." He quickly opted for a subject change once his story had been told, and she played along, sensing that dwelling on his past was painful for him. She told him almost everything there was to know. She kept her promise to Grace and did not reveal that she could see beyond the Fae's magical glamour to their pointy ears, sharp teeth, and glowing eyes underneath. She admitted that she had read some books about Fae folklore and was eager to learn the truth about the Fae while she was there. Alfie helped her select a history book and encyclopedia of Fae abilities and terminology to help her understand the basics of the new world around her.

He walked her back to her room when she was finished and insisted on carrying her books until they reached her destination. Of course, there was a guard at the beginning of her hallway, not too far from her room. This one had bright red eyes and short black hair in a military-style cut. He inhaled deeply and licked his lips as she walked by. Alfie insisted on bringing her books inside her room, where he deposited them on her desk.

"Be careful of that one out there." He motioned in the direction of where she had seen the guard with bright red eyes. "Any one of them, really, but especially those with red irises. They restore their magic by feeding on human blood or energy, and you would be quite the temptation. I doubt they would touch you based on the declaration the king issued this morning, but best to always keep your guard up. I definitely recommend you read the encyclopedia first so you learn which of us can be the most dangerous." He winked at her. "I'll come to get you tomorrow for your studies." He turned to leave.

"Alfie?" she called out after him. "Why did the king

put me in the queen's quarters?"

"I think if you search your heart, you already know the answer to that question." With a smile, he closed the door behind him, and she was once again left alone.

She spent the remainder of the afternoon reading her new books, learning about all the different races of Fae and their abilities. Most of the time you could tell what a Fae's abilities were based on their eye color (as Alfie had mentioned about red irises). Those Fae had a dominant type of magic they inherited from one of their parents. However, if a Fae inherited both of their parents' magic, their eye color could be misleading. Thankfully, inheriting two different abilities was rare, but all the information was a lot to take in.

Corydon had dinner delivered to her room and ate with her as promised. He confessed how much he missed her and filled her in on everything that had happened since they parted ways. She in turn filled him in on finishing school and graduation, applying for colleges and getting accepted. When they finished eating, he tugged her to the bed to sit and talk more. She had forgotten how much she missed having a best friend to share everything with, especially with him. It had always felt so easy.

He confessed his insecurities about leading his people, how he was afraid their expectations and the responsibilities would change him, how he needed her to remind him of who he was and wanted to be. They lay side by side until he pulled her closer, content only when she was snuggled against him.

"I missed this. I missed this so much," he confessed, kissing her hair, her cheeks, the tip of her nose, and finally her mouth. His hands skimmed across her back and her arms, leaving fire in their wake. When they slipped under her shirt and onto her to skin, she sighed into his mouth at the contact. It felt like she couldn't get close enough. She tugged his tunic loose from his leather pants, demanding to feel his skin. He moaned when her hands grazed his back under his shirt. Instantly she was transported back to the summer, when they spent many days lost in kisses and the feel of each other's skin. Having spent most of the day in their swimsuits, what they were doing wasn't anything beyond where they'd drawn the line back then. His fingers splayed across her back, pulling her closer and maneuvering her onto her back where he tugged her shirt up to her ribs and peppered her stomach with kisses until she couldn't stand it any longer.

She wiggled away from him laughing. "Mercy. Mercy!" she begged between giggles.

He brought his face up and grinned. "I always loved how ticklish you are."

She shook her head. "Whatever."

"Just one of the many things I love about you." He sighed and rested his cheek against her bare stomach. She ran her fingers through his hair and he closed his eyes. "This doesn't feel like it's real. I used to dream about this, about having you here. I'm scared I'll wake up and you'll be gone."

Her fingers stilled. She loved being with him, but she wasn't sure she wanted to stay there. Could they even make this work, or were they asking for a disaster of massive proportions? She stayed quiet while she mentally debated the pros and cons of staying. It was so easy to tune out the rest of the world when it was just the two of them, but how long could they do that? What would the consequences be?

"Cor, why am I here?"

"You're here because a Fae brought you."

She resumed running her fingers through his hair, hoping it would encourage him to keep talking.

"No, I mean why am I here in this room? In the queen's quarters?"

"So I can keep you safe."

"Couldn't you keep me safe in another room?"

He huffed a sigh and pulled himself up into a sitting position, scooting toward the edge of the bed and facing away from her. She could see his stormy expression in the vanity mirror.

"Yes, but I wanted you near me."

"Is it going to cause problems, me staying in this room?"

"Does it matter?"

"I don't know…does it?"

He tugged his hands through his hair. "Yes…no…shit. To me it doesn't. I don't really care. If I want you here, I should be able to have you here—that's the benefit of being king. I get to be the one who makes all the decisions. I'm the one in charge, and what I say goes. If I want you here by my side, everyone else can just get over it."

She crawled toward him and wrapped her arms around him from behind. "Do you want me here? In Fae? Or am I only here due to an unfortunate circumstance and now you're stuck?" She figured she might as well bring out the big guns if they were going to get serious. She needed to know if he wanted her there or was only dealing with the consequences of her actions. Once she knew the answer to that, she could be more levelheaded about her decisions—or so she thought.

He pulled her around so she straddled his lap, facing

him. He brushed her hair back from her face and tucked it behind her ears. "I want you here. I've always wanted you here—never doubt that for one second. I never stopped loving you, and now that I have you again, I can't imagine life without you. You make me want to be a better man." She stared deep into his violet eyes, reading the truth behind his statement, and it knocked the breath out of her. Hope fluttered in her chest. Maybe they weren't the doomed lovers she thought them to be; maybe they could somehow make this work. She decided for the time being she would try to be happy there with him until he gave her reason not to.

She crashed her lips against his, this time stealing his breath. She consumed him as if he were the air she needed to breathe. She tugged his tunic over his head, desperate to get her hands on his muscled chest and back. He tugged hers off, moaning when their skin met. She pulled back from his kiss and threw her arms around him, pressing herself against his chest and holding him tightly, savoring the connection and at the same time drawing her line in the sand, the line she wasn't ready to cross just yet. She placed a kiss against his neck before pulling back and climbing off his lap. She picked up her shirt and slipped it back over her head as he did the same. She loved that he didn't make her feel bad for putting on the brakes. He never did; he was so respectful of her boundaries and pace, and it warmed her heart further.

He stood, pulling her into a fierce hug once more and pressing a chaste kiss to her lips. "I suppose I should go to bed. I won't lock you in the room anymore if you promise not to go anywhere without Alfie or me for the time being, just for a few more days?"

"Thank you. I promise not to explore without an escort."

"I think tomorrow night I'll have you dine with the court. Alfie can prep you on proper etiquette and such, but I think it would be best if everyone got used to seeing you around here with me."

She bit her bottom lip. "Are you sure?"

"Most definitely. It'll be fine. I've given my official declaration and everyone knows what the penalty would be for breaking it, so there shouldn't be any problems."

She was afraid to ask about the penalty, figuring this might be an instance where ignorance was bliss, so she didn't question him further. "Okay."

"Wonderful! I'll have Alvina help you get ready and select a dress that will meet the court's approval." He cupped her cheek before resting his forehead against hers and breathing in her scent. "Good night, Ayanna. I love you." He pressed a kiss to her forehead and walked to the door.

"I love you too," she said as she exhaled, watching him close the door behind him. She collapsed on the bed. *Can I do this? Can I be what he needs? What about college and my plans? Can I really be the girl who throws it all away for love?* She sighed. If she was truly honest with herself she would admit that ever since she lost her parents, the only thing she wanted in life was a family to love. Her heart and her head battled for quite a while, running through many different scenarios before she attempted to fall asleep. In the end, her heart won.

The next day Alfie came and got her from her room. She asked that he give her a tour of the palace so she could become a little more familiar with her surroundings. He seemed hesitant at first, but she reassured him that Corydon had said it was all right. He took her to the first floor where he showed her the entrances for the dining hall and the throne room, both of which they did not enter for fear of disrupting anything. He showed her the kitchen, where they stole a quick snack before going to the counsel room where the advisors met to strategize. He pointed out where the stairs led down to the dungeon and ended the tour of the first floor by showing her the ballroom. It was massive and everything she'd imagined a ballroom to be. It reminded her of the ballroom from *Cinderella*, so grand and exquisite. The only thing missing were the steps at the top leading down.

Finally, they returned to the library where Alfie taught her as much as he could about court etiquette. All the formalities of which silverware to use when were confusing and she was sure she would somehow mess up that night, but she did learn the best way to fit in would probably be to ignore any small digs anyone would make at her, which she had plenty of experience in from dealing with mean girls at her old high school in the city.

Still, she was a bit of a nervous wreck. As the day grew later and evening approached, her nerves only intensified. It felt like she had a family of hummingbirds living in her stomach zipping around. Alfie escorted her back to her room when he was satisfied she had learned enough not to horribly embarrass herself or the king. She threw her arms around Alfie, hugging him to show her thanks when he dropped her off. He seemed startled at first but then returned her embrace and smiled.

Once she was in her room, she noticed a strapless gown had been lain out on her bed. It was navy blue, which would bring out her sapphire eyes, with a sweetheart neckline and a gold beaded lace applique material spanning from under the bust to right above her navel, from where it dipped down farther along the sides before meeting more of the blue fabric and flowing out into a long skirt. She gulped, noticing that the gold applique was see-through. This gown was one she would not have chosen for a first impression, but she was sure whoever had picked it out probably knew what they were doing.

"Your bath is ready. Hurry now, no time to waste." The older woman she had seen on her first day at the castle stood in the doorway to the bathroom, urging her forward. She gently placed the gown back on the bed and stepped into the bathroom, closing the door behind her, afraid the woman may want to bathe her as well.

"Don't wash your hair. I want it dry to style," the woman, who Ayanna assumed was Alvina, called through the door.

"Okay," she called back. She pulled her hair on top of her head in a messy bun before stepping into the tub. She scrubbed every inch of her skin with a sweet-smelling soap, and when she was done, she toweled off and wrapped the towel around her, tucking it in at her chest before stepping back into the room.

"Makeup first, then hair, dress last. Sit." Alvina pointed to the chair in front of the vanity where a variety of brushes and ribbons lay. Ayanna took a seat and let the woman get to work. Alvina picked up a makeup brush and Ayanna looked for the makeup but didn't see any.

"Relax," she ordered as she ran the brush across Ayanna's face, humming a sweet, soothing lullaby. Ayanna closed her eyes. A smaller brush ran across the lids of her eyes, and yet another over her cheeks and lips. The entire time Alvina hummed, getting louder at some parts and softer at others. Finally, the large brush swooped across her entire face, and she fought the urge to laugh from the ticklish bristles.

"There. You can look now."

She opened her eyes and gasped. Her makeup was flawless. It was as if she were ready for a photo shoot. Her cheeks looked perfectly blushed and her eyes had a black smoky eye around them, making her blue irises pop. Finally, her lids were topped with some sort of shimmering glitter that made her eyelids look like sparkling onyx. Even her lips had a rosy tint to them that she wasn't used to.

"How did you…?"

"Magic, of course," the woman stated, as if the girl were stupid for even questioning it. "Now, let's see about your hair." This time she picked up a hair brush and ran it through Ayanna's hair several times while humming a different tune. She also ran her fingers through it, twisting this way and that. When she was finished, it looked professionally curled. To top it all off, she pulled a few strands from the front and braided them back at each side of her head, the strands meeting in the middle at the back in an ornate swirling design. It was beautiful.

"Thank you," Ayanna whispered in awe.

"Dress now," the woman ordered, pointing to the gown.

"I need to grab some undergarments first." She blushed, trying to step around the woman to the dresser.

"Nope, no panty lines." The woman pointed at the dress again, more forcefully this time.

Her mouth suddenly went dry, but she took one look at Alvina and knew she wouldn't win this battle, so she picked up the dress and tried to walk toward the bathroom.

"You don't have anything I haven't seen before," Alvina complained, but Ayanna continued forward to where she could slip on the dress without watchful eyes. She dropped her towel and stepped into the garment, but of course couldn't lace it up by herself.

She stepped out of the bathroom, holding it up around her breasts. "Um, I can't lace it up."

Alvina rolled her eyes. "Of course not. That's why you should have just changed out here." She laced her up then fretted around the gown, picking off invisible lint for a few minutes before declaring her ready. She looked at herself in the mirror. She was stunning, looking like she could easily grace the cover of any magazine. The gown looked fantastic. The blue was the perfect shade and the see-through lace applique around her midsection was definitely eye-catching. She felt sexy, and it was just the confidence she needed.

She was slipping on a pair of strappy heels when there was a knock. "Is she ready?" Corydon's voice rang out through the closed door.

Alvina opened it. "As much as she can be," she muttered before leaving the room. Corydon stepped inside, and she could almost see the drool gathering at the corners of his mouth as he stared her over from head to toe.

"You look stunning," he said breathlessly, his voice a few notes lower than normal.

"Thank you. You look mighty fine yourself." And he did. He filled his rather formal uniform nicely, looking very much like a dashing Disney prince.

He offered her his arm once more and she took it, eager for assistance in the heels. He escorted her down the stairs and through two large double doors into the dining hall, where the guests were already seated. They all stared, some curiously, others more maliciously, but no one spoke a word as he pulled out the chair to his right for her. He was seated at the head of the table, his brother was straight across from her, and the rest of the rather large dining table was full of unfamiliar faces. Some of them were still staring at her, others whispering to each other. A few females shot her daggers while the men seemed more curious. The only other familiar face she could see was Casimir at the other end.

"Before we eat, I would like to propose a toast." Corydon's voice spoke for all to hear as he stood and lifted a goblet.

Everyone else retrieved for their own drink, so she picked up the one in front of her. She was pretty sure it wasn't water inside.

"To Lady Ayanna, may you all be as charmed with her as I am." He raised his goblet before bringing it to his lips and heartily taking a drink. She watched the others do the same, some rather reluctantly. They were watching her as well, and she knew refusing to drink would be an insult to the toast and the king, so she brought the cup to her lips and tipped it back. The red liquid danced across her tongue, sweet and fruity with a few floral notes. It was perhaps the most delicious thing she'd ever had to drink. She brought the goblet to her lips again and took another sip. She was about to say screw it and drain the whole thing when a hand on her right gently tugged the goblet down.

"Easy there, we'll have plenty of time for that. Best to get some food in you first or you'll be drunk before the meal begins," cautioned a man with pale orange eyes and jet black hair in a sort of pompadour style.

"Oh, thank you. I didn't realize there was alcohol in it."

"Of course not." He shook his head. "He really should have prepped you better," he muttered under his breath before continuing in a regular volume. "We call it ambrosia. It's our version of your wine and has similar effects as alcohol. For most Fae it takes quite a bit for us to feel the effects, but humans, on the other hand, seem to be effected rather quickly. I'd take it really slowly if I were you."

"Thank you," she whispered, surprised he had stopped her from making a fool of herself.

Corydon motioned a servant over and whispered something in her ear. She returned a few minutes later with a goblet of water and set it next to Ayanna. Ayanna smiled at Corydon, who raised his goblet toward her, and she picked up the water to toast him back.

Conversation flowed easily around the table. Rodric seemed to dominate Coyrdon's ear, but he kept a watchful eye on her, checking back in from time to time, asking what she thought of the meal and the palace and such.

The gentleman next to her eventually introduced himself as Lord Dante, and he kept her engaged in polite conversation, seeming fascinated with her human life and the advancements of technology. He was right about the ambrosia—she started to feel funny halfway through the meal. It was not like she had never been drunk before, so she knew what it would feel like, but she hadn't expected to feel it so quickly. She set her fork down and closed her eyes.

"Keep eating. Try some of the bread—it will help." She picked up the bread and nibbled on it, hoping it would do just what he said. "Now drink some more water," he instructed.

She blinked her eyes open at him more slowly than normal. "Why are you being ssssoo nicccce to me?" she slurred, frowning at her uncooperative mouth.

He smiled, dropping his voice to a whisper. "Believe

it or not, I know you mean well. I think you're both be-ing incredibly naïve about the whole thing, but I know he means well too. He's trying to live up to the expectations that were thrust upon him and not lose himself in the pro-cess. He thinks you'll help with that. Now, I may not be a huge fan of his plan, but he's already a much better leader than his brother will ever be, and as such, I will continue to assist him."

She furrowed her brow. "How do you know about of thissss?"

"More bread," he instructed when she hiccupped. Then he leaned closer. "Want to know a secret?" She nodded slowly, afraid the movement would be too much in her ine-briated state. "I can read minds," he whispered in her ear before leaning back to watch her reaction.

"Really?" She narrowed her eyes suspiciously. *Is that really his power or is he just messing with me?* She couldn't tell. She took another drink of water and nearly spit it out with his next words.

"I'm not just messing with you." He laughed.

Her eyes widened as she swallowed. *Oh shit!*

"Oh shit, indeed." He waggled his eyebrows, his or-ange eyes sparkling with amusement.

The thought that he could read what she was thinking was quite sobering. She preferred her thoughts to be kept private, so she decided to test just how well he could read her mind.

What's nine times seven?

"Sixty-three."

What color are my eyes?

"The same blue as a twilight sky."

"Shut up!" she joked a little too loudly, completely in awe of his ability. The noise around them ceased and it seemed they were the center of attention. She put a hand over her mouth, covering up her giggles.

Corydon raised an eyebrow. "Everything okay over there?"

She hiccupped in reply, still trying to swallow her laughter.

"I was just showing her my parlor trick, Your Majesty." Lord Dante smiled.

"Ah, I can see how that would be rather entertaining and hard to believe." He smiled back at both of them.

She still had the hiccups so she politely asked to be excused then asked Corydon where to find the nearest restroom. She had just gotten her hiccups under control when she left the bathroom. She'd debated splashing water on her face to help her sober up, but she didn't want to ruin the makeup.

As she was leaving, she found a gorgeous blonde with dark green eyes waiting outside the restroom. She looked amazing in her skintight red dress and heels, her sharp features making her even more ethereal.

"Oh, pardon me," Ayanna said, but the woman grabbed her arm.

"You don't belong here," she hissed.

Ayanna smiled. "Let me go please."

"I'd watch out if I were you. He won't keep you around very long when he could have any Fae. I mean, look at you and look at me—it's quite obvious who the better choice is."

Insecurity swam under Ayanna's skin, but she kept her

features neutral. The woman laughed and released her grip.

"Run along, little pet. Run back to your master."

Ayanna held her head up high as she walked calmly back to the dining hall and took her seat.

"Everything okay?" Dante whispered.

"Fine," she replied, grabbing her goblet of water and bringing it to her lips. She took a small sip and immediately spit it out, causing gasps around the table. Something wasn't right. It tasted bitter, and water doesn't taste bitter.

"Ayanna?" Corydon asked.

"Are you okay?" Dante asked.

"Water…something…wrong…" She coughed, her throat growing itchier by the second.

Dante reached for her goblet and brought it to his nose. "Poison!" he exclaimed.

The crowd gasped and Corydon jumped to his feet. "Guard the doors! No one leaves except my brother!" He turned to Rodric, who was already on his feet as well. "Healer, now!"

He sprinted out of the room as Ayanna continued to cough, finding breathing to be difficult. When Corydon reached her, he pulled her out of her chair and laid her down on the ground, kneeling at her head, his eyes wild with fear.

"Shallow breaths," Dante urged. He brought a goblet over from the table. "I know you don't want to drink this, but I think it in this case it may help."

"No!" Corydon yelled.

"It's just my ambrosia," Dante replied, taking a sip to show it was fine. "I think it may help her relax enough to get her breathing back under control until the healer can arrive."

Corydon nodded and helped her sit up so Dante could pour the liquid down her lips. It was hard to work it down her throat, but it soothed the itch as it went down.

"I need you to find out who did this, Dante. Use whatever means necessary."

"Of course, sire."

After a few minutes, she felt like she could finally draw in a deep breath. In fact, she felt almost as if she were floating outside of her body. It was heavenly. She reached a hand up to Corydon's face, which was frowning above her. "Don't frown, you're too pretty to frown. Sssmiles, only sssmiless," she slurred, pressing her fingers against the corners of the mouth as if to push them up.

"Where is that damn healer?" he growled just as the door flung open and a man rushed in behind Rodric.

The healer knelt next to her and took one of her hands. Through the haze, she remembered how Enora had touched the area that needed to be healed, so she brought his hands to her throat just as she coughed again.

He murmured words she couldn't make out as he pressed his hands to her neck. It felt deliciously warm and tingly. Then he moved them down to her chest, focusing on her lungs, and his eyes flashed silver.

Ayanna sniggered. "He just touched my boob," she whispered loudly.

Corydon ground his teeth back and forth while Dante chuckled lightly and said, "I think she may be feeling better."

The healer ignored her inappropriate comment, still chanting and focusing on her lungs before moving down to her stomach. He pressed his hands to her soft belly and murmured for several moments, a light sheen of sweat beading on his forehead from his concentration. Finally, he rocked back on his heels.

"I think I got it all, Your Majesty, but someone should stay with her tonight to make sure. If you'd like me to stay, I can."

Corydon growled. "No, she'll stay with me. If I need you, I will send for you."

"Very well." He bowed. "I'll check on her again in the morning to look for any lasting effects." Corydon hissed at the reminder that they may not be in the safe zone just yet.

He stood and his voice boomed "No one is to leave until the culprit is found. You know the penalty for defying an order from the king!" Several of the guests fidgeted nervously.

"Rodric, Dante, find out who did this."

"Of course, brother," Rodric replied, placing a hand on Corydon's back. "I'm glad she'll be okay."

"I'm ssssleepy," Ayanna mumbled through a yawn.

Corydon bent and picked her up, cradling her in his arms just like he had done the first day she had arrived.

"You're sssso ssssstrong. Have I ever told you ttthh-hat?" She smirked.

Corydon didn't say a word as he carried her upstairs and into his room. He placed her gently on his bed.

"Thissss isn't my room," she stated.

"I know, but I need to keep an eye on you and make sure everything is okay, so you're going to stay in here with me tonight."

She kicked her feet. "Why am I wearing shoes in bed? Get these shoes off!"

He gripped her ankle, stilling her kicking feet to remove each of her heels.

"Isss it bed time?" she asked, yawning again.

"Yes, it is."

"Where are my pajamas?" She sat up.

"Shit. Do you want me to get Alvina to help you change?" He ran his hand through his hair.

Her brow furrowed and she stuck her lips out, pouting. "No. She doesn't smile." She reached back for her laces but had a hard time grasping them and tipped over.

"Here, let me." He pulled her slowly up from the bed and stood her next to it. Then he turned her and untied and loosened the laces on her back, groaning as he did so. "Seriously?" His knuckles skimmed her bare back.

"Mmmmm, that feels good," she moaned.

He stepped back, quickly crossing his room to retrieve a shirt for her to sleep in, all the while avoiding looking at her. He slipped the shirt over her head and tugged the rest of the dress to the floor. Before he could help her, she was already climbing back into the bed. Unfortunately, that gave him a flash of what was underneath his shirt—or rather, what wasn't.

"Ayanna…" He took a few deep breaths. "Are you wearing underwear?"

"Nope!" She popped the P at the end of the word. "No panty lines!" she sang.

He dragged his hand over his face and groaned loudly then whispered, "I'm going to kill Alvina." He opened the door and called to a guard. "I need a female servant immediately," he ordered. Within moments there was a light knock at the door and he opened it.

"What do you require, Your Majesty?"

"I…um…" he stammered, turning a lovely shade of pink.

Ayanna tittered from where she lay in the bed. He was cute all flustered. She decided to try to help him out. "Panties!" she squealed, laughing as Corydon turned a deeper shade of red.

"Um…yeah…she needs that…from her room."

The servant girl blushed, leaving the room without a word and returning moments later with a scrap of violet silk in her hands. She walked over to the bed and handed them to Ayanna. "There you go, milady."

"Oooo pretty," Ayanna said, setting the panties across her lap and running her fingers over the silky material.

Corydon drew in another deep breath, fortifying his resolve to be a gentleman.

The servant girl blushed again and hastily exited. Corydon closed the door and turned around just to be smacked in the face by silky violet fabric.

Ayanna giggled from the bed. "Panty fight!"

He removed the undergarment from his face, breathing deeply a few more times. "No panty fight. Put them on." He handed them back to her and turned around, knowing if he watched her, his resolve might crumble.

"Party pooper," she pouted. He heard the rustle of blankets and dared to peek around. It seemed she had slipped on the panties and now rested her head on the pillow, her eyelids drooping.

He bent down and kissed her forehead. "I love you, Ayanna. I'm sorry about tonight. I don't think I could live with myself if you were hurt because of me."

"Love you, too, sssexy pants," she whispered right before she started to snore. He sighed and changed his own clothing, slipping into a pair of pants and a t-shirt before crawling into bed next to her. The more clothes between them, the better. In fact, he decided to sleep on top of the covers to provide them an additional barrier of fabric. He sighed and rolled over on his side, studying her as she slept. He had come so close to losing her that night, and whoever was responsible would pay with their life. His retribution would be swift and severe so his people would understand just what awaited them if they dared to defy him.

Chapter 12

SHE BLINKED HER eyes open slowly, hissing at the light. She moved her hand up to wipe off a bit of drool from the corner of her mouth and realized her pillow was warm and hard. She pulled her head up to see a small dot of saliva on his shirt—her pillow was his chest. She flopped onto her back with a muffled groan; of course she would drool on him. Could it get any more embarrassing? Suddenly the previous night's actions came rushing back to her and she covered her head with the sheets to hide her mortification. *Did I really flash him? Throw my panties at him? Oh, sweet baby Jesus, I did, and now I've drooled on him.* She wished the bed would just swallow her whole.

His hand tugged the blankets down and she peered into his violet eyes. "How are you feeling?" His gaze held no accusation, no teasing about her behavior, only concern.

"I've been better," she mumbled. Her voice was hoarse and her throat ached. "Can I get some water?"

He rushed over to fill a glass for her and brought it

back while she pulled herself up to sit against the head-board. She hesitated for just a moment, giving it a light sniff as she remembered how the last time she had a glass of water, it had tried to kill her.

He sighed just as a knock sounded at the door. "Come in!" he called.

"How is our patient this morning?" asked an unfamiliar man, his silver eyes studying her.

"She seems to be okay."

She swallowed the water, relishing its cool feel against her throat.

"Anything still hurt?" he asked, directing his question at her this time.

She nodded. "My throat," she croaked.

He approached the bed. "May I?" He reached to place his hands on her neck.

"Of course. Thank you," she whispered.

He closed his eyes and concentrated, a familiar warm tingle radiating from his touch. She closed her eyes. When she opened them, his silver irises blazed back at her. "Better?"

"Yes, very much. Thank you."

He then turned his attention to Corydon. "I believe she'll recover nicely. If there's any other concern, please let me know." He bowed and exited the room.

"You okay?"

"Besides being mortified about my behavior last night?"

He waved a hand dismissively. "There's nothing to be embarrassed about."

"Oh really?" She arched an eyebrow.

His lips quirked up in one corner. "Okay, maybe a few things, but that's not what I'm talking about." Just as quickly as it had appeared, his smiled faded. "Someone tried to kill you last night, Ayanna." He took her hand, sitting next to her. "I can't even protect you while you're in my home. How did I ever think this was going to work? If I send you back, you could get hurt. If I keep you here, you could get hurt. Either way seems to end up with you getting hurt."

She tapped her fingers against his lips. "Shhhh, it's okay. I'm okay. It'll be fine. I will be fine." She removed her fingers and pressed a kiss in their place.

He gladly accepted, pulling her into a tight embrace. He held her close. "I was so scared. I'll do everything in my power to make sure nothing like that happens to you again."

"I know." She rubbed her hands up and down his back in a comforting gesture, sensing just how close he was to cracking.

A knock at the door interrupted them. He pushed her back onto the bed gently and stood. "Enter!"

"We've found the culprit, your highness." Lord Dante had dark circles under his eyes and looked as though he would gladly collapse into the nearest chair, couch, or bed.

"Excellent. Gather the court and send an invitation to the people to see what we do with traitors. I will be down in a few minutes."

Dante bowed. "I'm glad to see you are well, milady." His eyes weighed heavily upon her.

"Thank you, Lord Dante." Then he left just as quickly as he'd entered.

"I need you to go to your room and get cleaned up. I'll have Alvina pull a suitable outfit for the trial and meet you down there." He kissed her once more and walked her back to her room, peeking around, probably to see that everything was as it should be. He called for a servant, requesting breakfast for her.

Her stomach rolled at the thought of eating. "Maybe just some toast and water," she suggested. The servant nodded and they both left. She was alone in the room. She managed to get herself into the bath before she broke down as the seriousness of what had happened struck her, a million what-ifs running through her head. *What if the ambrosia hadn't helped? What if I'd taken more than just a small sip of the water?* In reality, she could have died, but she knew what he said to be true: if someone dared attempt to hurt her there, under his watchful eye, being away wouldn't stop them, not as long as he loved her.

When she finished bathing, Alvina was there to help her dress. While Alvina quickly braided her hair, she munched on her toast. Then Alvina brushed some makeup over her face, handed her the red dress, and stepped out of the room.

Ayanna stepped into the dress and pulled it on. It was a long A-line dress with a deep plunging neckline. The blood red material shimmered under a black lace overlay that gave it a sort of gothic appearance, and there was a leather strip of fabric around the waist that required Alvina's help to lace and tie. It hugged her curves and hid her imperfections all at the same time. Her makeup was a little more subtle than the previous night, except for her lips, which were the same red as the dress. There was very little talking between the two women, mostly comments made by Alvina under her breath that made it quite apparent she despised being the one who had to help her. She seemed to have something against humans, but Ayanna didn't want to question it. The fewer enemies she had, the better.

Alvina led her down the stairs and handed her off to Lord Dante, who was waiting just outside the front door. He escorted her outside to a more secluded courtyard to the side of the castle. There was a large crowd of people, but as they neared the front, she could see a chained man kneeling on the cobblestone. His clothes were ruffled, his face bruised, and blood spattered the front of his shirt. She remembered briefly seeing him at the other end of the table at dinner the night before, glaring at her for most of the evening when he thought no one was looking.

She was so focused on the man that she was surprised when they reached a raised wooden enclosure like box seats at a baseball game; she didn't find this entertaining. Corydon was seated on a throne while Rodric was standing next to the smaller one instead of sitting on it, as he had in the throne room the other day. Dante lead her over to the empty throne before stepping back down and off to the side of the crowd.

Her eyes were wide, wondering about the implications of sitting on the throne next to the king, but she knew better than to deny the seat. Rodric rested a hand on her shoulder and bent down to her ear. "Your job right now is to look as stoic as possible. Try your best not to show a drop of emotion on your face. I know it will be hard for you, milady, but you must." He gave her shoulder a slight squeeze before returning to his position to the side of her chair. She schooled her features to the best of her ability, trying to convince herself that she was acting in some sort of play. It was not that hard to do, since she already felt as if she were on the set of the king's castle in *Braveheart*, only the man kneeling in front of them was definitely no William Wallace.

The king rose, and the crowd silenced immediately, all eyes turned toward him. "We have a traitor in our midst. I made an official proclamation that he chose to ignore. Before we listen to his defense, I would like to remind you that a strike against Lady Ayanna is a strike against me." He sat and gestured lazily for the man to offer up some sort of explanation.

"You are making a grave mistake, Your Highness," the man sneered as more of a threat than a request for reconsideration.

"Lord Dante has already dug around in your mind and we know your intentions. There is no denying you are the one who poisoned and tried to kill Lady Ayanna."

"And I would do it again!" the man roared as he spat on the stone in her direction. "Your father would roll over in his grave if he knew you had a human sitting in your mother's seat."

Ayanna flinched at the insult, and Rodric's hand went to her shoulder once more, giving it a gentle squeeze, reminding her she needed to remain indifferent.

"That's enough!" Corydon yelled. Ayanna could see the fire in his eyes. "Your judgment has been made. For the act of treason and attempted murder against your future queen, I sentence you to death!" His voice roared above the murmuring crowd.

Ayanna felt like she was going to hyperventilate. *Did he just say future queen?*

She had no time to fully process the weight of that statement because the guards tugged the man to his feet. It was only then that she noticed the stained slab of stone off to the side of him. She swallowed hard. They thrust the man forward so he bent over the flat rock and held him there, his head dangling over the edge.

Corydon rose and drew his sword from its scabbard at his side. Her heart pounded and her stomach rolled. Her hand unconsciously flew up to her mouth, but it was caught midflight. Rodric gripped it painfully and lowered it. He inched closer to her and moved his hand back up to her shoulder, squeezing firmly. "No emotion," he hissed. "It is essential. You will ruin us all if you cannot stomach this. This is part of what you have to do when you are queen. Isn't that what you want?"

At that moment, she wasn't in the mood to argue with him, because honestly, she'd never once thought about being queen. She had mentally separated Corydon from his position, never fully understanding the responsibility that came with being with him.

He continued, "Any emotion right now will be considered weakness and we will not survive it." She gulped and gave a slight nod, indicating that she understood.

The crowd went wild, hungry for blood. It didn't seem to matter that it was the blood of one of their own.

"Do not close your eyes—do not even flinch if you can help it," he whispered in her ear, his tight grip a firm reminder of what she had to do. She sat helplessly as she watched the king—the boy she loved—take his sword and bring it down on the Fae's neck in a smooth arc, severing his head from his body. Her chest rose and fell quickly with her breath, the only indication of her internal battle with the brutality she had just witnessed. The crowd roared. Corydon wiped his blade with a rag before sheathing it and then walked around to lift the man's head by his hair.

Bile crept up her throat and Rodric's grip tightened.

"Let this serve as a reminder of what happens when you cross your king!" The crowd applauded and cheered as if he had just finished a five-star performance. He tossed the head into the crowd, which made them crazier. It reminded her of feeding time at the zoo, some sort of crazed animal instinct whipping them into a frenzy. Her calm mask slipped when she watched one of the Fae take blood from the head, smear it across a female's neck, and then proceed to lick it off.

She closed her eyes. "May I be excused now?" she whispered.

Rodric released his grip on her shoulder. "You may if the king wishes it so," he replied in a normal voice.

She looked toward Corydon, who was watching the crowd with a smile of satisfaction, his sharp teeth glinting in the sunlight. He turned toward her. She had never seen his eyes glow so brightly, the normal violet now a stark lavender. He simply nodded in reply. She rose and stepped off the platform carefully, suppressing her instinct to run.

A hand grabbed hers gently at the bottom. She looked over to see Conall, the boy with green eyes, studying her with concern.

She felt her panic and revulsion subside, almost as if she had released a deep breath and, with it, the weight of the moment. "Can I escort you back inside, milady?" he asked politely, and she nodded, grateful for the help. He dropped her hand, choosing instead to place his on her arm to guide her.

"Aren't you a little young to be here?" she asked, even though he only looked around her age.

"I could ask you the same thing," he teased, his lips drawing into a tight line when she didn't take the bait. "I'm training to be first in command to the king," he replied. Noticing that she still didn't understand, he continued, "That means someday soon it will be my job to carry out the executions if the king deems it so." He opened the door, allowing her to enter before him.

"Oh." She frowned. *How awful that must be.* Her mind unwillingly played back the execution she had just witnessed. She staggered to the side and leaned against the nearest pillar, the marble cooling her skin. He stepped in front of her and placed both hands on her arms. She watched as his emerald eyes swirled neon green, and a sense of tranquility washed over her body, putting her at ease.

Only when he removed his hands did she realize the emotion was coming from him. She really needed to study that encyclopedia so she knew what to expect from her encounters with the Fae, as she knew this would not be the last one and it would be best to be as prepared as possible. "Thank you," she whispered. "How did you do that?" She pointed back and forth between them.

"Oh…" He blushed. "I'm an Incubus, which means I can take away emotions and replace them. I just took away your fear, revulsion, and panic, and replaced them with serenity."

"Can Corydon do that?" she asked, not realizing until it was too late that it might be strange of her to talk about the king with such familiarity, although he had just announced that she was his future queen. That reminder shortened her breaths again, and Conall placed a gentle hand on her back, leading her back to her room while at the same time removing her panic once more.

He frowned. "That's probably a conversation you should have with the king, milady."

She sighed. "Of course. I just wondered…" It hadn't even occurred to her that he could possibly control her emotions, but now she wondered if what she felt for him was real.

"He's not an Incubus, if that's what you're wondering. Your emotions are safe with him."

She nodded, thankful that they had reached her room. "Thank you, Conall. I appreciate your help. You've been very kind." She smiled sadly.

"I hope you don't need my help again any time soon, but it's always there for you—although I'm sure the king would prefer if I didn't touch you." He smiled and winked before leaving her at the door to her room.

She opened it and stepped inside then leaned against it, unsure of what to make of her morning. She was thankful her tray from breakfast had already been removed as her stomach rolled. She closed her eyes only to see the gruesome scene replay itself against her eyelids. She staggered toward the bathroom where she emptied the paltry contents of her stomach then curled up on the cool marble floor and wept.

She had just managed to dry her tears, brush her teeth, and straighten herself when her door flew open and Corydon stepped inside, his eyes still glowing eerily bright. He didn't speak as he stalked toward her, backing her against the wall. He leaned in, pressing his nose against her neck and inhaling sharply. She wasn't sure what to do. Part of her kept screaming that he had just killed someone, and the other part countered that he had only done so to protect her.

"You're safe now," he whispered. "No one will ever hurt you again." He pressed kisses against her throat and then her lips, devouring her before moving back down to her throat again. He tipped her head to the side and sucked on her skin, his fingers tugging the laces at the back of her dress until they came undone. She moaned.

"Cor, stop…we need to talk about this."

"No talking." His hot breath against her skin made her shiver. He continued to kiss her neck, working his way down to her collarbone.

"Corydon." She gave him a slight shove and his hands slammed against the wall on either side of her before he pushed himself away.

He huffed, turning and walking toward the door. "You'll need to get changed for the celebration tonight. I'll send Alvina up in a few hours."

"Celebration?"

"Yes, we have a feast and celebration after every execution—provides everyone with a release."

She wrinkled her nose in distaste and his brow furrowed slightly, disappointed by her reaction. "We still need to talk, Cor." She needed to know what he was thinking, what he was feeling, but he shut her out.

"Later," he replied, leaving the room and taking with him her opportunity to argue. To make matters worse, when she went to chase after him, she found he had locked her inside. She growled, frustrated with his avoidance, and threw herself on the bed to pout. Eventually she picked up the encyclopedia with the different races of Fae and started to read.

Several hours later, Alvina came in the room. She picked out yet another dress for Ayanna to wear, but she was so over the idea of a party when they had just watched someone get beheaded that she didn't even pay much attention. She didn't even bother to make Alvina leave before she changed. She was in a sort of daze as she was dressed and primped. Of course, Alvina seemed happier with her more complacent attitude.

She joined the merry crowd at the dinner table for a

feast, and it seemed they had already been partaking in the ambrosia before she got there. She ate dinner without really making conversation, so withdrawn inside her own head. She even ignored Lord Dante's attempts to engage her. Finally, Rodric politely excused himself and stopped by her seat, asking her to join him in the hallway for a moment. She reluctantly agreed after Dante promised to watch her beverage carefully.

The second she exited the room he manhandled her, tugging her to the counsel room where he closed the door behind them.

"Do you love my brother?" His blue gaze scrutinized her reaction, his question like a bucket of ice water.

"With all my heart," she declared defensively.

"All your heart?" He quirked an eyebrow.

"Yes!"

"Then you must love all of him, even the parts you don't like. He is the Unseelie king, and if you can't handle that and all the responsibility that comes with it, perhaps you should leave."

His words stung with truth. "I can handle it," she whispered.

"Are you sure? Because you're currently doing a really shit job of it. We are at a celebration and you are sitting there like someone just drowned your kitten. Snap out of it! If you'd rather throw in the towel, you'd better figure that out fast."

"I don't think I have a choice, do I?"

He shook his head. "Of course you do. If you want to leave, I will happily find you a way out, because I'm going to be honest with you here: I don't think you're what he needs. You may make him happy now, but you will never help him be the king he needs to be for his people."

She took a few deep breaths, his words voicing her own insecurities, and then she tightened her resolve, remembering how much Corydon needed her. "I can handle this," she repeated, this time like she meant it.

"If you change your mind, you know where to find me, but let's keep this conversation between us, shall we?"

She agreed, knowing she would keep his offer a secret if only because she may need to take advantage of it in the future. He left the room and she followed behind a few minutes later as to not make it look suspicious.

When she returned, she smiled at Corydon and the rest of the room, feeling like she should be an award-winning actress.

"You all right?" Dante asked as she took her seat.

"Just peachy." She smiled again then took her goblet of ambrosia and drained it.

He arched an eyebrow at her curiously but chose not to comment. The drink helped loosen her up and before she knew it, she was laughing along with one of Rodric's stories about when he and Corydon were little boys.

After dinner, the king escorted her and the rest of the crowd into the ballroom. There was a band of some sort with instruments ready to play. The music began, thrumming throughout the room. It was heavy with drums, the beat echoing through their bodies. She watched as the Fae danced, much as humans did at a club, bodies writhing against each other to the beat. A waiter came around with more drinks, and she plucked a flute off a tray. It was a different drink, lighter in color, more of a pale pink and bubbly. She sipped it, savoring the strawberry shortcake flavor.

She had drunk probably half the glass when Corydon took it from her hand. "Easy there." He drained the rest of it then stood behind her, pulling her against him. He kissed the shell of her ear. "I like my marks on you." He traced a finger down her neck, skimming it back and forth across the skin below her collarbone where she was shocked to see he had indeed left a few marks on her.

She mentally kicked herself for not paying more attention while Alvina was dressing her. There was probably a row of hickies leading down her neck to her shoulder. She was surprised Alvina had chosen a strapless dress and not covered them with makeup.

"Dance with me." He kissed her neck again and she moaned her reply.

He took her hand, leading her to the middle of the dance floor. The tribal beat vibrated within her bones and she swayed to the rhythm, a slave to its beat. They danced and danced and danced, bodies rubbing together, hands roaming, lips stealing kisses. She was losing herself to the music and the sensations. She felt like she could feel everything, see the beauty in everything, and do anything. She felt alive.

She wasn't sure how long they danced, only that she almost collapsed from exhaustion when they stopped. It swept over her in a fierce wave, and Corydon carried her to his room. She may have protested if she had been in the right state of mind, but she was too tired and happy to care. He helped her change out of her dress, acting less of a gentleman than the night before. It seemed she wasn't the only one who was lost to the delirium of the festivities.

His lips traced down her shoulders and her back as he slid the dress down, every touch sending lightning through her body and stirring a fiery blaze within her. She lost herself in the feel of his mouth, her body begging for her to give in. "I love you so much, Ayanna," he whispered, his hands and mouth worshiping her skin, showing her how he felt. She was overwhelmed in the feeling of him and the moment, and it felt euphoric, so she gave in, letting herself have him and him have her. They got lost in each other, in the touch of skin on skin, the sharing of breath and heartbeats and whispered words of love and devotion.

CHAPTER 13

THE NEXT MORNING came far too soon and she lay there for quite some time pretending to be asleep while running through the events of the evening in her mind. She ached in places she hadn't even known were possible, and even though she might have taken things much slower if she hadn't been so lost to the rapture of the party, she didn't regret it. It was beautiful and came from a place of love. She smiled as she felt his lips against her bare skin.

"I know you're awake," he teased, and she opened her eyes to meet his gaze. "You're beautiful. Thank you for loving me as I am. I never thought it was possible to feel something like this." He placed his hand over her thundering heart.

She smiled at him before tugging his mouth to meet hers and losing herself in him once more.

The next few months passed with her in a mostly blissful bubble. Her days were spent learning as much as she could about Fae (including their history, abilities, hierarchy, wild creatures, lands, and the court), war strategy, and diplomatic policies from Alfie. Her nights were wrapped up in Corydon. She was free now to wander most of the castle except for the dungeons, which she really had no desire to see. They didn't have any more problems from the court, most of them taking his threat seriously after the execution. There were still a few snide comments and sneers here and there, but as long as they weren't trying to kill her, she was willing to let it go. She still battled her insecurities, knowing she would never quite fit into their world as a human.

There were also questions she knew she should ask, things she should discuss with Corydon, but she didn't want to ruin their bliss with her concerns until she absolutely had to. She was more than grateful her studies with Alfie kept her out of court proceedings during the day. She didn't have to watch any trials or deal with the politics, but she knew the longer she stayed, the sooner that day would come, and the thought of attending another trial turned her stomach.

At least once a week she woke up in a cold sweat from a nightmare. Sometimes it was her being poisoned and no one lifting a finger to save her, just watching and laughing. Other times she saw the execution on loop. The worst was when she dreamed of the execution, only she was the one on trial and Corydon was bringing the sword down on her head. That night she woke up screaming and startled half the castle. After that Corydon had the healers prepare a draft for her to help her sleep without dreaming.

She missed Grace fiercely, and sometimes she would write her letters, but she never sent them. She figured it was for the best if her aunt knew as little as possible. Probably the biggest problem for her was that when she closed her eyes and let herself picture her future, it was back in the human world with a normal family. Yes, Corydon was still by her side as her husband, but they were not in Fae ruling the Unseelie together. If she were truly honest, she had no desire to be queen and wished there was a way he wouldn't be king anymore, but after a conversation with Alfie about royal heritage, she knew her wish would never come true.

"Why is Corydon the king and not Rodric? I mean, wouldn't it make sense for Rodric to be the king since he's the oldest? That's how it used to work in the human royal families," she asked her teacher one afternoon.

"Well, my dear, you have just posed a rather interesting question that has caused lots of debate amongst my people. It all has to do with the eyes, the correct color of eyes, to be exact. We do know it has something to do with genetics, with just the right blend of traits. It could possibly have started as a mutation and was passed down from there. The eye color has yet to be seen outside the royal family, unless the king has had a secret affair..." He waggled his eyebrows and she chuckled. "Although there are some who believe it's part of the magic, that the magic chooses its next leader. Others believe it may be a combination of the two. I find myself being one of those, a believer in science and magic."

"So how come one child and not the other? Why not both children? What happens if the king dies before he has a child to pass it along to? Has it always been a boy, or has a girl been chosen before?" she asked, flipping through the pages of the book in front of her on the family trees of past kings and queens.

"My, you are curious this morning. Any particular reason?"

"Just trying to understand how it all works."

"Well, I'll try to satiate your curiosity the best I can. As I said before, there are a few different beliefs and theories on which child inherits the violet eyes and why only one, as we have yet to see it occur with more than one child in a family. Some believe it is merely the child who inherits the correct combination of traits, but others believe it's the magic's choice, that the magic evaluates someone's fate and who they are or will become at their core. Only once before we have come across the king dying without children, and in that particular case, his cousin took the throne. Things did not go well for the people. The times were full of turmoil and there was much debate over whether it was because he did not possess the royal eye color or if it was from his lack of preparation. Eventually the cousin's sister had a son who was born with the royal eye color, and he was given the throne as soon as he was of age. That son was Corydon's father, and he ruled for a very long time. The ones who are old enough to remember that time still harbor some hesitation about allowing another to hold the throne, just in case it is tied to the magic. We can be a superstitious folk." He smiled sadly. *"As for your last question, yes, a girl has been chosen before. It's rare, but it did happen with the Seelie, and she was a wonderful queen—a sight to behold, fiercely protective of her people, always putting their needs before her own."* His features almost transformed in front of her, appearing much younger as he talked more about the Seelie queen. Then suddenly his eyes grew misty, lost in some memory. *"We were happy for quite some time under her reign."*

"What happened?" she whispered, curious to hear the story there, because by his expression, she knew there was

one.

"As what happens with most of our kind, war between the two courts. The Unseelie captured one of her men, and she loved him more than she should have, too much to see reason and let him go. So, she tried to save him and ended up sacrificing her own life trying to save his." Heartbreak and longing etched every wrinkle.

She reached across the table and squeezed his hand. "Oh Alfie, I'm so sorry."

He squeezed her hand quickly then released it. He sighed. "Nothing to be sorry for. It was a lifetime ago." She knew enough to let it drop, although she had her suspicions about just who the queen had been trying to rescue.

She yanked herself back into the present. That night was an important one. They were throwing a bacchanalia, which Corydon described as a large celebration for a milestone in a royal's life, this one being for the official announcement of their engagement. Even though they had talked about it, she was a little disappointed Fae didn't propose like humans, with a grand gesture or heck, even asking her the big question. It was more like entering a business contract, a merger of entities, only in her case, she really didn't bring anything to the table.

The castle was buzzing with preparation, and while she was walking to meet Alfie, she bumped into Conall. He apologized profusely and turned a shade of red. The guards nearest to them looked over and almost sneered as he fussed over her. To make up for his fumble, he offered to escort her to the library. It seemed everywhere they walked the servants whispered and guards turned their noses up at them. It was odd. She hadn't quite experienced anything like that before. Most of the time they ignored her or seemed to tolerate her much as one would tolerate an overly curious child.

Conall noticed her frown. "It's me, milady. It's nothing to do with you." He shrugged as if to say, *What can you do?*

"I don't understand."

He sighed. "It's because I'm half Fae," he stated, as if that would answer all her questions.

"Oh, I see." She pretended to understand so she wouldn't appear stupid.

They walked the rest of the way in a comfortable silence, and he bid her farewell when they reached the door. Alfie greeted her and she began her studies, but her mind was still stuck on what Conall had revealed.

"Alfie," she interrupted, "I have a question." He stopped his lecture and waited for her to continue. "Conall was walking with me today and I noticed the servants and guards were acting a little weird as we passed. He explained that it was because he is half Fae, but I know he's frequently here at the castle and has dined with the high court. I would think the servants would treat him with a little more respect. Why does being half Fae make that much of a difference?"

He sighed. "Our people are a stubborn lot, and in many ways stuck deep in the traditions and ways we have always done things. I think it's the curse of our long life spans." He took a deep breath and exhaled. "There are some who feel humans are beneath them, especially the Unseelie. They treat humans more like pets or toys."

She remembered the blonde woman who'd called her 'pet' and her kidnapper calling her 'little mouse', as if she were something to be hunted. She swallowed thickly.

"However, some Fae enjoy the frailty of humans, their unique views on things, and from time to time, it has become common that one may enjoy the company of humans…in the, um…romantic sense." He blushed lightly, and she nodded to show she could connect the dots to what he meant. It seemed Fae didn't mind getting busy with humans, which of course reminded her of the previous night with Corydon, causing her own cheeks to flame.

He cleared his throat. "Well, some see the half Fae as less powerful, so they look down upon them. I personally don't see things that way. I think the human half of them offers a unique perspective that can, in fact, strengthen their magic in ways we can only begin to imagine. However, I suppose I'm an oddity in my beliefs.

"In regards to Conall, his mother is Fae and a member of the court, but his father was human."

"Was?"

Alfie smiled sadly. "Yes, was. He passed away many years ago. See, the main problem with human and Fae relationships is that our life spans are so vastly different, so what might seem like a full human lifetime is only a small part of ours."

Her heart stopped. She knew he didn't mean for his words to hurt her, but she hadn't even really considered what that would mean for her. She knew Corydon was much older and time worked differently so they would age differently, but she hadn't considered just how much her life would be a fast-burning flame compared to his. It was usually one of those things she chose to not dwell upon, to remain in ignorant bliss.

Alfie noted her expression. "Now I will say that when a human is in Fae, things tend to work a little bit better, as our realm operates at a slower pace than the human one," he offered in a comforting tone.

"It's okay, Alfie. I've always known this wouldn't be easy, I just hadn't really thought…" She let her words trail off, unsure of how she could explain to him how naïve she felt. "I think I should go. Alvina has a lot of primping to do to prepare me for tonight. Thank you for all of your help and your patience, as always."

She gave him a hug before leaving the library and walking back to her room, her mind heavy with the contemplation of time. After what felt like an eternity of pulling, prodding, and primping, Alvina declared her ready. She looked in a mirror and was astounded by what she saw. Her gown was like the midnight sky filled with stars, covered in glittering crystals set against a deep blue. It had a fuller skirt than the other gowns she had worn along with a long train, but the plunging neckline kept up with the Fae fashion. Her neck was adorned with even more crystals or diamonds, she wasn't sure which, and her golden locks were curled and twisted back. A small tiara of sorts sat against her forehead, its silver curling and curving in an ornate design above her ears to the back of her head. In the very center sat a violet jewel the same color as Corydon's eyes. Her makeup was flawless, and she felt like a queen.

The minute he laid eyes on her at the feast, he couldn't take them away. "You look ravishing, my future queen," he professed, kissing her flushed cheek. The night was filled with laughter, drink, and dancing. She knew her limits with ambrosia, but the drink that evening was the same pale pink one that had induced her euphoria the night they first made love. It made her smile to remember, and it also made her less cautious with her drink.

She pretended not to notice the humans sprinkled throughout the crowd. They seemed under the spell of the Fae and their drink, as she was, and she pretended not to notice when the crowd's dancing transformed into more than just dancing. She pretended not to see them feed, to hear the screams over the crowd. She downed more drink to drown them out. These were the creatures she was going to be queen of. The thought turned her stomach, but all it took was one look at Corydon and her negative thoughts would slip away. She got lost in his touch, in dancing with him and being held in his arms, in the euphoria of the night, until she was too dizzy to stand and he carried her to bed.

She awoke a few hours later, reaching for him only to find the bed cold and empty. She was still in her gown; her tiara had slid into her hair and she worked to tug it free. "Cor?"

No answer.

She rose, the tiara clutched in her hand, and placed it on the table next to the bed. She had kicked her shoes off in her sleep, thankfully. She crept barefoot outside of the room where there were no guards to be seen. *Strange.* She continued down the stairs, and she could hear voices from the ballroom. *They must all still be at the party...how late is it?*

She heard cheers from the crowd still gathered inside, and it sounded like they were chanting Corydon's name. She edged around the outside of the room, not wanting to draw attention to herself but curious to see what the fuss was about. She froze the moment she saw him. He was standing in the middle of a circle, the green-eyed blonde woman plastered to his side like she belonged there, and there was a human kneeling at his feet.

"Please let me go," the man pleaded. The crowd laughed, Ayanna's stomach clenching at the man's words and the sight of the blonde pressing her breasts into Corydon's side. *Am I hallucinating?* She hoped it was just another nightmare, but when she pinched her own arm, she felt the sting.

"I think you should show him what you can do, Your Highness," the woman cooed, running a finger down Corydon's chest. Ayanna swallowed hard. She kept hoping that at any moment he would throw the woman's hand off, but he didn't. He smiled at his companion instead, and Ayanna's heart cracked.

Corydon took a step back and unlaced his boots. The crowd murmured their agreement. Next, he tossed his shirt over his head, and a few whistled. Finally, he shucked his pants, and the crowd roared. He stood in just his simple undergarments before shaking his shoulders and bouncing on the heels of his feet like a fighter gearing up for starting bell. The crowd backed up and Ayanna ducked behind a curtain, afraid of what might happen if she were to be seen. She knew she wouldn't be able to pretend this wasn't happening, to smile and agree with whatever they were about to do to that poor man, and she also knew she couldn't do anything to save him.

What she saw was like a punch to her gut. The air around the king shimmered with magic. He was there one minute, and the next a large, familiar, jet black stallion stood in his place—her stallion. She couldn't breathe. Her mind flashed back to all those nights, all the things she had told Midnight…and it had been Corydon all along. The crack in her heart spread.

"Isn't he beautiful, pet?" the woman said, teasing the human. "A fierce, magnificent creature?"

"Yes." The man's eyes were lost in wonder of the beast in front of him. The stallion—*Corydon*—huffed, pawing the ground ferociously.

"A thing of dreams, isn't that right, pet?" The woman's

voice oozed as she circled around the man. "The thing is, we're not the creatures of your dreams." She paused as the crowd began to chant a sound like the thrumming of a drum. The woman's voice grew with the beat of the crowd. "We're the creatures in your nightmares!"

Just like that the crowd roared and the air shimmered around Corydon. She stared in horror as he became some sick combination of goat and man that can only be described as a demon. He had large horns that curved up and behind his goat head. His eyes glowed violet, the only reminder of who he truly was.

The man's expression probably matched her own. He was utterly terrified, and the crowd was eating it up.

"Aw, pet, what's wrong?" The woman laughed, clearly enjoying the moment. She placed her hands on both of his shoulders and closed her eyes smiling, feeding off his terror. "My, your fear is quite delicious." She licked her lips.

Ayanna had seen enough. She stumbled from the room as quietly as she could. Her eyes blurred with tears and the minute she was back in her room, she stumbled to the toilet just in time. She closed her eyes, but all she saw was him as a demon, and she heaved until there was nothing left. She fought to tear the gown off her body then ran a bath, hoping it would help her feel clean again. There she scrubbed her skin raw and filled the tub with her tears. *How could I love such a monster?*

She cried herself to sleep, relieved he didn't crawl into her bed or demand to know why she'd left his. When she awoke the next morning, she didn't know how she was going to act, how she could just go back to pretending everything was okay. *God, I'm an idiot.* Her stomach heaved and she barely stumbled to the sink before she lost what little was left. She saw a note with her name scrawled on it in his handwriting with her breakfast tray but didn't have the heart to read it, not when she knew it wouldn't ease the ache inside her chest. She worried his words would only cause the pain to intensify, because as much as it killed her to admit it, a part of her still loved him.

She nibbled on toast while she scoured her encyclopedia, arming herself with whatever information she could find that may help her figure out what to do. She learned that Corydon was a Pooka, able to transform himself into a few beasts of the night, such as the stallion and the goat demon. She lost her breakfast after that. She couldn't believe he had been her comforting confidant, that he would keep that from her when he promised to tell her the truth, but even worse was the look on the Unseelies' faces as he tormented that poor human. They wanted more; they fed off it. It matched everything she had read about Unseelie, and she wanted to kick her own ass for ever being so naïve. She couldn't lead the Unseelie—she could never stomach it. The truth was a knife straight to her heart. As much as she loved him, she knew it wouldn't be enough. She knew with complete and utter certainty that no matter what, she couldn't be his queen. She could never be *their* queen.

She had to be careful about this. Was it even possible for her to leave? She knew her thoughts could be dangerous if he, Lord Dante, or any number of Fae were to grow suspicious of her. She trusted Alfie, but she doubted he would be able to help her with this. It was then that she remembered Rodric's offer to help her leave after the execution. *Would he still be willing? He was the one who pointed out that he didn't think I was the right one for the job.* She chewed on her bottom lip, debating back and forth with herself, but the fact of the matter was that she didn't have much of a choice. She knew she had to get out, and she couldn't do it alone. She would have to feel him out, find a way to see if he was still willing to help without giving away her intentions in case she would be condemning herself. It would take some time. Luckily, she had some sort of a grace period with the engagement bacchanalia having just occurred; they wouldn't expect them to wed for a few months at least.

In the meantime, she would have to act like nothing was wrong. Her life and any hope of escape depended upon it. She gathered her strength and reached over to the table to pluck his note off her tray.

My love,

My bed was cold and lonely without you. I hope your slumber in your own bed is merely a result of your overindulgence in drink last night, although I seem to remember leaving you in mine.

She heaved a sigh, realizing his suspicions were already complicating things. She rubbed her forehead and continued reading.

I have matters to attend to this morning. I expect you may need a day to recover, but now that you are officially my betrothed and the future queen of the Unseelie, you will be expected to attend meetings with me and sit at my side while I rule on any judgments and oversee our people. I will make sure Alfie briefs you today on all that may entail so you are prepared to begin tomorrow. We are to dine with the court this evening, so Alvina will select a dress for you.

That was another thing she would have to talk to him about—she didn't need someone else picking her clothes out for her. The less people she had in her business, the better. She would have to convince him she was perfectly capable of dressing herself.

See you at dinner if I can't sneak away sooner.

With all my love,
Your soon-to-be husband

She figured it was as good a time as any to join Alfie. Her nausea had dissipated, and the library would provide her with a good escape to attempt to formulate some sort of plan for what to do next.

"Is everything okay, Ayanna?" Alfie's voice tugged her away from her internal plotting.

"Huh?"

"You seem distracted—is everything all right?"

"Oh, yeah. I, um, just don't feel too well. I think I

drank too much last night." She blushed knowing that was partially the truth. She did feel like crap and figured it was some sort of evil hangover.

"Ah, yes. Would you like for me to send for a healer?"

"No, that's not necessary." She smiled politely. "I think it's best if I feel the full effects to remind me not to drink so much in the future."

He smiled in return, but his eyes still held concern. "Good point. Shall I continue?"

She nodded, and he returned to explaining everything her new role entailed. It was a lot—quite overwhelming, actually. She was expected to help the king hear cases from the people, carry out execution orders if necessary (which she knew in her heart she could never do), and sit in on his advisory council and war strategy meetings. While she did not hold as much power as he did, it was quite apparent that she would hold more than anyone else. It was rather intriguing that they would value the queen almost as much as the king, but she remembered Alfie's story about the violet-eyed Seelie queen, that the genetics and magic could choose either. Every responsibility he explained weighed on her as one more requirement she knew she would not be able to fulfill. Eventually, he could see he had overloaded her with information and called it a day, his eyes still filled with concern as she wearily made her way back to her room, the weight on her shoulders slowing her steps.

She sighed in resignation when she saw a gold dress laid out on the bed. She changed for dinner and tried to dismiss Alvina, insisting she could do her own hair and makeup, but the woman would have none of it.

Dinner was an interesting arrangement. A chair for her almost as grand as Corydon's had been placed next to his at the head of the table, whereas before she had always sat around the corner off to the side. The blonde who had haunted her nightmares was around the corner, followed by Conall. Rodric and Casimir were seated across from them, and various other members of the court filled the rest of the table. Lord Dante was nowhere to be seen, which she had to admit was a little relief, knowing her thoughts for once may be safe. Of course, that didn't mean she was going to let her guard down; she still wasn't sure exactly what other types of Fae were around the table.

She drifted in and out of the conversation around her, participating when required while also attempting to think of a way to send a message to Rodric discreetly. Corydon noticed her distraction, but she claimed she still felt a little hungover, just as she had with Alfie. She requested water to drink with her meal instead of ambrosia and was re-lieved when no one questioned her action. It was hard to shut down her racing mind, but fear of what someone may be able to discover helped. She would wait until she was alone to do her plotting.

Still feigning illness, she requested an early leave from dinner, which garnered a looks of concern from Corydon and Conall and curiosity from Rodric. She was hoping he might make it easy on her and offer to escort her back to the room, but he did not, merely quirking an eyebrow in her direction. She would have to find another way to seek him out and fast if they were going to pull this off. The longer she stayed, the more she risked being discovered, and she shuddered to think what would happen to her then.

She made her way back to her bedroom and changed into a nightgown. She worried what Corydon might think when she chose to sleep in her own bed again, but per-haps not feeling well would be a good enough excuse. She wasn't so lucky, for she was tugged from her slumber in the middle of the night by warm, strong arms lifting and cradling her.

"You're in the wrong bed," he growled in her ear. She could hear the mix of emotions behind his accusation, concern laced with frustration.

"I didn't feel good," she replied weakly against his shirt.

"So you chose your own cold sheets instead of my warm, cozy bed where I could keep an eye on you? Is something else wrong?" He placed her gently on his bed, his eyes filled with worry. She could see his insecurities looming under the concern, and it chipped away another piece of her heart. No matter what monster he was becoming as king, she still loved him, and she knew she would be breaking his heart when she left.

"No, of course not. What could be wrong?" she lied.

He sighed, rubbing his hand across his cheek. "I don't know. I just feel like you aren't as happy as you should be. We just celebrated our engagement last night. We should be continuing to celebrate tonight. I should not arrive in my room to find my bed empty when you have shared it with me for the last several months."

She exhaled slowly. If he was already suspicious, would he then be overly concerned? Would he watch her more closely? She tried to forget everything she had seen the previous night, the pleasure he'd gotten from torturing the human, the fact that he was her midnight stallion, the blonde touching him. She focused instead on the boy she had fallen in love with.

"What if I can't be the queen you need me to be?" she whispered.

"Nonsense! You will be a magnificent queen! You are everything I need you to be—*everything*. Is that what has had you so distracted?"

She nodded sheepishly, admitting the partial truth. He cupped her cheeks and pressed his lips to hers, reassuring her that she was everything to him. He whispered words of love and devotion as he worshipped her, and when a few stray tears managed to slip through her barrier, she claimed she was overwhelmed by the moment, not by her own heart breaking.

The next few days passed in a blur. She woke feeling slightly better than the previous day, this time able to keep all her food down. When she attempted to locate Rodric, she found he had left to settle a negotiation with the Seelie king. She learned a lot about the tedious peace arrangement the two courts had and what had to be done to maintain it. She couldn't help but feel slightly defeated, knowing she couldn't make an immediate escape. To survive without detection of her possible actions, she would have to act like nothing was wrong. The only stroke of luck was that Lord Dante was expected to be gone for a little bit, too, although no one would say why. She was kept busy most of the days, still learning about her queenly duties with Alfie or sitting next to Corydon as he made decisions. It was rather tedious and boring but helped keep her mind off her inevitable plans for escape. She finally insisted that if she was going to be queen, she should be able to start dressing herself, only allowing Alvina to help with her hair and makeup when it was necessary.

At night she even drank ambrosia with her meal several nights in a row, not until the point of needing to be carried up the stairs, but enough that she could let her stress and cares slip away, finding it easier to pretend when she could forget what she'd seen that night and the thoughts that always weighed heavy on her chest.

Naturally, the following morning, she always regretted her actions, having woken many times feeling nauseous or barely making it to the bathroom before puking. Corydon seemed concerned, but she brushed him off, claiming it must be a human side effect of consuming the Fae wine.

One of the days that week, he decided it was finally time for her to see some of the village surrounding the palace. She was equal parts thrilled and terrified to be leaving the comfort of the space she had grown accustomed too, but he insisted seeing more of her would help the people come to terms with her as their queen. His wording caused her nerves to rise, knowing the truth behind them. She knew his people would never come to terms with her as their queen, and he was blinded by love to hope so.

Just like the palace itself, the village surrounding it was like stepping back in time, or into a Disney movie like *Beauty and the Beast*. The homes and shops varied in materials, from wood to stone and brick. The one thing most seemed to have in common was a thatched moss roof. They rode his horse all around the town with her seated in front and him whispering in her ear, explaining everything.

While the town itself looked inviting, the chilled air and even chillier reception from the people caused her to shiver. They stared at her, some with open disgust, others lasciviously or with mild curiosity. Corydon seemed oblivious to it all and made no comment other than to tell her about the different shops or to greet people as they passed. Even more disconcerting than the Fae were the few humans she saw. She was shocked to see them there, following behind Fae like a puppy dogs or obeying their commands, many even wearing collars around their necks.

Her stomach churned the more she saw of the town, the now familiar nausea resurfacing at the worst time. Corydon noticed the stiffening of her spine and her silence but didn't question it until they returned and were in his room.

"Is everything okay?"

"No."

His brow furrowed and he tugged his hand through his pale hair. "What is it? I thought you would like to see the town."

She sat down in a chair, not wanting him to sit next to her. *Did he really not know?* She cocked her head to the side. "Why were the humans wearing collars?"

It took a moment, but she saw when the question sank in, the slight paling of his cheeks and the flash of lavender in his gaze. "Oh."

"Oh? That's all you have to say?"

"What do you want me to say? I'm pretty sure you know the answer to the question you're asking." He threw his hands up, knowing the truth would not appease her this time.

"I do, but I want to hear you say it," she growled, outrage simmering under her skin at seeing her people treated like slaves.

He sighed, rubbing his temples. "Not all of them were wearing collars."

"You think that makes it better?!" she yelled.

"No, it's just…" She arched her eyebrows sharply, warning him to choose his next words carefully. "Some of them were wearing collars because they belong to those Fae."

"Belong to them?"

"Yes." He swallowed hard.

"You allow humans to be owned by Fae, to be forced to wear collars like some sort of pet, but you expect your people to accept one of them as their queen?"

"I…" He seemed at a loss for words, and she waited while he gathered them. She saw the resolve settle over his features, transforming his face into a mask of stone. "They will. They will accept you as their queen because I tell them to, and I am their king. My word is all they need." She opened her mouth to point out the many flaws in his explanation, but he silenced her with a single gaze that left no room for argument, his eyes glowing with the authority behind his words. "Do not question me again on this matter." Then he left the room, slamming the door behind him.

She collected her jaw off of the floor only to have the outrage that was simmering under her skin boil over. She grabbed the nearest object, a vase from the end table next to her, and threw it against the door where it shattered. She knew just what that felt like, and she left the pieces there to show him just how she felt. She left his room and locked herself in her own, refusing to come down for dinner or to see him at all. She slept in her room and cried herself to sleep. She begged whoever might be listening to make Rodric return soon so she could make her escape.

The next morning, she still wasn't feeling like herself. She thought perhaps the recent revelations were weighing heavily on her soul, and as much as she wanted to hide away in her room all day, she knew it wasn't possible. She would just shove it all down inside of her until Rodrick came back, and she could process it all after she left.

She ignored the note and flowers that were sitting on the table in her room, not wanting to hear his apologies or read his excuses. She gathered all the strength she had to face him and walked downstairs. When she entered the throne room, she almost froze. The people gathered were so quiet, watching a chained man kneeling on the floor with a sword pointed at his neck. The man pointing the sword was explaining that he had caught the thief stealing from the king's garden. Corydon spared her a glance when he noticed her entry, sharply tilting his head to indicate that she should take her seat beside him in the throne Rodric had sat upon the day she'd arrived. She nodded and quickly made her way to the throne, careful not to draw too much attention to herself.

"What do you have to say for yourself?" Corydon asked, his features set in a mask of indifference.

"I only took a few vegetables, sire. My family is hungry. I thought only of them and the food they needed. I—"

"Enough!" The king's sharp voice echoed through the hall.

Ayanna's heart speed up with the vibration of his voice bouncing off the walls. She felt a hand upon her shoulder and tore her gaze away from them to see Conall next to her. "Calm, milady—you must remain calm." Warmth radiated from his touch, slowing her heart back down to normal. She remembered then that some of the Fae could pick up on her emotions, and sure enough, at least two of them were staring at her hungrily like lions stalking a baby gazelle.

"Thank you, Conall," she whispered, and he remained next to her but moved his hand to the side of her forearm where it was less noticeable to the gathered crowd.

"Do you know the price for theft?" Corydon asked,

standing from his throne and walking toward the man.

The man nodded and swallowed hard. "I do."

"Very well." He plucked a sharp knife from his belt as the man behind the accused used his foot to push the kneeling man to the ground. He kept his foot on the man's back while a guard approached and stretched the man's arm out in front of him. The energy of the crowd grew with the tension. When she felt as if she were going to jump from her chair, a warm wave of tranquility washed over her, taking her anxiety with it, and she sat and watched, unable to feel the horror she was witnessing.

In one swift move, Corydon raised the knife and brought it down against the man's wrist, instantly severing his left hand from his arm. The man wailed as the crowd cheered. Her stomach dropped, and only the false sense of calm coming from Conall kept her in place, apparently undisturbed by the event. Corydon took a handkerchief from his pocket, wiped the blade clean, and slid it back into his belt. When he climbed the dais, his eyes were fixed on his own throne, not flicking over to Ayanna, and she was grateful.

She closed her eyes, not wanting to look at the man who continued to wail for the loss of his hand. "Keep them open. Watch with indifference, milady. You must. Do not let them see you as weak," Conall whispered in her ear, and she nodded as she complied.

"Your punishment is complete. This is your only warning. You may see a healer to stop the bleeding." With that the thief was dismissed, and a guard helped pull him from the room. Corydon then addressed the accuser. "Feel free to keep his hand as payment."

The Fae smiled, his red eyes glowing brightly as he snatched the bloody hand off the floor before bowing.

"Thank you, Your Majesty." A few servants scurried over to clean the evidence of the scene from the floor before the next citizen stepped forward with an issue to present to the king.

The rest of their time, Conall stayed close to Ayanna, offering her what she needed with a casual brush or whisper that would seem to the common observer as words of advice. Corydon barely looked at her, and she wasn't sure if she should feel relieved or disappointed. When they broke for lunch, she claimed she needed to freshen up and retreated to her room. Conall's touch had helped calm her rolling stomach, but she didn't know how much more she could take. *Dear Lord, Rodric needs to return soon.* She prayed he would return quickly and almost wept with relief when she went down for the meal to find him seated at the table.

"You're back!" she exclaimed, unable to contain her relief.

"I am." He tilted his chin slightly.

She recovered quickly. "I just didn't know how long you would be gone, is all, so I'm surprised to see you."

She sat down, still ignoring Corydon, and they began to eat.

"You've been faring well in court, I hear."

Her fork paused for just a moment before she forced it to continue toward her mouth. The food tasted like sawdust on her tongue as she chewed. She smiled. "Alfie trained me well."

Luckily, Rodric then turned his attention to Corydon, eager to get caught up on any events he'd missed. She pretended to eat the rest of her meal by taking tiny bites and pushing the food around on her plate until she was "full".

She drank only water, the wine looking too close to the blood she had seen spilled on the floor earlier that day. She tried to think of a way she could let Rodric know she needed to talk to him without anyone getting suspicious, but it was near to impossible.

She retreated to her own room after dinner that evening, still having yet to talk to Corydon after the day's events. Of course, she knew he would not let it be, and sure enough, there was a knock at her door that night then he stepped inside.

"I'm sorry." He hung his head down, unable to meet her gaze. "I know today was hard for you. I don't enjoy distributing punishments to my people, but sometimes they must be done." He approached her cautiously, his eyes begging her to forgive him, to understand. "Sometimes I wish I could just go back to the summer we met, before I had to deal with any of this, when it was just you and me." He cupped her chin, forcing her to meet his gaze. His violet eyes were mesmerizing, and she could almost feel his longing for a simpler time. It was wishful thinking, a thought they both shared, but she knew it could never be.

"Me too," she whispered, leaning into him as he wrapped his arms around her.

"I'm sorry about yesterday, too. I know it was hard on you, as many things are, and I wasn't very understanding of that. I'm trying, I really am." He kissed her forehead. "I missed you in my bed last night. It was empty and cold and I woke searching for your warmth only to remember how badly I had messed up because you were nowhere to be found."

She blinked and stared into his eyes. No matter what a monster he had become for his people, he still broke through her armor when he came to her so vulnerable. She could see the boy she had first fallen in love with, and she missed him so much. She didn't move when he went to kiss her, instead losing herself in the feel of him, in the memory she knew she was making. She knew it would be their final time together.

He lifted her into his arms, carrying her to his room. When he placed her on the bed, his kisses became frantic, eager to show her just how much he missed her, and they lost themselves in each other, in a final act of love. She let all the love she had for him bleed through her, spilling out of her heart and onto his skin, and he soaked it up, feeling as if they were making up for lost time, but to her, it was goodbye. She was saying goodbye to the future she had envisioned for them, knowing reality would never come close, saying goodbye to the first man she had ever loved and who had unknowingly shattered her heart. She knew then that she would have to leave quickly. She could not keep pretending with him.

The next morning, she woke to the smell of sausage from the breakfast platter sitting on their table and it turned her stomach. She stumbled out of bed and barely made it to the bathroom before she threw up. This time she knew it wasn't the wine, as she hadn't had a drop to drink the night before. Corydon was there in a heartbeat, gathering her hair away from her face and rubbing her back soothingly. When she had finished, she leaned back against him. She could feel that he was already fully dressed and she wondered what time it was, how much longer he would linger. While she took comfort in his presence, it was also now intermingled with paranoia and fear.

"Are you not well?"

"Maybe just the flu or something I ate not agreeing with me. Common issues for a human," she replied, trying not to let her own misgivings leak through.

"Do you want me to get a healer?"

"No!" she blurted out before smoothing her expression and tone. "I mean, no. I'm sure I'll be fine." She smiled reassuringly. Her hands trembled and she stilled them against the tile, using them to push herself up. She rinsed out her mouth at the sink before climbing back into his bed. "I'm sure I just need to rest. Usually that's what it is."

He studied her, his eyebrows drawing together. His lips thinned into a tight line. "I'll give you today, but if you're not well by tomorrow, you *will* see a healer." He kissed her forehead and she opened her mouth to protest, but he placed his fingers against her lips. "It is not up for discussion." His eyes softened and he kissed her cheek before heading to the door. "Stay and rest. As soon as you are well, join me downstairs. I'll send Alfie to check on you later. If you change your mind and want a healer, just let one of the guards know." She nodded.

Once he left the room, she collapsed against the pillows. Too many days in a row of throwing up, nausea, and fatigue had worn her out. She closed her eyes, running through the possibilities—flu, food poisoning… Her mind stopped, screeching to a sudden halt along with her heart. *No, no. It can't be.* She shook her head. "Impossible," she whispered, while knowing it was entirely possible—Conall was proof of that. She jumped out of bed and reached the toilet before vomiting again. *Shit, shit, shit.* She slumped back against the wall next to the toilet and started the mental calculations, counting back to her last period. *God, how could I be so stupid?!* she screamed in her head. *I'm a complete and utter moron.* She knew the consequences of sex; she'd learned about it in health class, and hell, her own mother had given her the talk when she was alive. *Why did I not think to use protection?* That was the problem—she hadn't been thinking things through at all. She'd been living through her emotions, and now her actions had caught up to her. She guessed an ignorant part of her had thought that perhaps with Fae there was some magic behind it, since Corydon hadn't shown any concern about the possibility of her becoming pregnant.

She couldn't fight it and the sobs broke free, her panic exploding. *What the hell am I going to do now?* Unconsciously, she placed her hand over her stomach. She let herself wallow in her own self-pity for maybe half an hour before knowing she needed to get a plan together more quickly than she thought possible. If it was morning sickness, as she believed, she wouldn't be better by the next day and the minute the healer laid his hands on her, he would know what was causing her symptoms. She shuddered. If she was pregnant, there was no way she could stay. She could not waste another minute. She had to get out, and she had to do it that night.

CHAPTER 14

S HE DRESSED QUICKLY and formulated as much of a plan as she could on her own. She opened her door, relieved to find no guard posted in her hallway, and she saw no servants either. She debated how she would draw the least suspicion and settled on moving with purpose and confidence. She wasn't sure if Corydon had told anyone else about her illness, but she knew she had to avoid him, if possible, and somehow find Rodric.

She marched through the hallways, hoping Rodric wouldn't be with Corydon but knowing that was most likely where he would be. She was lost to her internal mission when she practically collided with Conall at the bottom of the stairs.

"Oh, milady, I apologize." He placed his hands gently on her shoulders to steady her.

"It's fine, Conall." She shook his hands off but frowned when his brow furrowed. She smoothed her expression, realizing it was her snippy words and actions that were drawing his reaction. He had only ever been kind to her, and she to him in return. She smiled gently. "It's my fault. I wasn't paying attention."

"Is there anything I can help you with, Lady Ayanna?"

She hoped this was the right thing. It felt right to trust him a little after he had shown her such kindness in a cold place. "Actually, I think there is. Do you know where Rodric is?"

"Rodric?" He repeated, his nose wrinkling.

She hoped her gut wasn't wrong about him. "Yes, I need to speak with him in private." Conall frowned. "I want to get a gift for Corydon and I need his help, but I want it to be a surprise you see, so I can't let Corydon know." She winked and prayed he didn't question her further, prayed her explanation would be enough.

He grinned widely in return, seeming oblivious to her lies. "I see. I can get him for you. I'll have him meet you in the library. No one should be in there right now."

"Oh, that would be perfect! I'll be forever grateful." She placed a hand on his shoulder and squeezed.

"Not a problem. He'll be there shortly." Conall's green eyes sparkled with amusement as he turned to complete her task.

She sighed and turned, ascending the stairs and making her way to the library. She passed a guard or two along the way, but no one questioned her. It was routine to see her head into the library, and the suggestion had been very smart thinking on Conall's part.

She was chewing her bottom lip, wringing her hands, and pacing the room when the door opened and Rodric stepped through, his pale white hair pulled back into a ponytail. "Conall said you wanted to see me about a gift for Corydon." His right eyebrow was raised, realizing his words did not match her actions.

She stopped, smoothing her hands down on the skirt of her dress, trying to appear less nervous. "Please." She motioned toward the chairs. And he closed the door behind him as he took a seat. He studied her like a cat watching a moth, taking in all its sudden movements and waiting for the right moment to strike. His gaze tracked every one of her nervous ticks, which only amped her up more. "I need to know if you were serious."

"You're going to have to be more specific than that." He crossed his arms over his chest and reclined into the chair.

"If…" She took a deep breath, knowing her next words would either condemn or save her. She cleared her throat. "I need to know if you were serious when you offered to help me leave."

He scratched his jaw and leaned forward, resting his elbows on his knees. "That depends—is your question serious? Have you thought through exactly what consequences merely asking this question could have?"

She sat down across from him and stared him straight in the eyes. "It is, and I have. I realize simply asking you is risking my life."

"And yet, you ask."

"I do." She nodded.

"I thought things were going well. We just celebrated your engagement. Surely, I would think that had you honestly wanted to leave, you would have done so sooner, when you were less involved, when there was less to risk."

She sighed. "I…" She closed her eyes. "I was so swept up in him and in love, I didn't realize exactly what I had gotten myself into. I know you warned me, but I was so naïve." She shook her head. "I was an idiot to think I could ever be queen to your people."

"Why the sudden change of heart?" He studied her closely, weighing her reactions and answers.

"It was the party, the engagement bacchanalia. I..." She licked her lips, her mouth suddenly dry. "I woke up later and snuck back downstairs when Corydon wasn't in bed. I saw...I saw him...*change*, and the way the crowd took pleasure in tormenting the human man."

"Ah, so he had not told you about his type of magic, and you had not bothered to ask."

She shook her head. "He always seemed to avoid the question, and I was content to remain in blissful ignorance. You don't have to say it—I know how stupid I've been, but I also know I could never be the queen he or your people need, not when the thought of carrying out a court punishment makes me want to throw up. I need to get out, tonight, if possible."

"You do realize it won't be easy."

She nodded and swallowed hard. She had figured as much.

"You will have to be careful—we *both* will—and once I get you out, you must keep going. He'll look for you where you first met, and he will not be happy. You'll be breaking his heart."

"I know, but I can't stay. It'll be worse for me to stay."

"I'm not going to argue with you there. If you are certain, I'll find a way, and you will leave tonight. We cannot have anyone discover our thoughts. Luckily, Dante is still out of town, which should help things. You will need to pretend everything is fine so Corydon does not suspect anything. Can you handle that?"

She nodded. "I can. He already believes me to not be feeling well today."

"Very well. Do you know where you will go?"

"My aunt's house first, and she will take me somewhere else."

"Okay. I will gather the necessary supplies, including a horse that knows the way to the gateway and back."

"Thank you."

He scoffed. "Don't thank me yet. We aren't in the clear, and there are a million things that could go wrong." He stood and strode toward the door, pausing as his hand reached for the handle.

"Oh, and Ayanna"—he stared directly into her eyes—"for this to work, you're going to have to slip something into his drink, just a little something to help him sleep, to make sure he does not wake before we have gotten you safely away."

She nodded. "I understand."

"I don't think you do." He cocked his head to the side. "He won't just let you go, sweetheart. He *will* come after you, and if he thinks you did not leave on your own, he will pursue you to the ends of this earth. You're going to have to find a way for him to know you left on your own, whether you fight with him before or leave a letter after. The fact of the matter is, you're going to have to break his heart, shatter it into a million pieces." His aquamarine gaze pierced hers. "Can you do that?"

She took a deep breath, sharp pain radiating from her own heart. She knew what it would take to break his, and she only hoped someday he could forgive her and might be able to understand why she had to do it. She hoped it wouldn't completely change him, but it was not the time to be selfish. She had someone else to think about. She closed her eyes, clenching her hands against her dress to keep them from drifting to her belly. She didn't know how to describe what she was feeling, but it was almost as if love flooded through her being. Even though no one had confirmed it, she knew. She just knew she was with child. Call it mother's instinct or whatever, but she knew and would do anything to protect her unborn child, even if it meant breaking her heart and the heart of the man she loved.

"I can." She met his gaze head on, letting the fierce protectiveness she was feeling fuel her resolve, and whatever Rodric saw satisfied him enough to turn back to the door.

"Be ready to leave around midnight."

She was glad to have the illness as an excuse not to have to be around court that day. Of course, Corydon came to check on her several times, as did Alfie. Each time she reassured him that she was feeling much better already and did not need a healer. His concern was touching and a bit smothering at the same time. In order to not draw suspicion to herself, she claimed she was well enough to eat with the court and joined him by his side. Her mind was elsewhere and it was a constant battle to focus on the moment at hand, to not let her thoughts wander lest someone be able to read them.

Corydon didn't seem to question her behavior as she laughed at the appropriate times and engaged in conversation. She did request water instead of ambrosia, but given her illness from earlier, it was understandable. As she excused herself from dinner, Rodric stealthily slipped a small bottle into her palm—the sleeping draft, she presumed. She kissed Corydon on the cheek and begged him not to be much longer, throwing a flirty wink his way. She requested that the servants also bring a nightcap for two to his room, and he smirked at her when he overheard her request. She blew him a kiss before slipping out of the room.

She snuck into the kitchen with the excuse of grabbing a bowl of strawberries to have in her room, and while Alvina wasn't looking, she slipped a knife into the ribbon she'd tied around her thigh when she was getting dressed. She thanked Alvina, who just rolled her eyes in return, and then she climbed the stairs to the king's room with the bowl of fruit in her hands. She placed it on the table next to the glasses of ambrosia the servants had left. Then she poured out her own glass into the sink and refilled it with water. Finally, she tipped the sleeping draft into his wine and swirled the two together with her finger before slipping out of his room and into her own. She hastily grabbed the pack she had stuffed full of supplies earlier and hidden in her wardrobe. She retrieved the rock Enora had given her months before from its hiding place and slipped it into the pack along with the knife then concealed the bundle once more. When she was finished, she poked her head out of her room and waited until the coast was clear to sneak back into his room. There she changed into her nightgown and had just sat down on the bed when Corydon opened the door, smiling at her.

"Feeling better, my love?" he asked, kissing her lips.

She nodded. "I'd like to talk to you for a minute, Cor. Would you like a drink first? It might help." She smiled nervously.

His jaw clenched for a minute before he released it and nodded, going over and picking up his wine. He drained the entire goblet quickly. "And yours?" he asked, pointing to her goblet of water.

"Oh, I already had my liquid courage." The corners of her mouth lifted.

"Do you need courage to talk to me?" he asked, tilting his head to the right.

"Um…in this case, I think I do. I need to ask you something, and I'm not sure how you're going to take it or how you're going to answer. I mean, I've tried to ask you before, but you always seemed to avoid it. However, I think now that we are to be married, you should tell me the truth." She had thought this through, considering what would convince him that she left of her own free will. The only way she saw fit was if he blamed himself enough for her departure to let her go. "What kind of Fae are you?"

He sucked in a breath and winced. Her heart stopped, waiting for his answer. It took him a few minutes, but eventually he spoke. "I'm a Pooka." He walked over and sat next to her on the bed.

The truth struck a chord, bringing her back to the moment she'd seen him as her midnight stallion and the betrayal she felt. *What will he have to say for himself?*

She continued to stare at him with innocent doe eyes. Although she had already looked up the information on what he was, she wanted to hear the words from his mouth. She dipped her chin, encouraging him to continue.

"With my magic, I'm able to change into something else."

"Like a shapeshifter?"

"Sort of. I can take the form of a large dark feathered eagle…among other things." He studied her reaction closely, knowing she might make the connection.

"What others?"

He sighed. "One is something I never wish you to see. It's not pretty." The demon with the curved horns snarled in her mind and she blanched.

"The other…I'm afraid." He took her hand and held it in his own.

"You're afraid?"

"Of what you might think of me after I tell you. It's probably something I should've told you a while ago." He took a deep breath, and she squeezed his hand, knowing his answer would've been a knife to her heart if she hadn't already seen it with her own eyes. Her chest ached.

He sighed. "The other is a large black horse."

She feigned the appropriate amount of shock, curiosity, and anger. "A…black horse? Like a stallion? Like Midnight? "

He nodded sheepishly. "I…I'm sorry I didn't tell you sooner. I was worried how you would react."

She withdrew from his touch and began to pace the room. "And how did you think I would react? By being pissed to find out you had been lying to me? That you let me believe I was confessing all my secrets and feelings to a horse when in fact it was you?

"I thought we promised we wouldn't lie to each other anymore, Cor—did you not mean it when you told me you would be honest with me?" She threw her hands up, letting him feel her frustration.

"Of course I meant it, I just…" He stood to approach her, his hands reaching for her.

"You just what?! Decided it would be okay to break that promise? Did it mean so little to you? I feel like I don't even know you right now!" she yelled.

He dropped his arms and shook his head to the side as if she had slapped him. "I'm sorry."

"You lied to me!"

"I didn't lie, I just didn't tell you the truth," he protested.

"It's the same thing! And you did lie—the minute you made that promise knowing what information you were withholding from me, you lied." Her heart ached, and while she would have liked to say the argument was merely to set up the reason for her escape, it wasn't. It was a conversation she had been waiting to have with him, and every word that came out of her mouth, every emotion that overwhelmed her was genuine. "I don't know who you are anymore."

He grabbed her then and pulled her against his chest. "You know who I am. You're the only one who knows who I am in here." He placed her hand over his heart. "I love you, Ayanna, so much. I never meant to hurt you, and I promise to make it up to you."

"I think I might need some time...please understand."

"I'll give you time, but please stay tonight, just to sleep. I don't want you in your room after you were sick last night. I need to make sure you are okay."

He pulled her tight against him, breathing in her scent.

She sighed. "Okay, but that doesn't mean you're forgiven."

"Thank you." He pressed a quick kiss to her lips before she could push him away.

She climbed back into bed and he quickly followed. He gathered her in his arms and she closed her eyes, soaking up his scent one final time, knowing what it was to be wrapped in the warmth of his love. It wasn't long until his soft snores filled the air.

After an hour or so, when she was certain he was sleeping peacefully, she crept out of bed. She slid an envelope with his name on it from under her side of the mattress and tiptoed toward the table. Setting the letter down gently, she turned to look at him one last time. She drank in his sharp jaw and pointed ears, his pale moonlit hair spilled across the pillows and the peaceful rise and fall of his breath. She took a deep breath knowing it was the last time she would ever lay eyes on him then amassed all her courage before gently closing the door behind her. She rested her head against it, waiting for any sign of him stirring, but thankfully he did not. The sleeping draft she'd slipped into his glass was working well. She wished things could've been different, but they weren't.

Luckily there was no sight of guards in the hallway, no one to notice as she slipped back into her old room. She closed the door behind her with a soft click before taking a few deep breaths to gather her strength. The letter should help things. She had given him her reasons for leaving, the many ways she felt she could never be the woman he needed her to be, and begged that if he loved her, he would let her go because it was the best for everyone in the long run.

Ayanna rested her hand over her belly, knowing she wouldn't be able to hide the truth much longer. Either a slightly protruding baby bump or someone's Fae magic would reveal the secret she was hiding, and she had to escape before it was too late.

As much as she loved Corydon, she didn't love the man he had become since assuming his father's seat on the Unseelie throne. The power, responsibility, and need to be the uncontested ruler were all changing him. He was no longer the man she had first met and fallen in love with two years before. Had it really been so long? It felt like she had only been there a couple months, but she sighed knowing a few months could equal a year back home. She knew her birthday had mostly likely come and gone in the time she'd stayed; she very well could have been nineteen already and not even known it. *Nineteen and soon to be a mother—too young.* She focused her thoughts on her baby, using her love and protectiveness to fuel her determination.

She rubbed her hand against her flat stomach. "Don't worry, my precious baby, your mommy will protect you. I will do whatever I have to do to keep you safe. I'm sorry you will never know your true father, but trust me, this is for the best."

She dressed quickly and started braiding her golden blonde hair. She was glad, then more than ever, that Alvina had listened when she insisted she didn't need anyone to help her dress anymore. If that woman ever found out… She shuddered to think of it. Alvina would probably insist that it would be better for the baby to be raised by a pure Unseelie like herself, and Ayanna couldn't let that happen. She would die before she let anyone take her baby away.

She slipped the knife she had smuggled from the kitchen into her right boot then plucked her necklace off the vanity, the midnight blue one he had first given her. She carefully put it on, tucking it underneath her tunic. It made it easier to leave knowing she still had a piece of him with her, something that might help protect her. She checked her pack to make sure she had all the necessities and quietly closed the door. Tiptoeing her way through the castle, she hoped her plan would work and she and her baby would soon be free.

She removed the grey stone she had kept safe all this

time from the pocket of her pack. It wasn't hard for her to urge her heart to reach for Enora; it was already desperately reaching for anyone who would help. The rock shimmered a bright silver as she pressed it into her palm, closing her fist around it. It glowed, leaking light between her fingers. She wasn't sure how it worked, but she thought about Enora's powers and how she could feel others' emotions and used them to heal, so she took everything she felt and willed it to transfer into the rock—the fear for her safety, for the safety of her unborn child, her broken heart, and her panic about her escape. When the rock's glow dimmed, she hoped her message had been sent. She knew it would take some time for Enora to reach her depending on how far away from the castle she was, but it was the only hope she had, and she could not just wait around for her to show up, not when so much could go wrong, not when Lord Dante could return at any moment and discover the secret she was hiding.

Rodric had said he would make sure the guards wouldn't notice her escape, but she had no clue what that meant. She was surprised to find the ones normally posted at the stairs spread prone across the floor. She worried briefly that they might be dead, but then one of them snored loudly. She breathed a sigh of relief, continuing her flight down the stairs. She went as quickly and quietly as she could. She knew Corydon was sleeping in his bed, but there were still many other ways she could be discovered. She was thankful Rodric had followed through with his promise to help her escape. She followed his directions and snuck out the side of the castle through a servant's entrance near the kitchen. She took the well-worn path toward the stable, and he was there waiting with a horse.

She knew Alfie had warned her about trusting him, but what choice did she have? "Ayanna," he whispered in greeting as he handed her a large black cloak. She put it on, drawing the hood over her head to hide her identity. When she was finished, he helped her mount the horse. "You understand that he will come looking for you. He will not let you go so easily. I'll dissuade him from pursuing you as best I can, but we both know how pointless that may prove to be."

"I understand," she replied.

"I don't think you do, fully. After you return to your aunt's house tonight, you must leave immediately. It's best if she does not know where you are, but I understand if you need to involve her. However, you should not return to her house for any reason, lest he discover you. Wherever you go, if you wish to see her, make her come to you. I'm sure she'll agree with me on this if she is as logical and protective as you have led me to believe."

She nodded reluctantly, understanding just what was at stake, even if he didn't know the secret she was harboring.

"Know that you are doing what is best for him and for his kingdom. Our people would never accept you as our queen, and you're doing all of us a great service by leaving."

His words did little to ease her breaking heart. She wasn't leaving Corydon to do what was best for him or for his people; she was leaving him to do what was best for her baby. It was best if her baby never found out who her father truly was, and that truth shattered her heart into a million pieces. While she loved him with every breath she took and loving herself may not have been enough to make her leave, her love for her child was a fierceness she had never experienced and she was determined to keep them both safe for her baby's sake.

"Thank you for your help, Rodric. Please..." She

sighed, unsure of what she wanted him to do. "Please help him heal, help him understand."

"I'll do my best." He bowed his head formally, accepting her request. She wasn't sure how the others thought Rodric to be so cruel, a mirror of his father, when he had only been kind to her. "This horse will lead you home. He knows the way. When you get there, he'll sense his way back, so you need not worry about that. Safe travels, Ayanna."

She nodded once more and leaned toward the horse, grabbing ahold of the reins tightly. "Go!" she whispered, and the horse took off. It took all her strength not to look back, but she resolved to only move forward from that point on. Had she taken a moment to glance back, she may have seen Rodric smiling widely with a triumphant gleam in his eye.

She rode for quite some time along the dirt road, letting her horse lead the way while urging him to do so as quickly as possible. She pulled him up short when she saw another rider approaching in the distance. She made sure she was covered, her face hidden within the shadows of the hood and the night sky. She pressed him on at a more casual pace until the rider passed by. As the other rider neared, she could see a head of long mossy green hair illuminated in the moonlight, and she brought her horse to a stop. "Enora," she said, breathing a sigh of relief.

Enora quickly drew her steed next to Ayanna's horse, grabbed her hand in greeting, and then frowned at what she felt. Their eyes met, Ayanna's filling with tears as Enora's glowed a bright silver. She gasped, releasing her hand, and leaned over her horse to place her hand across Ayanna's belly. "How long?"

"I'm not sure. I just figured it out. In fact, I didn't know for certain until just now. If I had to guess, a few weeks at least, probably more." She was not an expert at pregnancy, and wasn't like the castle library had books lying around about it or that she would have had the guts to read them, afraid of letting anyone in on her secret, but she'd known the minute she contacted her, Enora would be able to tell.

"Is he…she okay?" Ayanna asked. She wasn't sure what to call her baby.

Enora smiled. "*She* is fine. Healthy as can be."

"She?" Ayanna asked, the tears she had held at bay now overflowing, overwhelmed as she was with love for her daughter. She placed her own hand on her belly, next to Enora's.

Enora nodded. "She knows you love her. She can feel it through you, but you need to be strong for her. This will be a dangerous journey, and if we have any hope of saving the both of you, we must do so quickly. I know you want to sink into all the emotion you are experiencing, but you cannot yet. Do you understand?"

Ayanna nodded her head, wiping her tears away with her hands.

"Be strong for her—she needs you." Once Enora was satisfied that Ayanna had shoved her emotions back inside and steeled herself for the journey ahead, she handed the reins back to her. "Quickly now, no time to waste. You can tell me more while we ride to your aunt's house." With that, the two raced off into the night.

While they rode, Ayanna started at the beginning and told Enora everything. She told her how she met Corydon, how they fell in love, how she'd known what he was since the beginning but hadn't care. She told her about the breakup, about going to their spot one last time, about being taken to the king and finding out he was indeed the boy she had fallen in love with, how she fell more in love with him until she discovered what he was, what he could do. She shuddered with the memory of that night. She recounted the court punishments and how she knew the only way he could be the king his people needed was if she were to leave, how she'd discovered she had life growing inside of her and finally how Rodric helped her escape. Only when she reached the end did Enora interrupt.

"Are you sure Rodric didn't have another reason for helping you?"

"What do you mean?" Ayanna asked.

"I have never known him to be generous or kind. In fact, he is known for being incredibly manipulative and conniving, just like his wife and his father were. I think he may have had other reasons for helping you leave."

"Does it matter? I mean, he did help me, and I'm safe now, so does it matter why he did it?"

"I suppose not," Enora said, but she didn't look convinced. Enora was quiet for a little while as they continued to ride. Finally, she spoke again. "I don't think you should tell your aunt. I think it might be best for her if we just let her believe he was some random Fae, and don't tell her about the baby, at least not yet. I fear if she knows, it will be dangerous for her. I'll encourage her to stay away from her home for a little while as well. I know you don't like keeping secrets from her, but in this case, the less she knows, the safer she will be. It'll also keep you and your baby safe. If he finds out about the baby, he will not stop until he has you both. Do you understand?"

"I do." Ayanna nodded, remembering how easily humans could be interrogated and toyed with, how the slightest prod on Grace's subconscious from Lord Dante could spill all her secrets at the feet of the king or his enemies. They continued their journey in silence, each of them weighed down by truths.

After a while, they veered off the road and into the woods. Her horse followed Enora's lead and slowed when they came upon a strange arch of entwined branches from two white sycamore trees that seemed to glow in the moonlight. They stopped right before the archway.

"This is the gateway from our realm back to your own. It may be uncomfortable for you to pass through. I just wanted to warn you before we continue," her companion said, and she merely nodded in acceptance before they trotted through. The sensation was strange, and she was grateful she had been unconscious the last time she went through. Her stomach rolled and she closed her eyes against the nausea. When she opened them, the world around her seemed a little dull, the moon not quite as bright. She held herself on the horse but leaned over to puke, losing the battle against the nausea.

Enora handed her a leather pouch filled with liquid and she raised it to her nose first before taking a drink. She swished it around her mouth before spitting it onto the ground.

"It's only water, but I am glad to see you take drinks from Fae with caution."

"Learned that lesson the hard way," Ayanna said, remembering the night she drank too much of the pink champagne. Her research with Alfie had revealed that the main ingredient of the beverage was zahra flowers, the vibrant pink ones that had made her high two summers ago. After that she was less eager to drink it, and only pretended for court appearances.

She took another drink of water, this time swallowing it now that the vomit taste was gone from her mouth. "Enora, how long have I been gone? I mean, I know it has been about four months for me, but I also know time moves differently in Fae."

"Over a year," Enora replied.

"That's what I was afraid of." She handed the water back. "What am I going to do?" Ayanna twisted her hands; she had been so focused on her escape she hadn't even considered what she would do after, where she would go, how she would live her life.

"We have a plan. Your aunt and I worked it out a while ago and were just waiting to put it in action, although your situation does complicate things a little. Don't worry, though. It'll be okay."

Ayanna smiled. She was worried about what Grace would say and how she would react to her return, but knowing she had already planned something with Enora only proved how loving and forgiving her aunt was. "Let's go then." She grabbed the reins and gave them a shake, urging her horse to continue on their path home. *Home?* She knew Aunt Grace's house would no longer be her home, and she fought once more to prevent her grief and fear from overtaking her. She pressed her feet gently into her horse's sides, allowing him race off into the woods, hoping she could outrun her feelings for the time being.

When they reached Grace's house, the sky was brightening with the light of dawn. They dismounted the horses quickly and raced up the porch steps. She pulled the door open, relieved to find Grace had left it unlocked. "Aunt Grace?" she called out. "Aunt Grace, are you here?"

Grace appeared at the top of the stairs in her green plaid pajamas, her curly hair wild with sleep. "Ayanna!" She raced down the steps and pulled her into a fierce hug. "You're here! You're really here!" She pulled back to look at her. "Are you okay?"

Ayanna was unsure how to reply. "Kind of…"

"Grace, we must put our plan into action immediately. The sooner we can get you both out of here, the better our chances are," Enora interrupted.

"Enora!" Grace smiled briefly at the appearance of her friend, but then her lips turned downward. "Of course. I understand." She turned her attention back to her niece. "Grab some snacks and drinks for the car while I grab our things, and be fast. You can tell me more when we are on our way."

Grace ran upstairs while Ayanna searched the kitchen, throwing bottles of water and what snacks she could find into a cooler that was sitting in the corner as if waiting for exactly that moment. When she returned, Grace was slipping on her shoes, two large suitcases sitting next to her in the entryway. Her curly hair had been haphazardly pulled into a sloppy bun and her clothes appeared to have been thrown on in a rush. As soon as her shoes were on, Enora rushed them both out the door, helping Grace with one of the bags.

They walked toward the truck and Ayanna noticed only Enora's horse remained in the clearing; her horse had already taken off back to his master. They loaded the cooler and suitcases into the truck and Grace bid Enora goodbye, thanking her for the help before climbing into the vehicle and starting it up. Enora hugged Ayanna once more. "Remember what I told you: only reveal minimum facts to Grace, and never tell her who the true father of your baby is, for *all* of your safety."

Ayanna sighed and agreed, but then a sudden thought struck her. "What about you? Won't they find out that you know? Will they do something to you for helping me?"

"Your concern is sweet, my dear, but Grace and I planned ahead. Since spending more time here with your aunt, we have made some interesting discoveries about how human medicine affects Fae. You should ask her to tell you about it. It's really quite interesting. Anyway, we found something that will help me forget, a common household pill used to treat pain for humans. It'll make my memories of the last twenty-four hours rather muddled and jumbled so that neither I nor anyone who might be tempted to interrogate me would find the proper answers."

"Thank you. I can't think of any way to repay you for all of your help."

"I can." She smiled. "Take care of yourself, and take care of that baby. Remember that she is half Fae, and half Unseelie at that, but that does not make her bad. We are all products of our experiences. Raise her to know her humanity, to value it beyond everything else, so that when the time comes and she can choose who she wants to be, she will make the right decision."

She hugged Enora once more before she climbed into the truck, and they both waved goodbye as they raced away into the night.

It turned out Enora and Grace did have a well-thought-out plan. The minute they were on their way, Grace started questioning Ayanna about everything, and Ayanna told her only the bare minimum: that she had met a Fae boy and fallen in love, that she hadn't set out that day intending to leave Grace but was taken by another Fae and then rescued by her boy. She told her how he convinced her she couldn't go home for her own safety and that of her family so she chose to stay with him for as long as she could, and how eventually he broke her heart. Grace could sense that there was more to the story but also that the memories were painful, so she didn't press further. She seemed placated by the web of semi-truths and omissions Ayanna spun.

After a few hours, Grace pulled over at a gas station, where she filled up the truck and told Ayanna to change. Ayanna looked down at herself, realizing just how strange she may look to others. Luckily it was still early in the morning so only the gas station manager sent her a curious glance as she fled into the bathroom to change. She removed the cloak and tossed it into the trash can, knowing any ties to the Fae would be a giveaway. She slipped the knife out of her boot, deciding to keep it for the time being. She removed the leather pants she had smuggled from the castle laundry, longingly running her hands against the soft buttery material before tossing them in the trash as well. She slipped on a pair of jeans, the material seeming rough in comparison to her previous pants. Lastly, she pulled the black tunic, one of Corydon's, over her head. She brought the fabric to her nose and inhaled deeply, cherishing the last bit of his scent, and finally the events of the night caught up with her. Her emotions burst forth in the form of heaving sobs and she curled up on the floor of the gas station bathroom, half dressed, and buried her face into the shirt, overcome with grief.

She wasn't sure how much time had passed, but eventually Grace came in to check on her and gathered her into her arms, letting her cry more as she rubbed her back. "I know, sweetheart, just let it all out. It'll be okay, you'll see." She held her until her tears dried and then helped her to her feet, plucking the tunic from her grip and placing it in the trash with the rest of the Fae garments. "I know it may not seem like it now, but our hearts are the strongest organs in our body. You'd be surprised how much pain they can take. Even when they feel like they have broken into a million pieces, they can be put back together. A few scars will remain to remember where you came from, but they do heal, and yours will too." She briefly fingered the necklace around Ayanna's neck, her final reminder of Corydon. "I understand if you want to keep some piece of him." She motioned for Ayanna to hold her arms up and pulled a t-shirt over her head. "But it's probably best if you keep it hidden until you are ready to let it go, to let him go." She smoothed the shirt on top of the necklace, hiding it from view. "Okay, let's get us some coffee, and maybe some donuts." She smiled comfortingly, pulling Ayanna out of the restroom.

They ate their donuts and sipped coffee in the truck, talking before heading back out on the road. Grace told her they were going to a trusted friend's house. He and his wife had a large home with a small guest house on its grounds where they could stay. He was a professor at the local college and would get her enrolled in classes, claiming she was his niece.

"I know it's not exactly what you had in mind, but it was the only thing we could think of to give you some sort of future." Ayanna was touched by Grace's thoughtfulness. "Of course, I'll be moving there too, although it will take some time to close up loose ends back at the cottage with my business and the house."

"No!" Ayanna yelled. She couldn't let Grace stay with her—she would find out about the baby too soon. It was best if she hid it for as long as she could, at least making it plausible that it could belong to some human boy instead of a Fae.

Grace looked alarmed at her objection.

"I mean…I don't want you to have to do that."

"I don't have to, sweetheart—I want to. There's a difference."

"I know you do, and it means the world to me, Aunt Grace, but I can't ask that of you. I've already caused you so much worry and problems, and it'll only make me feel worse if you pack up your life to move here with me because of my mistake."

"We're family, that's what we do. I'm not leaving you, not when I just got you back." She reached across the seat and squeezed her hand.

Ayanna's heart ached knowing the pain she was still causing her aunt, but she had to do this for all of them. "I know, Aunt Grace, I do, but I think I just need some time alone to deal with everything. I love you, and I'm not saying I don't want you to come visit me, but I don't want you to give up everything for me. I'll never forgive myself if you do. I know you're willing to give it all up for me, but I can't let you—I *won't* let you. You've already sacrificed so much for me."

"It's not up for discussion," Grace countered.

"Aunt Grace, I love you, but if you do this, I will never forgive myself. I can't sit by and watch you do it. In fact, I won't. I'll leave. I'm a legal adult now, and you can't make me stay. Please, just do this for me. Stay for a few days, but then go back, live your life, and let me live mine. You can visit whenever you want, I promise, just please don't move with me."

Grace sighed in reluctant acceptance. "If that's what you really want, Ayanna. I don't like it, but I will respect it."

"It is."

"You're right, you're an adult now, but I still expect a phone call every day or I *will* come check on you."

"Understood."

They spent the next few days driving across the country to her new home in Virginia, where she would start her new life. They made pleasant conversation but avoided any more discussion about her time with the Fae or Grace's desires to stay with her longer.

Eventually they arrived at their destination. The house was as grand as she had imagined, and the guest house was perfect. It was the size of a small apartment and had all the amenities. The couple, Sean and Kate, were very sweet and kind, and they were excited to have her at their house. Sean had spoken to the admissions office when Grace called them the first day they left and had already got her transcripts sent over from her high school. Thankfully, she'd been admitted and would start classes in just a week. Sean was even more excited because he was in desperate need of a research assistant that semester, and Ayanna was relieved to have some way to pay them back for their kindness. She was even more interested when she discovered he was a professor of folklore and anthropology. Grace winked at her when he revealed this information, knowing his research would interest her.

After a few days, she convinced Grace to leave her and start the long drive home. They said tearful goodbyes and she promised to call her aunt every day. She was glad it had taken them so long to drive out there as it had meant they'd gotten more time together and would give Grace more time away before she returned. She only hoped it was enough to keep her safe.

CHAPTER 15

THE FIRST TWO weeks of classes proved to be difficult for her. She was paranoid whenever she went out in public, worried that she might somehow run across a Fae and be dragged back to the Unseelie palace. She still cried herself to sleep every night, her heart aching for her to return. She wondered how he took the news of her departure. She was sure he'd probably thrown an epic fit of rage, but what about now? Was he relieved she'd left, stripping him of any obligation to her, or had she truly broken his heart along with her own?

She tried to pay attention in her classes, faking her way through the days, politely introducing herself to anyone who asked but not offering to put herself out there. As soon as she could, she'd escape to Sean's office. He and his wife had been amazing. They didn't question anything about her arrival. Grace had told them she was escaping an abusive relationship and needed a fresh start where her ex couldn't find her, which was somewhat true, so they decided the best way to help her move forward was to not talk about the past, which suited her just fine.

One afternoon during the third week of classes, she was so lost in her own thoughts on her way to grab lunch that she slammed right into someone. She stumbled backward as large hands helped steady her. "Oh my gosh, I'm so sorry." She blinked up at the handsome boy in front of her. He was maybe five inches taller than her with messy brown hair and an easygoing smile. Once upon a time, this type of boy would have made her heart race, but now she wasn't sure she had it in her. As if her heart were born to contradict her, it gave a slight thump. Even though it was still broken, it was nice to know there was hope of healing and returning to the girl she'd once been.

"I'm not," the boy replied. "It's not every day a beautiful girl throws herself at me." He chuckled, righting the dark frames around his hazel eyes, which she had knocked askew. She stared at him, studying him, trying to sniff out his motive and any indication of Fae. Only when her eyes met his ears were her fears appeased and she released a breath of relief.

He took her hesitation in stride. "I'm Joel, by the way." He extended his hand and she stared at it. "Joel Grayson, junior, business major." She still stared at his hand, unsure how to proceed. "This is usually where you shake my hand and introduce yourself." He smiled, urging her to take his hand.

She did, shaking it. "Ayanna...freshman...undeclared."

"Ayanna—that's a unique name." He still held her hand in his own.

"Thanks," she replied, easing her hand from his grip.

"So where are you headed, Ayanna, undeclared freshman?"

"The student union, to eat."

"What a coincidence—me too." He winked at her.

She narrowed her eyes. "But you were just headed away from the union when I crashed into you."

He blushed. "Yes, well, you just reminded me that I need to eat lunch. So, may I join you? I promise not to bite."

She debated telling him off, but the truth was, she was a little lonely for companionship. "Sure. It's a free country, after all." She shrugged and he turned to follow her to the union. She grabbed some food and found him waiting for her at a table with only a drink in front of him.

"I thought you said you needed to eat lunch." She narrowed her eyes accusingly as she sat down.

"Well, the thing is…" He shrugged sheepishly. "I kind of already ate."

"I knew it!" she exclaimed triumphantly, her lips twitching in an almost smile.

"In my defense, I wasn't about to pass up spending some time with a pretty girl, so I may have fibbed a little bit to get you to let me spend some time with you."

The corners of her mouth dropped. "I'm not available," she replied curtly.

He took her confession in stride. "Well, lucky for you I'm only looking to fill a friendship slot right now. I'm not looking for a girlfriend."

She flinched. "I didn't mean to assume…I only thought…"

He laughed. "So are you not available as a friend either?" His eyes sparkled with mischief and genuine interest. "Because if that's the case, I'm going to make it pretty impossible for you."

"You are?"

"Oh yes. I fully intend on making you my friend whether you want to be or not." He smiled.

She sat thinking for a few minutes while she ate. "You're weird, Joel."

"Weird is the best way to be—makes life more interesting." He grinned brightly.

They made small talk during the rest of her meal—well, mostly he talked, telling her all about himself, about growing up as an only child to two wealthy parents who still lived in his childhood home, back in Vermont. He told her about his fraternity and his frat brothers, about his classes, which professors he liked and didn't like. The whole time she just listened, offering pieces here and there that showed she was listening but not revealing anything personal. It was nice getting to know someone new, someone she wasn't worried had ulterior motives that involved her death, like so many of the Unseelie Fae she had encountered at the castle.

"So, what do you think? Are you still unavailable for friendship, or have my charms convinced you otherwise?"

"I suppose a friend would be nice," she conceded.

"Excellent! Well, as your newest friend, I'm required to give you my phone number in case you need to contact me for any…friendly reasons. Do you have a cell? Otherwise I'll need a pen." She nodded, digging in her backpack and handing him the Nokia phone Grace had purchased to keep in touch with her. He added his number as a new contact then handed it back. "I have to go to class now, friend. I've had a wonderful time sharing my life story with you. Oh, and my frat is having a party on Friday night if you'd like to come. You may even make more than one friend there," he teased.

She winced, not sure whether she was ready to handle a party or not, and he promptly saved her from an explanation by offering her an alternative. "Or, if a party isn't really your thing, we could hang out on Saturday, maybe go for pizza or a movie—you know, as friends." She thought on it for a few minutes. It wouldn't hurt to have a friend, and she certainly knew she'd be needing one in the near future, but what if he wanted more than friendship? She had warned him she wasn't available. Would he leave her once he found out she was pregnant, not wanting to deal with some chick with a kid?

As if sensing her hesitation, he continued, "Why don't you think about it and let me know later tonight or tomorrow? You have my number now." He smiled widely before giving her a slight wave and heading off to class.

She pushed out of her chair and gathered her trash, depositing it into the nearest bin. What would be the harm in getting to know him? It wasn't like she had anything to really offer him outside of friendship, not while Corydon still had a hold on her heart.

She waited until later in the evening to text him a quick yes to the movie or pizza on Saturday. Only after she sent the text did she realize he had somehow managed to get her to give him her number. "Sneaky bastard." She chuckled, knowing he'd now be able to pester her by phone whenever he wanted.

On Saturday night, they went out for pizza and a movie. She was worried he would think it was a date, but he threw the friend word around enough to make her relax. She enjoyed their conversation and for once could forget about her current situation. She still found herself unfairly comparing him to Corydon and had to mentally smack herself upside the head. The most entertaining part of their evening was when he came to pick her up and received quite the interrogation from Sean. His skills would have made any cop proud, and luckily Joel took it all in stride.

"So, your dad seems a little intense," he commented on their drive back to her new home.

She sighed, knowing it was only a matter of time before she had to reveal some things about herself. "He's not my dad. Both of my parents died in a car accident a few years ago."

"Oh, I'm sorry. That must really suck." He reached over and squeezed her hand in a friendly, comforting gesture.

"You have no idea."

"So, are they like your guardians or something?"

"More like the 'or something'. I lived with my aunt after my parents died when I was 16. I was supposed to go to college after graduation but…" She wasn't sure how to explain everything to him in a way that would make sense, so she stuck with what they had told Sean and Kate. "I fell in love with the wrong guy and unknowingly let him control the choices I made, which led to me taking a year off school. I was too blinded by love to see what was really happening. He…changed over our time together into someone else…and he made it really difficult for me to leave, so when I was able to get out, my aunt sent me to live with her friends…some place where he won't be able to find me."

He squeezed her hand again, and she noticed that she

didn't mind that he was holding it, his other hand tightening its grip on the steering wheel. "So, that's what you meant by not available." His voice was rough, but his grip on her hand remained gentle, tender almost.

"Yep. I don't want you to think this is going to go anywhere. I'm nowhere near ready to even try to date again, but I'd be happy to have a friend." She tried to smile reassuringly and squeezed his hand in turn, hoping her explanation hadn't scared him off.

He pulled up in front of the house and ran over to her door, opening it for her before she could hop out. He stayed by the car, most likely to not put any more pressure on her by walking her to the door, as that would make it feel too much like a date. "I'd love to be your friend, Ayanna, for as long as you will let me." He hugged her, and she hugged him back.

"Thanks, Joel. I could use a friend."

She walked up the sidewalk to the front door and stopped to wave back at him before she went inside. Once he saw that she was safe, she heard his car pull away. She sighed. The evening had gone much better than she had expected.

Over the next three months, she kept herself busy studying, helping Sean with his research, and hanging out with Joel. He somehow managed to become a staple in her life. He would meet up with her and eat lunch on campus when their schedules allowed, and they almost always hung out on the weekends. He even convinced her to attend one of his frat parties. It was quite the experience, all the drinking, dancing, and games, but the crowds started to get to her. Almost as if he could sense her building anxiety, he hardly ever left her side that night. He introduced her to his friends and seemed to take pride in showing her off. Eventually she relaxed and enjoyed the company without thinking about being watched. He never even questioned her request to only drink water, and he only sipped on two beers the entire night. She loved seeing him around his friends. It was easy to tell that his charm had won them all over, and they accepted easily because he had.

After the party, they joined his friends for pizza, and she had never laughed so hard in her entire life. The guys were hilarious—raunchy at times, but hilarious. She ignored their curious glances when Joel casually slung his arm over her shoulder. They all knew she and Joel were just friends, and yet not a single one of his friends made a move to show any interest in her either—not that she wanted them to. She was perfectly content building friendships and learning to trust men again.

As the days went on, she and Joel fell into a routine of talking every day, either by phone or meeting up to grab coffee or food on campus. He'd sometimes go with her to the library to help her study, insisting that the freshman requisite courses were easy, and they almost always hung out on the weekends at least one of the days, if not both. It wasn't unusual for him to spend the night on her couch or hide out at her place, which was much quieter than the frat house and more conducive to studying.

He quickly became her best friend, and she adored him for it. She didn't miss the fact that he wasn't dating anyone either. She often questioned him about it, seeing as he was so handsome, caring, and smart. He would laugh it off, saying he had too much to focus on with his class load and trying to graduate. Sometimes he'd jokingly say, "Besides, why do I need a girlfriend when I've already got the best girl as my friend?" She would blush furiously and refuse to admit how much those words meant to her, how sometimes when she looked at him, she found her heart wasn't dead after all, because it would skip a beat.

Fortunately, with fall fading into winter, the colder weather made it easier to hide her growing baby bump. She hid behind baggy sweaters and jeans or layers of clothes. She also took herself to the doctor, despite her fears. She didn't know what to expect from a half-Fae baby, but the doctor assured her that everything was fine and her baby looked healthy. She cried happy tears when she first heard her daughter's heartbeat and saw her on the sonogram screen. No matter how she felt about her time in Fae, she would never regret the life growing inside her.

She wasn't sure what she'd tell anyone, but she knew she was on borrowed time. Eventually someone would figure it out. She had never been more grateful that she was staying in a guest house and not at the main house with Sean and Kate so she could hide her rather persistent morning sickness and exhaustion.

Thanksgiving came and Aunt Grace visited. Joel stayed in town, so Kate and Sean invited him over, and it was nice to see how easily he fit in with the people she loved. They really seemed to like him too.

She knew Grace noticed she was no longer wearing Corydon's necklace but chose not to comment, and for that she was grateful. It had taken her a month or so before she decided she should part with it. She didn't get rid of it entirely, just put it away in her jewelry box. Joel helped with that; he was mending her heart so she found herself thinking of Corydon less and less, and more about him. He would make some girl very happy someday, but she doubted he'd want to be with her once he discovered the secret she had been hiding.

Christmas made it a little more difficult for her to hide things, but she did her best. Grace joked about her gaining the freshman fifteen and she just laughed it off, grateful that Grace drew her own assumptions. She only stayed a few days, which Ayanna was even more grateful for. She didn't know how long she would be able to hide her pregnancy from her aunt as Grace had always been able to read her so well. Thankfully, her aunt also assumed her strange mood was because Joel had gone home to visit his parents for the holiday. She had to admit she did miss him with a fierceness that took her by surprise, but she tried to convince herself it was only because he had become such a constant part of her life so it was weird to not have him around.

The afternoon Joel got back in town, he almost immediately came over to see her. They were sitting on the couch and watching a movie when she fell asleep. She awoke to see him sitting across from her in a chair with a small piece of glossy paper in his hands.

"When were you going to tell me?" he asked, his voice cracking with emotion.

She realized it was the sonogram picture she kept by her bed. "Why were you in my room?" she demanded instead of answering his question.

He sighed. "I went to get a blanket off your bed to cover you with. I didn't mean to find it, it was just sitting right there."

She noticed the blanket he had draped over her and she used it to cover herself up, drawing her legs closer to her chest as if she could create a protective bubble around her body. She wasn't sure what to say.

"Is it *his*?" She knew by the way he growled the word that he meant her ex, the one she never named, the one he knew she was running from.

She nodded, swallowing hard against the tears. This is it—he's going to leave me just like everyone else.

He stood and began pacing the room, his movements rough and jerky, the sonogram still clutched in his hand. "How far along are you?"

"Almost 5 months." Her voice cracked on the last word and she blinked rapidly, hoping the tears would go away, but they fell anyway.

Joel stopped abruptly and swooped down on her, wrapping her in his arms, his anger dissolving with the appearance of her tears. "Shhh, it's okay, Ayanna. We'll figure this out."

"*We'll*?" She dared not breathe as she waited for his clarification.

"Yes, *we* will. I may not be happy about it, but that doesn't mean I'm going to abandon you. You're going to need all the help you can get." He swallowed hard and took a deep breath before his next confession. "I love you, Ayanna."

"I know, and…I love you too, Joel. You're my best friend." She smiled sadly through her tears.

He huffed out his breath. "I mean, I'm in love with you. I have been for a while, and I'm pretty sure deep down you already knew that." With that she opened the floodgate and let the tears pour out of her. He wasn't going to leave her, and yes, if she were honest with herself, she would admit she'd known for quite some time how he felt about her. They did almost everything a couple does, they just hadn't crossed any physical boundaries, pretending that would keep her emotional wall up when in fact she had been fighting her feelings for quite some time.

"Are you going to tell him?" Joel asked once she had calmed down to just a few sniffles.

"NO!" she yelled, pushing out of his embrace. "No one can know it is his, Joel—*no one!*" Her chest rose and fell rapidly with panic. What was she going to tell others? Would Grace try to convince her to come home if she knew? He read the fear written plainly all over her face.

"Shit, I didn't know it was that bad." His face darkened.

"He can *never* find out. If he does, he will take her from me."

"He can't do that. There are laws and things in place—"

"It doesn't matter. He would. He'd take us both, or worse, he'd just take her and I would never see her again. No one can know who her father is."

He took a few deep breaths, processing her words and the terror etched across her face. "Okay, it's okay, Ayanna. I get it. No one will know it's his…" He paused and his eyes widened. "Wait a minute, did you say her? You're having a girl?"

"I don't know for sure, it's just a feeling I have," she confessed, knowing she would have to wait for her next doctor's appointment to receive confirmation of what she already knew thanks to Enora.

"Can I?" He motioned toward her belly with his hand, and she nodded in agreement. He placed his hand over her growing bump. A weird expression passed over his face and he jumped up. "I've got to go. I…I just need a little time. I'll call you." He left, glancing back at her one last time.

She didn't know what to make of it. She was so confused by everything that had just happened. Had he really confessed that he loved her after finding out she was carrying someone else's child? She knew it was a lot to process, especially when he was clearly worried about her insistence that the father never find out. She didn't know what he was thinking. He'd told her he wouldn't abandon her, but then he had just left. She screamed into the couch cushions knowing that whatever happened, she only had herself to blame. She didn't fault him one bit for leaving; it was what any guy would have done in his place.

She cried herself to sleep that night when the phone call he'd promised to make never came, chastising herself for even hoping he'd stick around once he found out. It made sense that he would run away from her as fast as he could. It didn't matter if he claimed to love her; she knew the truth—she was ruined goods. Hell, she hadn't even told him how she felt about him. She wasn't sure how she felt, and she didn't feel the overwhelming passion she had with Corydon, but she definitely cared about Joel. He had somehow worked himself into her life so seamlessly that she couldn't imagine living without him. He was her best friend, and if she let herself admit it, she did feel more for him, more than she should have. She hadn't realized how much of her heart was invested until she was holding its pieces together, waiting to see what he decided.

He didn't call the next day, or the day after that. She wasn't sure how many pints of Ben & Jerry's ice cream she consumed. When she went over to Kate and Sean's house for dinner, they took one look at her and Sean scowled while Kate threw her arms open. "Oh, honey, come here." She cried into the woman's arms, telling them she'd had a fight with Joel and messed everything up.

"I think you underestimate that boy," Kate replied. "We've seen the way he looks at you."

Ayanna pulled away, drawing her eyebrows together,

unsure as to what Kate was referring.

"Don't tell me you didn't know. You may claim you're just friends, but that boy looks at you like you are his sun, moon, and stars all wrapped together in one package," Kate explained. "Besides, he's a good guy. Sean *may* have done a background check on him when you first started bringing him around."

Sean snorted. "Don't act like you didn't want me to. I had to make sure he was good for her. She's had a rough go at things and needs someone good."

Ayanna sniffled. "I appreciate it, Sean. Thank you, guys, for everything, really—for letting me stay here, for caring."

"Hush," Kate replied, waving a hand at Ayanna and going back to setting food on the table. "We love you, and we've enjoyed having you around these last few months. In fact, we consider you family now."

"Now, let's not let this beautiful meal get cold," Sean interrupted, clearly slightly uncomfortable with the emotional chatter.

They ate and talked about everything except Joel, and when they finished, she gave them both a goodnight hug.

"Don't give up on him just yet. I think he may surprise you," Sean whispered as he returned her embrace.

She walked back to her home and stopped short when she saw a hunched figure sitting by her door, toying with something in his hands. "Joel?" she called out.

He swung his head up and shoved whatever he was playing with into his pocket. "Hi."

She walked toward him. "What are you doing here?"

"I'm sorry I didn't call like I said I would. I had to figure a few things out." He ran his fingers through his hair, something he did when he was nervous.

"I know." She sighed sadly as she reached him.

"I don't think you do, Ayanna."

"What do you mean?"

"Have you been crying?" he asked now that she was close enough to look into her eyes. She hadn't thought about cleaning herself after crying with Kate, and she probably had mascara tear trails down her cheeks. He brushed his fingers them, wiping away some of the smeared make-up. "Why? Why have you been crying?"

"Does it matter?" she asked. If he was there to end things, she would rather not let him know how much it would hurt her.

"Yes, it matters."

"I thought you left me…thought you were done with me."

"And that made you cry?"

She nodded her head.

"Why?" His hazel eyes studied her, begging her to explain.

She took a deep breath, deciding to take the risk and give him the truth. "Because the thought of you leaving me kills me, Joel. I didn't think I had a heart to give until it broke when you walked out the door, and by then it was too late because somehow without knowing it, you stole my heart," she confessed.

He grabbed her then and pulled her toward him, pressing his lips against hers and giving them both what they so desperately needed. The kiss was passionate and sweet, and it stole her breath.

When he pulled back, he rested his forehead against hers. "God, I've been waiting so long to do that." Then he stole another quick kiss.

"Was it worth it?"

"Most definitely. I would've waited longer if I needed to. Do I need to?" He pulled back, searching her eyes, asking her indirectly if she was finally ready to admit they were more than friends, to let him be more, or if she still needed time.

She answered him by wrapping her hands behind his neck and pulling him down for another kiss.

"Thank…God," he said breathlessly in between kisses. Finally, he picked her up and twirled her around, squeezing her tight before setting her back on her feet.

She gasped in surprise when he then proceeded to get down on one knee before her. "I know we're still young and we're still figuring things out, but for a while now, I haven't been able to see my life without you in it. Now when I close my eyes and picture my future, the only two things I see clearly are you and her." He placed a hand on her belly, causing a fresh round of tears to spill over, this time from happiness. "What I'm trying to say is that I don't want you to have to worry about your future and what you will tell her about her father, because I want to take the job if you'll let me, and I will do my best every day to live up to the title."

Her shoulders shook with her sobs. How had she gotten so lucky as to have this beautiful, amazing man in front of her, offering her his entire world?

"So, Ayanna, will you be my wife? I know you're not ready right now, and I'm willing to wait as long as it takes if you say yes. I just want to be there, for both of you." He reached into his pocket and plucked out a black velvet box, opening it to reveal a small, simple diamond solitaire engagement ring.

"You aren't doing this just because you feel some sort of obligation to me, are you?" She had to ask even though her heart revolted at the thought. She didn't want him to stay only because he felt some weird sense of obligation to take care of her.

"No, you silly, stubborn girl. It's because I love you. You stole my heart the moment you literally crashed into my world." His hazel eyes pleaded for her to say yes, and she could see the nervousness behind them, the worry that she might say no.

"Okay," she whispered. "Yes!" she said more loudly as she threw her arms around him, kissing him over and over again until the sound of applause and cheers drew her out of his embrace and she saw Kate and Sean cheering from the back porch.

Joel slipped the ring onto her finger then placed a kiss to the palm of her hand. "I love you."

"I love you too."

He took her hand and pulled her over to Kate and Sean, who were obviously anxious to congratulate them. As Kate admired her ring, she noticed Sean and Joel chatting chummily. It was then that Sean's words made sense.

"Sean, did you know?"

He shrugged sheepishly. "Maybe."

Kate looked affronted. "And you didn't tell me?"

"Now, don't get all upset, dear. I didn't tell you because we both know how awful you are at keeping secrets." He pulled her into an embrace.

Ayanna was still confused as to how Sean had known,

so she looked to Joel for answers. He smiled shyly. "I wanted to ask for permission, but since your father wasn't here to give it, I figured Sean would be the next best thing."

She fell even more in love with him at that moment. She had never felt so blessed to be surrounded by people who loved her, and she hugged him tightly.

"Besides, I hoped this way Sean might be less mad when he finds out about the baby," he whispered in her ear. "Maybe he'll be less inclined to kill me," he joked. Ayanna held him, soaking it all in, every single moment. She hadn't thought she could be this happy again, but Grace was right—hearts do heal, and eventually you can fall in love again, which reminded her—

"Oh my gosh! We have to call Aunt Grace and tell her!"

"Oh yeah, about that…Sean may have already given her a heads up so she could be here to congratulate you in person. She should be here in the morning." He shrugged sheepishly before dropping his voice back to a whisper. "Then we can figure out how to tell them about the rest."

She pressed a finger to his lips. "Shhh, let's not think about it anymore tonight. I want to enjoy this moment with you and not ruin it by worrying about tomorrow."

After an appropriate amount of time celebrating with Kate and Sean, they politely excused themselves and walked back to the guest house, where he kissed her good night and told her he would be back first thing in the morning.

CHAPTER 16

GRACE ARRIVED THE next day, and when Ayanna had gathered her courage, she and Joel sat down and broke the news to Sean, Kate, and Grace. There was plenty of outrage and some anger, which Joel handled in spades, considering he wasn't even the one who had knocked her up. They both calmly explained that while they were young, they were adults and capable of becoming parents. Joel may have reminded them a few times that they were going to get married and nothing was going to change that, and he reassured them that the baby was not the only reason he was marrying Ayanna, that he truly loved her.

Eventually they all calmed down enough to see reason and think things through. They agreed it would be best if Joel moved into the guest house with Ayanna so he would be there to help her through everything. Kate offered to help watch the baby so they could both continue school, and that was the condition Sean placed on them: they could only live in the guest house rent-free as long as they both agreed to stay in school and finish their degrees. Overall, it went much better than they'd anticipated, and they were both thrilled to have such a great network of support around them.

Telling Joel's parents was much more difficult. To say they were upset would be quite the understatement. They even went as far as to accuse Ayanna of getting pregnant on purpose to trap Joel and take their fortune. It was then that Joel snapped and told them they needed to pull their heads out of their asses and accept his decision or he would have nothing to do with them in the future. That shut them up quickly, because when it came down to it, he was their only child and they were not about to lose him over this. Ayanna was glad they had decided to tell them over the phone instead of in person. She wouldn't have been able to handle the verbal insult in person, because the truth was, sometimes she did feel like she was trapping him, like some morning he might wake up and realize exactly what he had gotten himself into and regret it all then just leave them because he didn't really have any obligation to stay. Her baby wasn't his, after all. He might say things now, but what about when the baby actually arrived? *If my daughter looks nothing like him, everyone will know the truth, and how will he handle things then?* The reality of what they were about to go through weighed heavily on her shoulders.

The rest of her pregnancy passed in a blur. She couldn't help but fall more and more in love with Joel once they started living together. How she had been so blind to the way he worshipped her for so long, she wasn't sure, but now he didn't hide it at all. He always wanted to be touching her in some way, rubbing her feet when they were swollen after class, resting his head on her belly, and reading stories to the baby before they went to bed every night.

He was in awe the first time he heard the baby's heartbeat and grinned with pride when they officially found out the baby was girl. He couldn't stop showing off the sonogram pictures to strangers as they were walking to the car. He was so genuinely excited that part of her wished her daughter could have been his. She could already tell he was going to be an amazing father to her baby. He insisted on being the one to assemble all the furniture they purchased for the nursery (although she did sneak over and convince Sean to "drop by" to see if he needed any help, which thankfully he graciously accepted, or the furniture would still probably be in pieces). Who knew furniture could be so difficult, especially furniture for a baby?

Joel's parents eventually came around, flying in from Vermont to meet their future daughter-in-law in person and apologize for the poor way they'd handled the engagement-slash-pregnancy news. She was beyond relieved, as the last thing she wanted to do was cause any sort of rift in any of Joel's relationships.

Kate threw her a baby shower, and Grace was there too. It was perfect. She had made a few friends in her classes that attended, and they cooed every time Joel poked his head into the room to check on her, asking if he could get her anything. Joel's mother even came to show her support.

Everything was truly amazing. She was beyond blessed, but deep within her heart she still held on to some of her fear—fear that he might leave once the baby came, fear that she could still be discovered by a Fae. Any time the fears surfaced, she did her best to push them down and bury them, but they always lingered in the back of her mind.

Within that time, she also decided to declare her major, following in Sean's footsteps by pursuing a degree in folklore and anthropology. She focused her studies more specifically on Fae folklore, soaking up all she could, arming herself with knowledge she may need when the time came. She scribbled everything she had learned about Fae from her time in the realm into notebooks, filling their pages with her words. Sean did his best to supply her with all the research he had available and provided her contact information for others who may be able to help. She wasn't sure how she would be able to use her knowledge when it came to getting a job, but it didn't matter, and she knew that while Joel found it interesting, he didn't quite understand her obsession with Fae. She wasn't sure if she would ever explain it to him.

She studied as hard as she could, as did Joel. With graduation only a month away, Joel already had an interview set up with a major business where he had interned the summer before they met. It would mean a move, but she would do anything to support him as much as he had supported her. He wanted a job that would allow him to provide for their little family while she finished her degree. It was touching and sweet, and she couldn't deny him the opportunity.

She was in class the day she went into labor. The contractions started, causing her discomfort. She quickly stood to leave but had to stop and grab a desk as another one hit. Luckily her professor was an associate of Sean's and had a student run to grab him as quickly as possible. She sent Joel a text, knowing he was in class, but would be checking for her text message, and sure enough, by the time she made it to the front of the building (with Sean's help), Joel was there panting as if he had just run a marathon. He helped her to the car as fast as he could and drove her to the hospital.

Kate and Sean arrived just after they got her checked in and settled into a room. They didn't have to wait very long, her labor progressing quickly, and she wasn't sure if that was normal, but no one questioned it. Unfortunately, it also meant the normal drugs could not be administered, but she put on a brave face and focused on delivering her baby girl into the world. Joel was a mess, a ball of nervous energy who kept doting on her so much she snapped at him and then immediately apologized. He paled when she screamed in pain but held her hand and whispered loving words into her ear the entire time, until the doctor held up the baby and placed her on Ayanna's chest. Seeing her daughter, they both burst into tears. She kissed her head and held her close until the doctor let Joel cut the cord. He grinned and followed behind the doctors as they took the baby away to clean her up and check all her vitals.

Ayanna was exhausted, but she had never been so happy. Joel was cooing and talking to the baby the entire time he carried her back over to the bed. Her daughter was wrapped up in a tight little pink blanket, her wispy pale blonde hair covered by a pink cap. She took a minute to breathe in her baby scent, showering her with kisses. "I love you, my precious darling," she whispered, so over-come with emotion she felt like she was going to burst with love. It was then that her baby blinked her eyes open, causing her heart to stutter. The fear she had kept close inside her heart during the pregnancy blossomed in her chest.

"The doctors think it might be some sort of genetic mutation, but we won't know if there's a real problem with her eyesight until later," Joel whispered, pressing a reas-suring kiss to her forehead. Ayanna knew the truth, though:

her daughter's eye color had nothing to do with a genetic mutation. She had her father's eyes, the violet eyes of a royal Fae.

She swallowed hard and nodded, her heart thudding as she lifted the pink cap to peek at her ears. Noticing the rounded tips, she released the breath she had unconsciously been holding. The eyes they could deal with; the other features would've been harder to hide until she could learn to glamour.

"She's perfect," she whispered, kissing her baby once more.

"What are we going to name her?" Joel asked, scooting into bed next to her so he could hold both of his girls in his arms.

She'd thought long and hard about this and had a few names in mind, one specifically for the possibility of her violet eyes. "Ianthe," she replied softly.

"Eye-an-thee?" he asked, having not heard the name before.

"It means violet flower in Greek."

He chuckled. "Well, with eyes like that, it definitely seems appropriate. What about the rest?" he asked nervously. They had talked about it so she wasn't sure why he had to ask, but it warmed her heart knowing how much he wanted her baby to have his last name. She gave him something even better.

"Ianthe Lola Grayson."

"Lola? After my mom?"

She nodded as his eyes filled with tears.

"Are you sure?"

His smile lit up the room, filling with the happiness she

could read so plainly on his face.

"Well, little miss Lola Grayson, you will definitely be loved," he whispered to the sleeping baby. She didn't miss that he used Lola instead of Ianthe, but she knew it would be okay. Lola would be less strange. She'd had enough of people mispronouncing her own name over the years to think that perhaps it may be for the best if they call her by her middle name, but to her, she would always be her little Ianthe.

True to his word, he loved that little girl as if she was his own. It warmed her heart every day to see him fuss over the both of them. He took a few days off but somehow managed to return to school just in time to gear up for his last finals and pass with flying colors.

Kate, Sean, and Aunt Grace joined her to cheer Joel on at graduation. He nailed his job interview and they were set to move to Colorado in just a few weeks. She didn't know how she was going to do it, as Kate had been such a lifesaver since she'd come home from the hospital, but Grace had graciously agreed to stay with them for a few months to help them get settled. She was so grateful, and a little scared to be on her own. She found a school she could transfer to and continue her own studies while Joel started his new job. They found the perfect house, a small starter home, and he promised her that once he was making the big bucks, he would move them somewhere larger, but she didn't need large. She had everything she could possibly need.

They married shortly after Ianthe turned one in a small ceremony at the courthouse. Grace, Kate, and Sean all flew in, as well as a few friends they'd made since moving. Even a couple of his old frat brothers and her classmates managed to show up. They followed the ceremony with dinner and drinks at a local restaurant then danced the night away. Grace took Ianthe home when she crashed, and they'd booked a hotel room to fully enjoy the start of their honeymoon. They didn't want to be away from Ianthe for long, so their honeymoon was only a short weekend away at a bed and breakfast in a quaint little town. They spent most of the time lost in each other and their blossoming love. It was perfect.

They had four wonderful years of marriage, raising their beautiful, blonde-haired, violet-eyed daughter. Joel was amazing, a truly great father. He loved them both so fiercely and worked just as hard to provide for them. Ayanna finished her degree and spent her time as a stay-at-home mom, continuing to compile what she could about Fae folklore now that she knew her daughter would need it. She planned on getting a job once Ianthe was in school, and Joel agreed. He was smart and ambitious, quickly climbing the ranks in his company. They'd just moved into that much larger house he had promised her and it was huge, too large for what they really needed, but it made him happy.

They had their share of ups and downs, as no marriage is perfect. When they were ready to have more children, they tried many different fertility treatments without success, and the news that they were unable to conceive devastated Joel. She knew how much he wanted more children, and while she shared his sadness, she also couldn't help but be a tiny bit relieved. She'd never tell him, but she always worried if they had children together, he would unconsciously favor them over Ianthe, and her little girl was going to need all the help she could get. He recovered after some time, seeming to double his efforts to be the best father Ianthe could have. He always went out of his way to make family time and spoil his girls, and she loved him all the more for it.

While he was a fantastic husband and father, Ayanna still had moments where she would find herself battling her past, especially in crowds of people, almost as if she were constantly looking over her shoulder for Fae. He tried to reassure her that they were safe, that her ex wouldn't find them, and he tried to get her to open up, but she was terrified he'd think she was crazy if she told him the truth. He didn't understand her obsession with researching Fae folklore, finding it quirky and odd. When she tried to explain it, the possibility of magic beyond human understanding, the possibility that the folklore was based somewhere in truth and experience, he seemed to tolerate her explanation but didn't share her belief. It was more like he believed she believed it but couldn't see past his own logical, scientific mind to the possibility that Fae and magic could be real. She knew eventually she'd have to make him understand for Ianthe's sake, but they still had plenty of years until that day would come. If only she'd known how wrong she was, that just a few months after they celebrated Ianthe's fifth birthday, her past would catch up to her, ripping her world apart.

CHAPTER 17

S HE WAS OUT for her morning run while Ianthe was at a play date with their neighbor across the street who had a son around her age. She had run the same path at the local park for quite a few years now. It started as a way to stay in shape, along with the self-defense classes she took at Joel's insistence. He thought knowing how to defend herself would help stop her paranoia, maybe give her enough confidence to let down her shields, but he didn't know that her hand-to-hand combat training would be nothing but a laughable effort against a Fae. Still, she enjoyed the power she had, knowing she could put up quite a fight if she were to be found.

The path she ran wound in and out of wooded areas and grassy clearings, some with playground equipment, others just wide open spaces for people or dogs to frolic. It was Ianthe's favorite park, and Ayanna looked forward to taking her there more often now that the weather was warming up. She had just rounded a corner, her ponytail swaying with her steps, when she caught movement out of the corner of her eye—a man in the distance, his figure large and imposing, his jeans and hoodie giving him a menacing appearance. Her heart sped up like a rollercoaster starting its descent from the largest hill. She faltered a moment, unsure where to run, whether to stick to the path and appear unaffected, turn around and head back, or cut through the woods leading back to the parking lot. Her legs made the decision for her when the figure moved in her direction. She turned sharply and cut through the woods, her arms and legs pumping as fast as humanly possible, her blood roaring in her ears. She hoped her pursuer was human, because then she would stand a chance.

Luck was not in her favor, and she realized just how severe the situation was when the man was no longer a distance behind her, but only a few feet. She pushed herself harder, her heart in her throat, but he lunged and tackled her to the ground. She toppled, bracing herself for the impact. The wind was knocked out of her as she lay face down on the forest floor and a hand gripped her ponytail, pulling her head back gently, not roughly, which was odd. A second later, she was flipped over onto her back by gentle hands.

"Breathe, Ayanna!" A familiar voice echoed above the roaring in her ears and she gasped for a breath, her lungs filling and burning from being without oxygen. "Are you okay? Didn't you hear me calling your name?" Sharp, pointed features stood out from the shadows of his hoodie, framing his familiar aquamarine eyes.

"Rodric?" She didn't know whether to be frightened or relieved by his appearance. He had helped her escape all those years ago, even though she never quite understood why, especially when he hadn't ever been particularly kind to her, more like coolly tolerating her presence.

He smiled, but it wasn't exactly friendly, more like the smile of someone who was in on a secret no one else was privy to. He held out his hand to help her up, and she took it, unsure of what else to do.

Once she was standing, she brushed herself off, noting that her knees and the heels of her hands had taken the brunt of the fall. She had skinned them in several places, her left knee beginning to trickle blood, but not enough for her to be overly concerned. She took a step back from him, putting more space between them. "What are you doing here?" She looked around quickly to see if anyone else was near.

As if sensing exactly what she was looking for, he replied, "Don't worry, I'm alone. I, of course, was sent to find you by Corydon, but I won't let him know I was successful—although this isn't the first time. I thought he would have given up by now, but he's a stubborn one. If he ever does find you, I expect the reunion won't be a happy one. He's still quite angry. In fact, I believe you'd finally be able to see the dungeons at the palace firsthand." His eyes glowed brighter for a moment before he blinked, and then it was gone.

She paled, grabbing hold of the nearest tree to support her now dizzy frame. *He's still looking for me? I can't let him find us.* Her breath came in short pants with the realization that the paranoia that had plagued her was not unfounded and she could lose everything at any moment.

"Calm down," Rodric commanded forcefully. He huffed, realizing his abrupt tone was causing her panic to increase, not decrease. "He won't find you, I've made sure of it. Any time he tries, I feed him false information about your last known whereabouts. Most of the time he sends me anyway, saying I'm the only one he can trust." He rolls his eyes. "I don't intend for him to ever find you. I see that you've built quite the life for yourself. It didn't take you long to get over him, not with how quickly you got married and had a child. Was your bed even cold for a week before you invited someone else in?"

She gasped, his caustic words causing her to flinch. She could see now that his temper was just like Corydon's—so volatile. *Wait a minute, he's seen Ianthe!* Her stomach clenched and her mind raced, trying to throw him off the topic of her daughter so he wouldn't put the pieces together.

"What does it matter if I took comfort in someone else's arms? You told me to forget about him, so I did the best I could." She put her hands on her hips, gearing up to fight, hoping her anger would cover the terror she was experiencing.

He snorted as he pulled his hood back, revealing his white blond hair tied back in a ponytail and his pointed ears. "You humans are all the same, such fickle things, but you're right—you did do exactly what I told you to do, and based on what I've observed from afar over the years, you did so rather quickly."

"So, if you've been watching me for years now from a distance, why make yourself known now?"

"It seems you were rather careless in your selection of locations. This one is not too far from a Seelie portal."

"But I've lived here for almost five years. Why now?"

He leaned against the trunk of a tree, picking at his nails as if the conversation were boring him. "Our truce with the Seelie is shaky right now. They saw Corydon's infatuation with you as a weakness, just like I told you they would. I caught one of their spies a few days ago, and it seems his search for you has also not gone unnoticed. The spy confessed to a great many things while under my care, the main one being that there are others who may be trying to find you, to use you against him—although I'm not sure why, seeing as he's so angry he probably wouldn't lift a finger to save your life, but I'd rather not test out that theory." He eyes cut sharply from his nails to her eyes, piercing her gaze.

"So, what? I'm just supposed to pack up my entire life, my family, and move because you don't want to risk the chance that another Fae would find me? I can't just ask my husband to do that. He has a good job. We have a life here!" She threw up her arms in frustration. She'd known the cost of leaving, but she had never imagined an entire life with her family on the run. *Is there anywhere safe? What will Joel say?* She knew he wouldn't go. He would refuse to run; he'd told her that plenty of times over the years when she voiced her concerns about being found.

"A life you will see end shortly if you do not comply." His words were icicles against her skin, causing goose bumps across her arms.

"Is that a threat, Rodric?" She narrowed her eyes at him.

"No, it's a promise. I don't care what it takes, but you will move, and soon. I'll be back in a few weeks to see that you followed through, and if not, I will be ready to fulfill that promise." He spared her one last threatening glare before turning and walking away more quickly than any human could manage.

She swallowed against the lump in her throat and fought the urge to collapse right there on the ground. She hoped he meant a few weeks Fae time, as it would give her more time—she would need it to convince Joel to pack everything up and leave a job he loved to run across the country with her. *What the hell am I going to do?*

Her conversation with Joel that night went about as well as she expected, meaning it went horribly. They ate dinner together, but even Ianthe could tell something was wrong, even though she tried to act like everything was fine in front of her daughter. Finally, after their daughter went to bed, he confronted her about her strange mood.

She confessed that she was sure someone from her ex's family had found her and she had a feeling she was being watched all the time. She pleaded that they had to run immediately, before anyone found out about Ianthe. He tried to reassure her that they were fine, that there was no need to leave, that the law would protect them, that he would protect them. He seemed genuinely concerned by her conviction that they had to go and held her while she cried, telling her it would be okay, but she knew in her heart it wouldn't be.

A week had passed, and she stopped going running in the park, stopped taking Ianthe there. In fact, she stopped going out of the house at all, if possible, and refused to let Ianthe play in the front yard. She spent most of her free time researching new locations to move to, to run to. She knew Joel wouldn't understand, and she hoped it wouldn't come down to it, but she knew if she had to choose between staying with him and leaving with Ianthe for the safety of her daughter, she'd pack up and leave in a heartbeat.

Each night she tried to talk to him about moving, but he seemed to push the idea off until he finally got angry with her. "I'm happy at my job! Why would you want to ruin that? We have a good thing going for us here. Don't let your paranoia ruin it. Everything will be fine," he growled for the hundredth time. That was the night he also suggested she go see a counselor. She slept in Ianthe's bed, torn to pieces, knowing they had to leave and afraid Joel would never forgive her.

Another week passed and she had almost constant nightmares of being tortured by Rodric or some other faceless Fae, sometimes even by Corydon himself. She woke up, out of breath and disoriented, and she tried to avoid sleeping as much as she could, finding solace in short naps during the day. Her lack of sleep only compounded her paranoia and left dark circles under her eyes, causing Joel even more concern. He became more persistent in his request for her to see someone, and in turn she said it would all stop if he would just agree to move.

While he was at work, she played with her daughter or planned their escape. She reread everything she had learned about Fae, hoping there might be some way to fight if given the chance. She never had learned what kind of Fae Rodric was, which was a complete oversight on her part, so she tried to figure it out but only narrowed it down to a few options, none of which gave her much hope for escape. She needed to be prepared for him somehow if he were to show up before she could go. She was reluctant to leave without Joel, wanting him to see her way.

All her thinking was giving her a migraine, and she went to the cabinet to grab some medicine. She stared at the bottle in her hand when a memory resurfaced. She remembered the night she escaped, how Enora took some sort of painkiller to scramble her memory from that night, how she said human meds affected Fae differently. She grabbed the sink to settle her wobbly knees. She was so thankful for that memory she could've cried. It was exactly what she needed, something that might give her a fighting chance.

How can I drug Rodric? He wouldn't willingly take a pill, and she doubted they would be in the position to grab a bite to eat where she could slip it into his drink. She needed a needle and something she could inject; it was her only chance. She searched the bathroom cabinets and almost sobbed with relief when she found a stray injection needle from her fertility treatments when she and Joel were trying to conceive. She looked at the bottles now spread out on the counter. *What drug will work?* She had no clue, so she selected a couple of different ones and carried them to the kitchen where she kept the mortar and pestle Grace had sent her for grinding herbs. She ground several different pills up into a fine powder, and then following the general knowledge that mixing medicines was bad for humans so may be even worse for Fae, she dissolved the powder into a codeine cough syrup. Finally, she thinned the solution with a little water and prayed it would do the trick, testing it several times before finding the right viscosity to flow through the needle. When she was content, she capped the needle, tucked it into her purse, and cleaned up all evidence of what she had just done.

That night she tried a final time to beg Joel to understand her, to believe her. She knew her time was running out, that Rodric could show up at any moment. Her desperation was clear in her voice, and when the tears slipped out, it cracked Joel's resolve. He pulled her into his arms, unable to understand why she was asking him to leave a good job and uproot their family but knowing how much it meant to her. He finally conceded, telling her he would talk to his boss the next day about a possible transfer, which was enough to give her hope. She hoped that even if she did have to leave with Ianthe, he'd understand and would follow them. His concession gave her the strength to carry through the rest of her plan.

The next day she wrote two letters, the first to Joel, explaining why she had to go and take Ianthe with her. She laid it all out there, the absolute truth for him to read: what had happened to her before she met him, who—or rather *what* Ianthe was, and why she was so desperate to go. She begged him to join them after he settled things at work and told him how much she loved him. That way, if the time came and she needed to run, she would be ready and the letter would hopefully go a ways in helping him forgive her for what she had to do to protect her daughter.

The second letter was harder for her to write, but she knew there was a distinct possibility that things may not work out her way. If that were to happen, she also knew she'd do everything in her power to protect her daughter, including sacrificing herself. She didn't want to think about Ianthe growing up without her, but the reality was, the odds were against her. Even if she were to escape this time, who was to say it wouldn't happen again or she wouldn't eventually get caught. She dried her tears and sealed the envelopes, pressing a kiss to each one. She set them both on top of the dresser, knowing if things went according to her plan she'd be home in time to remove them before Joel returned, and if not…well, then Joel would find them and would know she'd tried her best to fight for their family.

She drew in a few deep breaths and called up her neighbor, Tonya, who had a son around Ianthe's age. She asked Tonya if she could watch Ianthe for her while she ran a couple errands, and Tonya was happy to help. They usually took turns having play dates and giving each other a little child-free time when they needed it. Her shoulders lost a little bit of their tension knowing Ianthe would be safe while she attempted to lure Rodric out, if he was indeed watching her like he said. She knew it might not work, that he might not be back yet, but she had to at least try before she went on the lam.

Walking Ianthe over to her neighbor's house knowing it might be the last time she ever saw her was hard. She fought to keep the tears at bay, soaking in the way her daughter's little hand felt in her own, the way her blonde pigtails bounced as she skipped happily, the way her violet eyes twinkled and her smile radiated joy.

She tucked a stray hair behind Ianthe's ear. "Be good for Ms. Tonya, my little violet flower."

Ianthe giggled. "I'm not a flower, Mommy—I'm a girl!"

"That's right, my darling, you are, and you're the best little girl your mommy could ever ask for." She hugged her close, feeling the tears swim behind her eyes. She took a deep breath, savoring the smell of her child before she kissed her on her cheek.

"I love you, Ianthe."

"I love you too, Mommy!" Ianthe replied before puckering her lips for a kiss, which of course Ayanna obliged. When she pulled back, Tonya had just opened the door. She attempted to wipe away the few stray tears that had leaked out.

"Hi, little Miss Lola! Owen is waiting for you inside. He was getting his dinosaurs out and ready for you."

"Yay!" Ianthe squealed before bounding through the door.

"Everything okay?" Tonya was studying Ayanna, noticing the wetness around her eyes.

"It will be," she replied vaguely, trying to muster up a smile. "Thanks for watching her. I should be back in a few hours. You know how to reach me if anything comes up." She left before Tonya could question her further, but she felt her gaze all the way to her driveway where she climbed into her car and pulled away. Only then did she let herself shed the tears.

She drove her car over to the park, wanting to have

a faster escape than her own two feet could provide if needed. She took a moment to pray to whoever might be listening for her safety and that of her family. She took a few fortifying breaths before climbing out of the car and slipping the syringe from her purse into her back pocket. She tugged her shirt down, concealing the evidence, and walked around the trail she had been running the last time she saw Rodric. She had just made her third loop by the playground when she saw him sitting on a bench, watching her. She approached cautiously, wiping her sweaty palms across her jeans.

"I thought I told you to leave," he growled, his light blue eyes glowing.

"You did," she countered.

"I thought the nightmares would have been enough to push you away, but perhaps you need a little more persuasion." He stood. Her eyes widened slightly, realizing he must be a Mara, Fae that controlled dreams—or in this case, nightmares.

"I…I just…I need more time. My husband is trying to get a transfer at work and there are things to arrange, like packing and selling a house. Just…give me a few more weeks," she begged.

His eyes narrowed, almost as if considering accepting her request, when a tiny voice caused her breath to catch.

"Mommy!"

She turned quickly, sprinting toward her daughter's voice, hoping to intercept her before she got too close. She swept her up into her arms and angled her away from Rodric's line of vision.

"Hey little flower," she whispered shakily.

"I didn't know you were going to the park! Ms. Tonya

said we could come play, and we haven't been to the park in *forever*!" Her little girl drew out the word to emphasize how long it felt to her.

Ayanna held her tightly, her voice strained. "I need you to listen to me, Ianthe. You need to go get Ms. Tonya and go home right now, okay? Can you do that for me?"

Her lower lip stuck out in a pouting motion. "But I wanted to play."

"I know, sweetheart, but right now I need you to go right home. Can you get Ms. Tonya and make her take you home? Tell her your tummy hurts, okay?"

"But I feel fine," she complained, confused by her mother's request.

"I know, baby, but I need you to do this for your mommy, okay? If you do, I will get you that puppy you've been asking for."

Her face brightened immediately. "Promise?"

"Promise."

"Okay." She wiggled her way down out of her mother's arms before running back toward Tonya, who thankfully didn't question whatever Ianthe said. She simply called for Owen and took both children back in the direction of their neighborhood.

Only after they had left her sight did she turn back to Rodric. His jaw was working back and forth as if he was grinding his teeth, and he gripped a knife so tight in his fist that his knuckles had gone white. She knew then that he had seen, that her daughter's gorgeous violet eyes had just condemned them both.

"You stupid, *stupid*, girl," he hissed before lunging toward her. She spun out of his reach and sprinted toward the more wooded area, away from where the children and mothers might see, in the opposite direction of where her daughter now walked.

He caught up with her quickly, tackling her. They were both out of sight of the playground, and for that she was grateful. She tumbled to the ground, her hands searching for anything she might use as a weapon against him and somehow managing to find a medium-sized tree limb. She scrambled up with the limb in her grip.

"I should've killed you a long time ago, before that abomination could have ever been born. She will never be queen!" he roared.

"She is not an abomination!" she yelled, swinging the branch in his direction. He caught it easily enough with his right hand but she was ready, hoping it was enough to distract him. She dropped the branch and plucked the syringe from her pocket, flipping the cap off behind her back. She gripped it tightly in her left hand and lunged toward him. In one smooth motion, she plunged it into his right side and pushed down, injecting him with her medical concoction.

"What the fuck?!" he yelled. "You'll pay for that, you and that little brat. You're both going to die." He swung the branch at her but she rolled out of its path, just to the right of where it struck the ground. She wasn't sure where his knife had gone but assumed he still had it. She scrambled away, knowing this was it, that if her drug mixture worked, she would be able to save her daughter. If only she had been able to save herself as well.

"I don't want her to be queen, I just want her to live… for her to leave…to get away from all this," she pleaded, pulling herself up to her knees.

"That will never happen, not when she has his eyes." He stumbled, and she hoped it was the medicine taking effect.

She glanced around and saw the glinting of his knife in the dirt behind him. She dove to the ground on his right side, toward the knife. He grabbed her calf, but not before her fingers closed around the handle of the blade. He dragged her across the ground toward him, and she tried to pull her arms closer to her chest to shield the blade. She felt her vision begin to blur around the edges, a force stronger than exhaustion pulling at her, but she fought with everything she had, focusing only on keeping her daughter safe. When he stopped dragging her, he flipped her roughly. Her back thudded against the ground, her vision blackening further, but she didn't hesitate. She put everything she had into one final motion and raised the blade, forcing it into the part of him she could reach—his thigh. He yelled loudly, stumbling back, and her vision cleared almost instantly. She didn't hesitate. She jumped up and sprinted for her car as best she could.

Her heart was pounding and she was out of breath by the time she reached her vehicle. Several people stared at her strangely as they noticed the dirt and grass stains on her clothes, as well as a few drops of blood—Rodric's not hers. She probably had grass in her hair as well, but she didn't care what they thought. The only thing that mattered was that she still had a chance since he wasn't following her. She sped out of the park, back to her house. Then she sprinted over to Tonya's house, ringing the doorbell impatiently several times.

Finally, Tonya opened the door, appearing as startled as the strangers in the park. "Ayanna?"

"I can't...I just need my daughter...we must go... emergency." She forced the words out between breaths as she panted.

"Lola!" Tonya called, and the little blonde head bounded for the door.

She swept her up into her arms and sprinted back to their house, only putting her daughter down when they were safely locked inside.

"Okay, my little flower, I need you to listen closely: we're going to go on a little trip, so I need you to get your favorite things you want to take and pack them in your little suitcase, the one we use to visit your grandparents."

"What about the puppy?"

"Later, honey. You need to pack right now."

"But you promised a puppy!" Her little chin began to wobble, so Ayanna took it in her hand.

"You're right, I did, and we will get your puppy when we get to where we're going on our trip. Go pack now." She patted her little bottom, sending her down the hall as she rushed into her own room, throwing what she needed into a suitcase. She knew she was running on adrenaline and fumes, but she had to get them out of there before Rodric had a chance to follow.

She flew into Ianthe's room next, throwing her clothes into her suitcase as well. Ianthe looked startled by her mother's frantic movements.

"Is Daddy coming on the trip?"

She paused in her movements, taking a deep breath. "No, baby, he isn't, at least not yet. He has to work. He'll join us when he doesn't have to work."

"I don't want to go without Daddy!" She burst into tears, running out of the room, sobbing.

It broke her heart to see her daughter to cry, to know she wouldn't understand, but she couldn't wait any longer. She kept throwing everything they needed into the suitcase, flying around the house and gathering essentials. She stopped back in her own bedroom last, pulling the envelope for Ianthe from the dresser and slipping it into the bag before adding a few more things she had forgotten.

She heard her front door open, heard Ianthe yell, "Daddy!" before bursting into tears again, heard him stop to comfort their daughter, but she didn't stop packing. She couldn't. They had to leave. They were out of time.

Joel stepped into the room behind her. "Tonya called me," he explained.

"No time! It's too late. They'll take her. We have to go. He's coming. I won't let him have her." She didn't look at him as she threw the last few items in the suitcase. She knew she wasn't making much sense, but she couldn't afford to stop and explain. It wasn't until she felt him behind her, his hands on the tops of her arms that she paused and looked up, straight out their bedroom window, to the familiar pair of glowing aquamarine eyes staring at her from the front yard. She opened her mouth to scream when Rodric smiled at her sadistically and closed his eyes. Her world went black.

CHAPTER 18

"**A**YANNA!" **SHE HEARD** Joel screaming her name, but it sounded as if she were drifting underwater, sinking farther away from him. She tried to answer, to tell him how much she loved him, to tell him to take care of their baby girl, but she couldn't speak. It was almost as if she were floating out of her body and into a deep black nothingness. *Is this was dying feels like?*

"You aren't dead yet, but you will be. I will make sure of it, and after I'm finished with you, I'll take care of that little half-breed. *Nothing* will stand in my son's way to the throne!" His voice jolted her out of the fog. She blinked her eyes open but was even more disoriented as she looked around. She was lying on a cold, dirty stone floor strewn with hay. Her jeans and shirt were gone, replaced with a dirty white nightgown, more like a medieval shift than any garment she was familiar with. She pulled herself up only to find her feet were shackled to the floor, and her ankles were bruised and cut where the restraints dug into her skin. *Where am I?* Her head swam when she noticed the crimson stains on the floor and bars across one of the walls of the room. It was like some sort of old prison.

"Have you figured it out yet? Where you are?"

She took a guess, piecing together what she could see with a reference he had made when she saw him the first day in the park. "The Unseelie dungeon?"

He stepped out of the shadows on the other side of bars and banged a piece of metal against them. "Ding ding ding! We have a winner!"

She placed both of her hands against the sides of her head, shielding her ears from the painful echoing clang of the metal. She tried to remember how she could have gotten there, but the last thing she remembered was packing the suitcase and seeing Rodric in the yard.

"How…?"

His chuckle slithered down her skin, biting into her bones. "You haven't guessed yet. Haven't figured out what I am?"

Of course! He's a Mara, capable of controlling and inducing dreams or nightmares. He saw the realization hit her and took joy in watching her face pale.

"That's right, sweetheart—I'm the creature of your nightmares. I can make you dream whatever I want you to, whatever will cause you the most pain." He snapped his fingers and a movie screen took up the better part of one of the walls. She watched in horror as images of her parents' car wreck flashed across the screen. She closed her eyes, hoping it would chase the images away, but it only made things worse, for when she did, she found herself inside the car, sitting in the back seat as her parents laughed, ignorant to what would happen to them around the next corner. She screamed, trying to warn them, but they couldn't hear her. She unbuckled her seatbelt and reached for them, but it was like trying to move a statue. She leaned over her father, reaching for the wheel when she found the same problem. She couldn't stop what was about to happen. Time seemed to slow down around her as she was incapable of changing the outcome, knowing what was about to happen. She braced herself for the impact, for the moment their car lost control, but she could never brace herself for watching in absolute terror as she saw them take the impact, the moment her mother's body slumped forward, the second the light left her father's eyes. She curled into a ball and cried for who knew how long then drifted off into the black nothingness once again.

She wasn't sure how much time had passed when she felt the cold stone underneath her limbs once more, only this time she wasn't alone in the prison cell. She rubbed her eyes, clearing the dried tear tracks, uncurling when she felt his comforting presence.

Joel.

She groaned; there would be no comfort here. She opened her eyes to see him chained to the corner of the cell, his skin pale and gaunt. Bruises molted across almost every inch of his bare chest, his lips were puffy and cracked, scabbed over in several places, and one of his eyes was swollen shut. She crawled toward him.

"Don't!" he yelled, as if her presence caused him pain. "It's your fault I'm here! It's all your fault." She crept closer, kneeling next to him, reaching to comfort him, but he lunged and tackled her to the ground. He straddled her chest and wrapped his hands around her throat. She flailed, attempting to shake him off, and pried at his hands with her fingers, but he wouldn't release his hold. She saw the rage in his eyes; he blamed her for everything, and perhaps he was right. When her lungs burned for a breath and her vision darkened around the edges, he vanished. Her cell filled with Rodric's laughter.

She gasped for breath, her tears falling of their own accord. "Stop," she rasped.

He only laughed harder. "Stop she says! Oh no, pet, I'm only getting started. You and I have *plenty* of time to spend here…days, weeks, years—we won't stop until I'm satisfied. See, there are things worse than death, and by the time I'm done with you, you will be begging me to die."

She knew he was right, could almost taste the words on her tongue. She didn't know how much of this torture she could take. She drifted away again into the nothingness, returning after an undefined amount of time.

"Wake up!" he seethed. "What the hell did you give me?" He kicked her in the stomach. "Wake up!"

She groaned at the sharp pain his boot left behind and gingerly sat up, curling her legs into her chest to protect herself from another blow.

"What did you give me? What was in that damn needle?"

She couldn't help but smile slightly when she saw that he was sweating profusely. She'd never seen a Fae sweat like that before. It was practically dripping off his face, which was red. His hands shook slightly and he gripped his hips to stop her from seeing.

"Why? Is something wrong?"

He growled. "What was in the needle? Tell me now!"

"A little bit of this, a little bit of that. It's hard to say since I mixed so many pills, crushed them up into a fine powder all together, stirred in a little cough syrup laced with codeine—you know, some *human* medicines."

"Do you think this is some sort of game?" he roared.

"No, but I think you do. You're certainly toying with me as if it was one, so why should I answer your questions? It's not like you're going to let me go."

"Fine, you want to play games, we'll play games." He snapped his fingers and Ianthe appeared on the other side of the bars, dressed in her favorite princess dress, pale blonde hair in wavy little pigtails. Ayanna choked back her sob, throwing herself toward the bars, only to recoil when the shackles yanked her back.

"Mommy?" Her violet eyes filled with tears as her little chin wobbled.

"Shhh, baby. It's okay. Mommy's fine." She tried to remind herself it was just a dream and her daughter wasn't there, but it was so difficult when she was just inches away. Ianthe reached her hand through the bars, and when her skin made contact, when that little hand gripped hers, she nearly broke.

"Come here, child," Rodric ordered. Ianthe glanced at her before letting go of her hand and complying.

"No, baby. Don't go near him!" she yelled.

He sat on a throne now, like the one she had seen him on the first day she ever laid eyes on him. He still appeared affected, sweating, the trembling now becoming more persistent, but she couldn't focus on that. All she could see was her darling little girl, the light of her life, approaching a monster. "Ianthe! Don't!" she screamed, but her daughter didn't listen. She approached Rodric, as trusting as a little puppy. He turned her in front of him so she faced Ayanna then he whispered in her ear. She couldn't hear what he said, but she knew it wasn't good by the way her daughter's face fell.

"Mommy, I didn't mean to be a bad girl. I'm sorry."

A sob burst forth from her lips. "No, baby, you were never a bad girl. You were always such a good girl, I promise."

Rodric placed both of his hands on her daughter's shoulders. "If I'm not a bad girl, why am I getting punished?" Ianthe squeaked.

"Don't touch her. Please! Stop! Let her go!"

"We're playing the game you wanted to play, the one you started when you wouldn't tell me what you injected into me." She watched as a shudder racked his entire body, and when it finished, he slid his hands up, resting on either side of Ianthe's head.

"No! No games. I can't remember, honestly. I just mixed whatever I had in my medicine cabinet—probably some aspirin, some meclizine, Midol, a few of Joel's old prescriptions from when he fell on the ice and hurt his knee. I can't remember! Please stop! Let her go! I can't remember!"

"Mommy?" Fear gripped her little girl's voice, and Ayanna closed her eyes, trying to remind herself that it was just a hallucination, but it was so hard when it felt so real.

"Mommy?" she repeated, her eyes pleading for her mom to save her.

She broke. "I'm sorry, sweetheart." She closed her eyes but very clearly heard the snap of bones and the small body's thud against the floor. She collapsed, threw her head back, and screamed for all it was worth, screamed until her throat was raw as the tears poured down her face. "This is just a nightmare, just a nightmare, just a nightmare," she whispered over and over to herself.

When she finally opened her eyes, she immediately

threw up all over the floor. The sight was something she wouldn't wish upon her worst enemy. No one should have to bear seeing the still, lifeless body of their child. It was only when the image flickered in and out that she could truly convince herself it wasn't real. She glanced at Rodric then. He looked awful. He was slumped over in the chair, his head resting in his hands.

"She's safe, she's safe, she safe," she said breathlessly, remembering what she had done to save her daughter, to ensure her safety, remembering that what she had just seen was merely a hallucination. Joel was with her daughter and he would keep her safe. He would protect her now.

"You don't look so good, Rodric," she whispered, knowing he would hear her. "How does it feel to know you're dying?" She hoped her assumption was right.

He lifted his head slowly and narrowed his eyes on her, but when he tried to stand and stalk toward her, he stumbled, collapsing back into the chair. "You think you've won? Let me tell you something, sweetheart: you're already broken. You are never going to wake up. If I'm going down, you're going with me."

"If it means keeping her away from you, I will gladly lay down my life."

He laughed weakly. "Do you honestly think she will ever be safe? She has his eyes…the royal eyes." His breath grew shallow. "She won't be hidden forever. Someone will find her."

"It doesn't matter. She'll always know who she is, who I raised her to be. She'll figure out what I did, and it will leave a mark. She'll be smart and strong. She'll be stronger than any of them."

"You're pathetic if you think she stands the slightest chance." He wheezed, his breath now causing him obvious pain.

She stood, her acceptance of her fate and conviction fueling her. "Pathetic? Just think, if her pathetic, *human* mother could take down the king's brother, what will she be able to do with royal Fae magic running through her blood?"

His eyes widened slightly before he was pulled into unconsciousness.

"I know one day, my little flower, you will become everything you are supposed to be. You. Will. Be. Magnificent," she whispered, hoping her words would somehow be carried across the realms of magic to her daughter. She closed her eyes, letting the love she had for her daughter fill every pore. Bright white light flooded the room behind her eyelids and she took her last breath just after she heard Rodric take his, opening her eyes to embrace the light.

EPILOGUE

12 and a half years later

IANTHE STARED AT her father, her mouth agape. She didn't know her jaw was open until Conall's hand gently lifted to close it. "You mean to tell me you knew…I mean, you've always known what I am?"

Joel nodded, his hazel eyes filled with regret. "I had my suspicions, but I didn't want to believe them. I know how your mother fought for you to have a different life, and I wasn't sure until now."

"But you didn't tell me!"

He sighed, having known this wouldn't be easy for her to accept. "I know I may have messed up here, but I was trying to do what I thought was the best for you, Lola. I didn't know what happened at the party was related to the Fae. I only knew what might happen after you turned seventeen. I was going to tell you…it was just so hard. You were already so lost to me." He inhaled deeply. "I failed her…I failed your mother so much." His eyes watered, dissolving any of her anger. Seeing his tears reminded her of just how fragile their relationship was and how he was trying to make things better.

Conall, her Unseelie Fae boyfriend and previous first in command to her biological father, the Unseelie king, squeezed her hand.

She sighed. "You didn't fail Mom, Dad. You did the best you could."

He wiped his eyes and shot her a wry look.

"Okay, well, I'll give you that—you could have done better, but you're doing better now and that's what matters." She released Conall's hand and walked over to her father, putting her hands over his and kneeling in front of him. "We can't change the past, we can only learn and grow from it to make a better future, and we're doing that right now. *You're* doing that right now."

He gripped her hands in his. "How did you get so smart?"

"I'm pretty sure I got that from you." She winked. She knew his wounds were still fresh, and even though they'd had their ups and downs, the fact of the matter was that this man had raised her, had been a father to her, far more than her bio-dad, and she wasn't going to let a silly thing like blood take away from the fact that he had stepped up and voluntarily taken the role of her father. Sure, he wasn't perfect, and yes, he'd lost his way after her mother died, but she was only beginning to understand how much the death of someone you love can change you so drastically. She shuddered, not wanting to think what she would do or how she would feel without Conall. As if sensing her dark thoughts, Conall smiled reassuringly at her from across the room. What mattered was that she and her father were making amends now; like a phoenix rebuilding itself from the ashes, they were rebuilding their relationship into something stronger. He loved her even though she wasn't his, even though she wasn't entirely human, and that unconditional love was a powerful thing.

"Hold on, let me get you something I should've given you a few months ago." He got up from his chair and climbed the stairs to his room. She stood, staring at the fireplace mantle that now held a picture of the three of them, her mom, her dad, and her. It was from her fifth birthday party. They were so happy, so much love and laughter in the photo you could almost feel it.

Her dad had surprised her the last few weeks after she was rescued. First, he'd accepted that her boyfriend was also half Fae. Of course, it probably helped that her boyfriend and two other Fae had been the ones to save her from the clutches of Casimir, her cousin. *Man, it sounds weird to call him that.* Then her dad surprised her even more by bringing out pictures of her mom he'd kept boxed up. He confessed that he'd stored them away because at first it was too painful to see her all the time and miss her so deeply, but he was finally ready. He felt it was time, and she was thankful. Conall came up behind her, resting his chin on her shoulder, staring at the picture with her. "She loved you, you know."

"How do you know?"

"It was just the kind of person she was. She had such a light and kindness inside of her. It was hard not to feel it when you were around her." He draped his arms around her, and she leaned back into his embrace.

"Thank you," she whispered. She knew he had met her mother once upon a time, and it was nice to hear about her.

"I'm proud of you, and she would be too. She'd be so proud of the magnificent woman you are today."

She swallowed against the lump in her throat when she

heard her dad clear his throat behind them. She shrugged out of Conall's arms, knowing there were some boundaries she didn't want to push with her father, and PDA with her boyfriend was a boundary she could respect.

He glanced briefly over her shoulder at the picture they'd been staring at. Then he smiled sadly and handed her an open envelope, her mother's familiar curly script on the front spelling out her first name. "I should probably apologize for reading it, but I'm not sorry that I did. It helped answer some questions I had when you left." His smile grew tight, a reminder of almost losing her. "She left this the day she fell into the comma. I have my own letter, and if you'd like to read it sometime I'll let you, can sort of make us even." He reached up and straightened his glasses, a thing he did when he was nervous. "I also have a box of her old notebooks that you may find useful hidden in the attic."

"Okay," she whispered, taking the envelope from his hand. She held it almost reverently. *These are the last words from my mother.* Conall grabbed her free hand and tugged her toward the couch so she could sit down to read. He sat next to her, pressing his legs against hers, radiating his magic comfort if she needed to take it.

"Thanks," she whispered to him as her trembling fingers opened the envelope and unfolded the pages. A necklace tumbled out, and she caught it before it fell to the ground. It was a simple silver chain with an almost but not quite heart-shaped stone at the end, the stone seemed to be made of small, dark blue crystals. *Interesting.* She handed it to an eager Conall, whose eyes sparked with recognition.

"You recognize this?"

He smiled. "I do. It's a sort of old Fae tradition, not seen much anymore. Most likely it was a gift to her from

Corydon."

She was too eager to read the pages in her hand to press him further for an explanation. She lifted the pages to her nose after catching the slightest hint of her mother's perfume. She closed her eyes against the onslaught of happy memories, memories of being read to and tucked in at night, of her mother kissing her scrapes when she fell and singing to her when she couldn't sleep, memories she thought she had forgotten but that were only waiting for a trigger to be released. She drew in a deep breath, opening her eyes, and began to read.

My dearest Ianthe,

I fear if you are reading this letter it means I am not around to help you at your time of need, and for that I am truly sorry. I did my best to protect you, most likely at the cost of my own life, but please don't worry! Would pay that price ten million times over if it means that you are alive and well.

There are some things I wish I were there to explain to you, things I know will be hard for you to accept, but know that you still have people there for you. You have my Aunt Grace, who will gladly answer any questions you have about what I am going to tell you, and you have your father, although I fear some of my news will not be what you want to hear, and I only hope it doesn't change how you think of him or feel toward him.

Let me start at the beginning. Once upon a time, I fell in love with a beautiful boy. He wasn't who I thought he was, although I didn't learn this until much later, but even after I learned the truth, it was too late, because I already loved him beyond reason. See, my darling, he wasn't exactly human. He was Fae (yes, like the pointed-ear Fae from the fairy tales I used to read to you), and even though Aunt Grace taught me not to trust the Fae, I couldn't help myself. He tried to break up with me for my own safety, which didn't work. I still ended up being discovered and dragged into a different world, into the Fae realm. When the boy saw me again, he remembered how much he loved me, and I remembered how much I loved him. We ignored everyone who told us we could never be, because he wasn't just any Fae, he was the unseelie king. Imagine my shock when I first discovered it, but to me he was just Corydon, the boy I had fallen in love with.

Over time, being a king changed him, and when I was no longer blinded by my love, I was able to see the truth of our situation, the impossibility of our relationship. When I discovered I was pregnant with his child, I knew I had to run away. See, my little flower, I loved you so much from the very first moment I knew. Knowing about you gave me the strength to leave. So, I ran away. Aunt Grace helped me and I moved in with some friends in Virginia, where I went to college.

That's where I met your father, and believe me, Joel is your father in almost every sense of the word. He was determined for us to be friends from the start, and he quickly became my very best friend. We had a special kind of love born from that friendship. When he found out about you, he loved us both enough to promise to raise you as his own, and how he loves you! You had him wrapped around your tiny little finger from the moment you were born, and I don't think he would have had it any other way. He gave you his name and legally became your father by claiming you as his own. I will always admire him for that.

I am writing this letter now because our safety has been threatened. Your biological father's brother, Rodric, has found me, found us. Please know that anything I did was to save you. I never wanted him to find out about you, because I knew what it would mean, what your beautiful violet eyes mean. You, my dear, are the unseelie princess, heir to the throne, chosen through heredity and a bit of Fae magic. I am terrified they will take you away from me, and I cannot bear the thoughts, so I've come up with a plan to keep you safe. If it works the way I want it to, we will both get to escape, but if it doesn't, I want you to know how much I love you.

I love you with every breath I take. I don't regret any of my past decisions or my relationship with your biological father, as it all led me to you. I never meant to keep such big secrets from you, but I wanted you grow up knowing lovehuman love. I wanted you to know what it is to feel compassion and kindness so when the day comes and you have to face your fate, you will be prepared, because I know fate has a lot in store for you. It chose you, a half Fae, to be the future unseelie queen, and that won't sit well with a lot of Fae. Your future will be filled with danger, and you'll need strength to get through it. You'll need to remember who you are inside so they don't change you.

See, my little flower, my darling Ianthe, I have seen into your heart, and I know. I know you have so much love and kindness to share. I know how smart you already are and can only guess at the woman you have grown to become. Know that I am proud of you, so proud. I can only imagine the hardships you have had to face or will face, but you are strong enough to pull throughalways remember that. I hope my love for you only succeeds in making you stronger, because I know deep within my heart that you will be magnificent.

Love always,
Your mommy

Acknowledgements

First I'd like to thank you, the reader, for taking time to read Ayanna's story. If you've been with me from the beginning, thank you for being part of this crazy journey, and I hope you continue to enjoy the Fae Realm series.

To my husband—thank you for cooking dinner, taking care of the animals, keeping the house clean, and making sure I was fed when I locked myself in the office to work. You are truly an amazing person and husband. Thank you for your never-ending support and encouragement. I love you.

Murphy Rae—this may just be my favorite cover yet! Your talent and eye for beauty continue to amaze me.

Haley Wolf—this book started because you started asking *What if?* You wanted to know the story behind Ianthe, what made Ayanna fall in love with Corydon, and what the hell happened to Casimir's dad. I love you so much for asking me these inspiring questions and pushing me to think about all the scenarios. We need more sushi/ movie dates!

My betas, Callie Vestal, Tonya Shaw, Kristann Monaghan, and my hubby—thank you all for your amazing feedback on my writing. You help me become a better author.

My mom and dad—thank you for teaching me to love books at an early age.

My friends (both online and IRL) and Southridge staff—your support and encouragement never goes unnoticed, especially Amalia Ayers. Your encouragement and enthusiasm has meant the world to me this year.

My brother and sister—I love you.

Caitlyn—I hope my overuse of that didn't drive you too crazy. Thank you for breathing new life into my work and helping elevate my writing with your edits.

Alyssa at Uplifting Designs—You've been such a help through this process. Thank you for making the interior of my books so stunning.

To the amazing authors who have welcomed me into this crazy world with open arms and are always willing to answer my questions: Manuscript Minxes, Colleen Hoover, Fisher Amelie, Teagan Hunter, Chelsea Mueller, Sara Ney, Jennifer Rebecca, Jeramey Kraatz, and my BS authors.

To the bloggers, like Unofficial Book Club, Garcia Sisters Book Blog, The BookAddict Mom, and T & G Book Boutique—thank you for supporting me and the Fae Realms.

To my BookSwappers and reader friends (especially Tacie Sterling, Jennifer Stiltner, and Shannon O'Neill)—I love you all! You help keep me sane and provide me with laughs, smiles, and hugs just when I need them.

To my students—keep reading and dreaming.

About the Author

Cathlin Shahriary lives in North Texas with her husband, cats, and dog. By day she is an elementary teacher, nurturing future book nerds and writers. By night (and weekends and school breaks), she is an avid reader, cat fosterer, and writer. You can usually find her fangirling over books, authors, and TV shows (like *Supernatural*, *Dr. Who*, and *The Walking Dead*, to name a few). She still believes in the existence of magic and the power of love.

Follow Cathlin on

Facebook
www.facebook.com/authorcshahriary

Instagram
@cshahriary

Twitter
@cshahriary

Turn to the next page to see a sneak preview of the next book in the Fae Realm series.

PROLOGUE

CALLIE COULD BARELY process how quickly her life had just changed. Could it be only a week ago that all she was worried about was high school and boys? It felt like a lifetime. She never in her wildest dreams would have imagined Fae were real and that her best friend, Ianthe, was half Fae, let alone that the guy that Callie had fallen for was a Fae who would kidnap her in some twisted revenge plot for his brother's death, but that's what happened. She knew from this moment her life would never be the same.

She shot a final glance at the boy Fae who had held her captive. Evin's honey colored eyes met hers, and as much as she tried to fight the pull, she felt it. *Must be Stockholm's syndrome*, she finally tore her gaze from his, but not before seeing the longing and regret on his face. His shoulders slumped forward as he walked out the door.

It wasn't that he'd been cruel to her, he'd been incredibly kind, but the fact remained that he lied to her and took her into a world of danger in order to use her. She couldn't stand to be used. Her parents used her all the time as a pawn in the divorce and it drove her crazy. She had friends use her before she moved to this town and boys who tried to use her. The one time she thought things would be different…she sighed. It was no use. He was no different than the others, if only her heart would believe her.

Conall paused as he passed by her, leaning in close. "For what's it worth, I think he'll regret it for the rest of his life—and for us that's a very long time." Her eyes met his emerald ones, and stupid hope fluttered in her chest. He smiled sadly. "He really does care about you, Callie." He patted her shoulder before walking away. Curse him for saying the exact thing she wanted to hear, and curse her heart for wanting to hear it.

She glanced once more at the closing door. It didn't matter, none of it did. They were from different worlds… literally, and she would never fit into his. This was all for the best. They could never be together. Now, if only she could convince her heart.